The Bull Slayer

Books by Bruce Macbain

The Plinius Secundus Mysteries
Roman Games
The Bull Slayer

The Bull Slayer

A Plinius Secundus Mystery

Bruce Macbain

Poisoned Pen Press

Poisoned Pen Press
6962 E. First Ave., Ste. 103
Scottsdale, AZ 85251
www.poisonedpenpress.com
info@poisonedpenpress.com

Printed in the United States of America

For Carol, Andrew, and Anthony

Versus quidem meos cantat etiam formatque
cithara non artifice alio docenteque,
sed amore, qui magister est optimus.

She even puts my verses to music and sings
them, accompanying herself on the lyre, with no
instruction from a music teacher but only love,
which is the best teacher of all.

(Pliny praising his young wife. *Letters IV 19)*

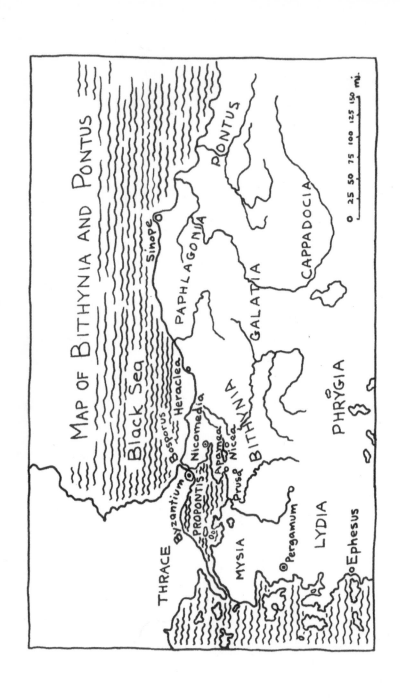

MAP OF BITHYNIA AND PONTUS

Black Sea

Sinope

PONTUS

CAPPADOCIA

PAPHLAGONIA

GALATIA

Heraclea

Bosporus

Nicomedia

Byzantium

PROPONTIS

Apamea

Nicea

Prusa

BITHYNIA

PHRYGIA

THRACE

MYSIA

Pergamum

LYDIA

Ephesus

0 25 50 75 100 125 150 mi.

Dramatis Personae

(in order of appearance)

Gaius Plinius Secundus (Pliny), Governor of the province of
    Bithynia-Pontus

Zosimus, Pliny's secretary

Gaius Suetonius Tranquillus, a member of Pliny's staff

Pancrates, a fortune-teller

Calpurnia, Pliny's wife

Ione, Calpurnia's maid

Atilia, the wife of a Roman businessman

Marcus Vibius Balbus, the Fiscal Procurator of the province

Fabia, Balbus' wife

Silvanus, Balbus' chief accountant

Diocles the Golden Mouth, a wealthy provincial, famous as an
    orator

Rufus, the young son of Zosimus and Ione

Timotheus, a Greek tutor

Faustilla
Memmia   the wives of Pliny's staff officers
Fannia
Cassia

Nymphidius, a member of Pliny's staff

Galeo, a *lictor*

Marinus, Pliny's physician

Caelianus, Pliny's chief clerk
Aquila, senior centurion on Pliny's staff
Aulus, Balbus' son
Baucis, Agathon's housekeeper.
Sophronia, owner of a brothel
Argyrus, Sophronia's half-brother
Glaucon, a wealthy provincial
Theron, Glaucon's brother
Didymus, a banker
Barzanes, high priest of Mithras
Lurco, Balbus' freedman

Chapter One

*THE TENTH REGNAL YEAR OF THE EMPEROR
TRAJANUS AUGUSTUS, CONQUEROR OF GERMANY,
CONQUEROR OF DACIA, PONTIFEX MAXIMUS,
HOLDING THE TRIBUNICIAN POWER,
CONSUL FOR THE FIFTH TIME, FATHER OF HIS
COUNTRY, BEST OF EMPERORS*

The province of Bithynia-Pontus

Through long weeks of instruction, the Father had taught him the rituals, the star-lore, and the incantations that he must pronounce when the moment came. All that study had made his head hurt; but he had a purpose that drove him. For the past week he had abstained from sex, meat, and bathing. And now at last he was drawing near to the cosmic cave, to a confrontation with the beautiful young god in his fiery splendor. He would see the mystery of the bull's death, he would be baptized with water from a living spring, his soul would soar up through the seven planetary spheres to the starry firmament where one day it would dwell forever. He would share bread and wine—the flesh and life-giving blood of the bull—with his brethren and be born again for eternity.

They emerged finally from the dark woods at the foot of a craggy upthrust of bare rock and, just as they did so, the sun broke over its top and bathed them in its rays. The Unconquered Sun. All-powerful Mithras. Lord and Savior.

No casual traveler could have stumbled upon the entrance to the cave; it was low and only some six paces wide and well concealed by brush. While the *mystae* busied themselves clearing this away, the Father, a frail old man with infinitely wrinkled skin, turned to him, grasped his hand in fellowship, and smiled at him. "Are you ready, my son?"

Following the Father, he ducked under the rocky overhang and descended the seven stone steps, worn smooth by the feet of the blessed, down into the earth's dark womb. The damp subterranean chill made him shiver. The stale air smelled of dripping stone and burnt pine. Now the *mystae* moved here and there in the cave, igniting incense and lighting the pine torches that stood in niches along the walls. He gazed around him in the guttering light. The cave was no ordinary one; it had been reshaped by men's hands. It wasn't large—forty paces long, fifteen across. Twenty men filled it full. A narrow nave ran the length of it with stone benches along each side where they would recline for their meal. The low ceiling was arched, painted midnight blue, and sprinkled with golden stars; the signs of the zodiac ran around the walls. The nave ended in an apse where curtains hung before the altar. The crash of a bronze thunder sheet shattered the silence and unseen hands drew the curtains back. Then he gazed for the first time upon the mystery of his new faith. Suddenly he thought his heart would burst—the intensity of his feeling took him by surprise. Sculpted in high relief from the living rock, the figure of Mithras, a serene and handsome youth dressed in a billowing blue cloak and red Phrygian cap, straddled a kneeling bull, holding it down with his knee, pulling its head backward with one hand, and plunging his dagger into its throat. A dog and a serpent licked the bloody wound, a scorpion attacked the bull's testicles, and from the bull's tail sprouted ears of wheat.

Bells chimed and the hollow eyes of the god blazed with sudden fire. The *mystae* began to chant the *Nama Mithras*. They raised their hands, each one holding the emblems of his rank—cup, spear, sickle, whip, thunderbolt. The torchlight threw their shadows huge against the wall.

Now hands removed his clothes, blindfolded him, and guided him down the nave toward the altar. Hands on his shoulders forced him down, pressing his forehead painfully against the cold stone. Other hands pulled his arms behind him and bound them with the hot guts of a chicken. The sharp point of an arrow pricked his neck.

"Take three deep breaths," spoke the Father close to his face. "You will rise into the air, you will look upon the face of our god, you will taste immortality."

And so he did, or thought he did at any rate, for a brief moment. And then it was over. His new brothers raised him up, removed his blindfold, clothed him. They pressed around him, shaking his hand. The Father beamed. The Sun-Runner, second in rank to the Father, hailed him in his rich baritone.

"You're a Raven now, my good friend, and soon to rise still higher in our ranks. You honor us with your patronage, a man of your rank and power. And now let us eat and drink to your good fortune. I should say to *our* good fortune."

The new-made Raven looked from face to face and was answered with smiles all around. Indeed, *fortune* was the word.

Chapter Two

Nicomedia, capital of Bithynia-Pontus. Two years later.
The 13th day before the Kalends of October

Clerks bustled back and forth in the great hall, carrying armloads of scrolls, making a great to-do of hunting for the missing documents, accomplishing very little. Gaius Plinius watched them with growing exasperation. The chaos of the archives, the slovenly habits of the staff he had inherited from his predecessor, the ruinous state of the old royal palace in which they were housed. Day three in his new post. He had expected bad: this was worse.

"Patrone." His freedman Zosimus touched his shoulder. "It's past midday. You'll want to eat something and then rest for a bit. Doctor's orders."

"What? It can't be so late already. No, just have a tray brought in." Zosimus frowned. "It's all right, my boy. I'll rest later, I promise."

What would he do without Zosimus? Secretary, companion, nursemaid at times. Friend. He had a head of yellow hair like an untidy haystack and the innocent, earnest face of a fool—but he was far from being a fool.

"See if you can't find Suetonius out there somewhere and ask him to step in. And stop looking so worried." Pliny waved him off. While confusion reigned around him, he busied himself arranging the objects on his desk—ink stand, styluses, sheaves of parchment, a carafe of watered wine, a bronze bust of Epicurus the philosopher inherited from his learned uncle, a cameo of his darling Calpurnia painted by her own hand. There was comfort in orderliness, even in small things. His passion for order amused his more exuberant friends.

Lately he had begun to be aware of his own mortality. He was nearing a half century of life—more than three-quarters of his allotted span. A half century that had seen the enlargement of the empire while rot set in at the center. By the grace of the gods they had survived Caligula, Nero, and Domitian and come at last to the present happy state of affairs—the reign of a sane and benevolent emperor who respected their liberty. He prayed it would endure at least as long as he did.

Pliny knew that others saw in him only a rather plump, rather domesticated, rather fussy man. He made no apologies. It was a lifetime of hard work, reliability, attention to detail that had won him, at long last, this extraordinary appointment: Governor of Bithynia-Pontus with overriding authority to clean up the most corrupt, mismanaged, seditious, and turbulent province in the Empire. The province had been a backwater for too long; a place for second-raters, governors from whom little was expected. That would all change now. Only a few people knew it, but Bithynia was to be the staging area for an invasion of the Persian empire. Restoring order and sound finances was now a top priority. Trajan, Best of Emperors, had entrusted this to him. And he would not fail him. Bithynia was a graveyard of governors. Pliny knew he had enemies who would relish his downfall. What man of importance didn't? He was determined not to give them the chance.

"There's a line of people out into the street waiting to see you. All clutching petitions in their sweaty hands." Suetonius, pink-cheeked and pink-scalped—at forty he was already losing his hair—edged through the mob of clerks, accountants, and messengers, and dropped into an armchair beside Pliny's desk. "Shall I send them all away?"

"On the contrary, I want you to interview them—unless you're otherwise engaged?"

"I was about to be. Research, you know. But it can wait."

"Ah, and which of your many works-in-progress are you researching today? Greek Terms of Abuse? Famous Whores? Physical Defects of Mankind?"

"Well, one never knows what will turn up, does one?"

They laughed easily together. Gaius Suetonius Tranquillus was one of Pliny's literary protégés: a talented writer, a man of restless curiosity, a bottomless repository of rude anecdotes, a tireless collector of backstairs gossip, a lover of the odd fact, fascinated by the grotesque—in short, an extremely useful man to have along in this hellhole of sedition. He was vain, too, and combatted his baldness with concoctions of horseradish, cumin, and worse things—all to little avail. No sooner had he arrived in the province than he'd exchanged his white Roman tunic with an *eques'* purple stripes for a colorful Greek outfit of sheer linen. *The better to blend in—you learn more.* He had jumped at the chance to come to Bithynia on Pliny's staff.

"Have you found what you wanted in the files?"

Pliny pressed his fingers to his temples and rubbed, feeling the skin move on his skull—for an awful instant imagining the skull bare of flesh as it might look ten, fifteen years from now if he lasted that long, if he husbanded his strength. He drove the image from his mind. "Beyond belief, the mess he's left us with! Six former governors of this province have been prosecuted and our friend Anicius is likely to be the seventh, for sheer incompetence, if nothing worse. Transcripts of trials, minutes of meetings with the local grandees—all missing. He's taken them home with him or more likely burned them. And the people he's left behind, this lot." His glance took in the room. They come in late, they leave early, they give you sour looks when you speak to them. I'm putting you in charge of the secretariat. Whip them into shape."

Suetonius winced. "Not really my—"

Pliny held up a finger. "What on earth is that racket?"

Through the open second-story window, carried on a soft September breeze, came a sudden shriek of flutes and a crash of cymbals. A parading army couldn't have made more noise. Pliny and Suetonius looked out and, as they watched, a mob turned the corner, marching along the avenue below them, men and women together, dancing, leaping, shouting something—a word, a name? Pliny strained to make it out but in the general din it was impossible. But there was no doubting who the focus of this adulation was. On a litter that swayed above the heads of the crowd, rode a handsome man whose hair hung down his back in long curls. He stared straight ahead, looking neither left nor right, motionless as a statue while eager hands reached out to touch his long, white garment as he passed. In his right hand he held a glittering scimitar, but what held everyone's eye was the giant python that draped itself around his chest and over his shoulder, its head swinging to and fro.

Pliny felt a stab of anxiety. Somewhere out there in this alien city was his wife.

◇◇◇

"'Purnia, don't let go of me!"

"Hold tight, Ione!"

Calpurnia, the taller and sturdier of the two women, gripped her maid's hand as they struggled to keep their footing in this crowd of madmen that surged outside the temple of Asclepius and filled the whole marketplace alongside it. Elegant matrons pressed against greasy-aproned shopkeepers, beggars contested with merchants for a glimpse of the holy man who rode above them in his litter like a raft tossed upon a sea of eager faces and outstretched arms.

A sharp elbow hit Calpurnia in the side, knocking the breath out of her. Her knees buckled and she thought for an instant she would fall and be crushed under the stamping feet.

"Pancrates! The god returns!" The shout rose up from five hundred throats, mingling with the din of cymbals, flutes, and drums.

Calpurnia and Ione had spent the morning going round the shops and stalls and ateliers of the unfamiliar city, escorted by a retinue of slaves and local guides—all of them now lost somewhere in this seething confusion of color and noise. The palace in which she and Pliny and all their staff were housed had once belonged to the ancient kings of Bithynia. Mithridates the Great—a name that could still strike fear in Roman hearts even after a century and a half—had ruled his bloody empire from here; and so had Pompey the Great, who defeated him and made the kingdom a Roman province.

The palace, which sat on a high hill overlooking the harbor, was vast: more than a hundred rooms grouped around two great peristyle halls. Impressive in size but disappointing in detail. All the portable works of art, all the splendidly wrought furnishings had long since been looted, first by Mithridates and then by a succession of Roman governors, culminating with the wretched Anicius, who had filled a whole ship with whatever was still worth stealing. The mosaic floors were original and fine, but the statues that populated the courtyards were now mere copies of copies. The tapestries and draperies were shabby, the brass work tarnished, the frescoed walls black with soot, the rooms littered with trash, the smell of mildew heavy in the air. Calpurnia sighed for her Italian villa, swallowed hard, and determined to turn the place into a home worthy of her husband. Worthy of Rome. The last governor, who had no wife, was so parsimonious that tradesmen had stopped coming to the palace, so she must seek them out herself. In a single day she had examined fabrics, contracted with cabinetmakers and painters and silversmiths. Thank the gods she had Ione with her. Her freedwoman spoke fluent Greek, while Calpurnia's halting kitchen Greek was not up to haggling in the marketplace. That was another thing she was determined to rectify.

It was the end of a long and productive morning. Hunger and the hot sun overhead urged that they return to the palace for a bath—at least the plumbing worked—and a meal with their overworked husbands, Pliny and Zosimus. And then suddenly they had found themselves swamped in this sea of frenzied celebrants.

"Long life to Pancrates! Oracle of Asclepius!"

The crowd surged forward as the object of their adulation was helped down from his litter—he and the astonishing snake. At that point she lost sight of him as he passed within the bronze doors of the temple. But a herald stood on the topmost step and cried out, "The god has returned to his house. Present your questions and they will be answered to your heart's desire for the fee of one drachma."

The crowd was mostly male but there were women too, Greek women modestly veiled as their custom was. But then, to her surprise, Calpurnia saw Roman faces too, unveiled and elaborately coifed like herself. One towering hairdo atop a whitened face and fat neck forced its way toward her through the press of bodies.

"You remember me, Lady Calpurnia? Last night—the reception—such an honor…"

"Yes, of course," Calpurnia murmured. *What was the woman's name?* "So many new faces—Atilia, isn't it?"

"Philomela, you stupid little bitch, where are you?" The woman looked around angrily as a little slave girl, who couldn't have been more than ten, struggled after her, fighting with both hands to hold up a large parasol.

The woman turned back to Calpurnia. "Impossible to find decent slaves in this country. But isn't it wonderful, he's returned at last!"

Calpurnia looked at her blankly.

"Pancrates, of course. Our oracle."

Chapter Three

That night. The villa of Marcus Vibius Balbus

Balbus snapped his fingers. Thick fingers covered with coarse hairs. Fingers that in their day had gripped a centurion's *vitis*, bringing it down hard across the shoulders of any legionary who didn't jump to attention quick enough. Fingers that lately wielded nothing heavier than a stylus—but even a stylus was a weapon in those fingers. Marcus Balbus snapped his fingers and a young slave boy ran up to refill his goblet.

"More wine, Governor?"

Pliny, reclining beside him in the place of honor, hastily covered his cup with his hand. He'd drunk too much already. Balbus preferred his wine unwatered and forced his guests to do the same.

"Another bite of turbot?" He held out the morsel dripping with sauce on the point of his knife. Eat." It was very nearly a command. Balbus' face, square, brown, and hatched as a chopping block, leaned close, smiling unpleasantly. He was a man made entirely of bone and gristle, a man who kept himself fit, with big-knuckled hands and a shock of stiff red hair speckled grey. Gaulish blood there somewhere, Pliny imagined, or even German.

Pliny waved the food away. The dishes were all too sauced and spiced for his frugal tastes. And he would not allow this man to bully him. After a long moment, Balbus withdrew his hand and shrugged.

Conversation, which had died momentarily, resumed with pretended gaiety. There were nine of them at table, the usual number for a *triclinium*. In addition to Pliny and Calpurnia, the guests included Suetonius, who was always reliably entertaining at affairs like this; two wealthy Roman merchants, one accompanied by his wife, and a man named Silvanus, who was Balbus' chief accountant. The merchant's wife seemed to know Calpurnia and conversed with her throughout the evening with great animation. "Thrilled to see you again…this morning…a god…miraculous man…you must ask him…yes, a snake…" Calpurnia had that fixed smile on her face that meant she was bored to tears.

Again Balbus brought his battered face close to Pliny and said in a whisper that was meant to be heard around the table, "We've met before, you know, you and I."

"Have we? I'm afraid I—"

"Don't remember my face? Well, I was younger and handsomer then, and I was only one of many. The night before Emperor Domitian was murdered. I was a Praetorian Guardsman then. We paid you a little visit, didn't we? Almost cost you your life, didn't it? And your charming wife's." He smiled at Calpurnia the way a crocodile smiles.

Pliny felt the blood drain from his face. That was a night that still, after fourteen years, haunted his dreams. And Calpurnia's. And why was Balbus mentioning it now? To make him squirm, why else? Suetonius shot Pliny a worried look. Calpurnia felt for his hand.

Pliny drew a long breath. "Those were difficult days, my friend. Thank the gods we live in happier times."

Eager noises of assent around the table. Then Fabia, Balbus' wife, a big-boned woman all bosom and jewels, hastily changed the subject to her favorite, her only, topic of conversation.

"These Greeklings," she said, "scoundrels every one of them. They don't love us." She spoke in a fluting, gentrified Latin that didn't quite disguise something foreign in the accent—Thracian, it was rumored. Pliny had heard that she concealed barbarian tattoos under her clothing. He could almost believe it.

"No reason why they should," he answered mildly.

"We've brought them peace, haven't we?"

"Peace, lady Fabia, has never been what they wanted. If the Empire were to disappear tomorrow they would all be fighting each other again and loving it."

"Strange words for a governor," Balbus struck in.

"I'm a realist. They pay a high price for Roman peace as you, of course, would know, Procurator."

Balbus eyed him suspiciously. "Is there a question buried in that remark, Governor?"

Marcus Vibius Balbus was not accustomed to being questioned. Trajan had appointed him Fiscal Procurator of the province. For over two years now he had wielded absolute authority to raise taxes and pay the soldiers, answerable to no one but the Emperor. He had his own office and staff and lived lavishly with his family in a spacious seaside villa south of the city, while Pliny and Calpurnia camped out in the shambles of their ruinous palace. Balbus' power had equaled that of the governor himself. Not bad for a man who had started life as a common soldier, and clawed his way up the ranks: Chief Centurion of a legion, then a stint in the Night Watch, the City Battalions, and the Praetorian Guard, and finally a succession of civil posts in every corner of the world. The typical procurator's career, it produced the tough, experienced men who made the Empire run.

Balbus was a man whom no governor questioned. Until now. Pliny's extraordinary commission from the emperor overrode his authority. Balbus knew it. Pliny knew that he knew it. How long would it be before they had to confront it?

The procurator pulled in his horns just a little. "You have questions about the taxes, Gaius Plinius, speak to my man Silvanus. You there, Silvanus, are you still sober enough to speak? Introduce yourself. Where're your manners, you ugly fellow? This is our new governor, come all the way from Rome to help us count our pennies. Show him some respect. Perhaps you've brought your abacus with you, show him how well you do sums."

The man addressed was short-necked, beak-faced, and bald but for a few sparse hairs combed ear to ear; he resembled, Pliny thought, nothing so much as a tortoise. His eyes were narrow and nearly without lashes. He blinked them myopically. He stared at his food, his jaws working, and said nothing.

"The man's as dumb as he is ugly," Balbus said in a loud voice and laughed.

But Fabia, Pliny noticed, did not laugh. What was it that crossed her face for an instant? A tightening of the jaw muscles, the eyes moving to Silvanus and then sliding quickly away. Perhaps it was only his imagination.

"But he's loyal," Balbus continued. "Loyalty's the great thing. Been with me for years."

Another uncomfortable silence. Broken by Suetonius, who asked, "What can you tell us about the former governor?"

"Anicius?" Balbus answered. "Excellent man. Excellent. Miss him already."

Pliny and Suetonius had met Anicius Maximus at the harbor where he was waiting, amidst a mountain of luggage, to sail back to Italy on their ship's return voyage. He had seemed almost pathetically eager to be on his way. The emperor had nothing against the man, or at least nothing he had shared with Pliny, and yet Anicius' jumping eyebrows, his fluttering hands, his muttered apologies for his hasty departure all seemed to signal some consciousness of guilt. Would he be the seventh governor of Bithynia to be indicted on his return for crimes real or contrived?

"We got along like brothers, each to his own sphere, no conflicts, no ruction." Balbus seemed to feel the point needed underlining.

"We're having trouble finding a number of documents in the—"

"Took 'em with him," Balbus cut him off. "Perfect right to. Governor's papers are his own, you know that. Mine too."

Pliny decided for the moment to let that pass. This was not the time or place.

Balbus swung his legs off the dining couch, stood and stretched. "Show you around the place." Dinner, it seemed, was over.

The villa and grounds were spectacular, crammed with first-rate statues and objects, although jumbled together and poorly displayed as though the mere having of them was all that mattered to the procurator and his wife. Calpurnia, who was an artist herself, made appreciative comments to her hostess and asked where they had acquired this bust, that vase. Fabia glowered and answered her with curt monosyllables.

It was growing dark now and they were returning from the garden, Pliny and Calpurnia walking ahead, followed by Balbus and his wife and the others, when a slender figure, half-hidden in the shadow of the doorway, suddenly bolted across their path and vanished into the dim recesses of the house. It was so unexpected Calpurnia gasped and grabbed Pliny's arm. "What on earth was that?"

Instantly, Balbus and Fabia were on either side of them, shouldering them back. "One of the slaves," said Fabia too loudly, "pay no attention." But her eyes said something else. For an instant, Calpurnia could have sworn, those agate eyes turned liquid.

It was all over in a moment and Balbus was eager to see his guests to their carriages.

◇◇◇

"Delightful couple," said Suetonius with a twinkle in his eye. He, Pliny, and Calpurnia had stepped down from their carriages and stood together at the palace gate. "You're going to have your hands full with Balbus."

"Balbus will open his books for me or find himself back in Rome explaining himself to Trajan. The emperor was very clear. There is too much money sloshing about in this province, misspent, unaccounted for, squandered on projects that never seem to be completed. Whether our friend Balbus has his fingers in any of that I do not know. But I plan to find out."

"Do they have children?" Calpurnia asked.

"Why do you ask?" said Pliny.

"I just thought—no reason, really."

"You, by the way, were wonderful, my dear as always. Putting up with that dragon."

"Fabia doesn't like me."

"Not surprising. She's enjoyed the highest rank among the Roman wives up until now. I know that doesn't matter to you but it does to a woman like her. You now hold that place, like it or not, 'Purnia."

If it had not been so dark Pliny would have seen the anxious look that crossed her face. Suetonius, with sharper eyes, perhaps did see it.

"Well," said Pliny. "Let's make an early night. Busy day tomorrow. We meet the Greeks."

"Just one thing more, Gaius Plinius," Suetonius said. "If you don't mind. What Balbus said earlier, something about the Praetorians visiting you the night before the unlamented Domitian died. Some danger to yourselves? Happens I'm gathering material for another project of mine, biographies of the Caesars from Julius to Domitian. I'd be grateful for anything you might…"

Pliny froze him with a look.

"Well, I mean, that is…" Suetonius looked from Pliny to Calpurnia, who gazed at him steadily.

"We don't speak of that night," she said.

"Yes, well—sorry," he stammered, "please forget I asked."

"Already forgotten, my friend." Pliny smiled and clapped him on the shoulder. "Sleep well."

◇◇◇

Not everyone slept that night.

In the temple of Asclepius, in a secret chamber beneath the great gold and ivory statue of the god, lamps burned late and a dozen sweating figures bent to their work: *Shall I receive the allowance? Will I be sold? Am I to be reconciled with my father? Will I get a furlough? Is he who is away from home alive? Is my partner cheating me? Am I to become a beggar? Will I become a fugitive? Will my son waste my property? Am I to be divorced from my husband? Will I get my money back? Is someone diddling my wife?*

Lads with nimble fingers inserted hot needles under the wax seals of the *tabellae*, opened them, and read out the questions. This was accompanied by a good deal of laughter. ("Yes, you old fool, half the town's diddling her!")

Pancrates permitted this. He paid them little enough, let them enjoy themselves. Better paid and more serious were his oracle writers, men with a smattering of literary education who composed the answers in crabbed poetic verses that could mean anything. The written replies were attached to the *tabellae*, which were then resealed so deftly that no one would suspect they had been opened. Often though, if the hour grew late and they were tired, they would simply attach stock answers without bothering even to read the questions. In any case, the next day the questioners would receive their responses for the price of a silver drachma. Hundreds of drachmas a day.

But that was for the common run of questioners. Seekers of higher status were vouchsafed an oracle from the mouth of the sacred python itself. Pancrates was careful to do this only rarely so as not to dilute the effect by overexposure. It was a complicated and tiring performance. He would sit in the doorway of the temple, the snake, asleep with drugged milk, hanging like a dead weight from his shoulders, its head under his arm, while he opened and closed the mouth of a canvas snake head by pulling invisible strands of horsehair. A confederate hidden behind him spoke through a tube made of cranes' windpipes.

For still more important clients—the Romans and their foolish wives—Pancrates would grant personal visitations: drawing out their secrets so subtly that he seemed, to their amazement, to read their unspoken thoughts. It was a talent he had perfected over years.

For the past six months he had toured the provinces of Greece and Asia, drawing immense crowds everywhere he went and putting to shame those shabby Christian proselytizers whom he encountered at every turn. Now he had returned in triumph to Nicomedia, all the more sought after because of his absence. It was time now to reactivate his network of informants. For in every great house there was some servant, some lowly hanger-on, who was on Pancrates' payroll. They sent him people's characters, forecasts of their questions, and hints of their ambitions, so that he had his answers ready. And sometimes the questions revealed that the writers were up to illegal activities. In these cases he didn't return the tablet with an answer but held on to it and used it to blackmail the sender. Here was where the real money was made.

Chapter Four

The next morning
The 12th day before the Kalends of October

"And so we entreat Almighty Zeus to favor our city, our province, our new governor and the benevolent Emperor who, in his wisdom, has sent him to guide us…"

Pliny, sitting stiffly, itching in his toga on this unseasonably warm morning, was moved in spite of himself by the thrumming baritone. Never mind that what was said was far less important than what was *not* said. He knew that Bithynia—like every land inhabited by Greeks—was a cockpit of warring factions, who agreed on only one thing—resentment of their Roman masters. In Nicomedia, in Prusa, in Nicaea and the other cities of the province, their ancestors had once debated questions of war and peace, life and death. Roman domination had put an end to that, yet their fractious spirit lived on, the more bitter as the stakes were smaller. Each city was a stage where the grandees waged constant battle for honor and influence. The rise of one meant the downfall of another and, like the all-out wrestling matches that these Greeklings were so fond of, there were no holds barred. Their world was a taut, vibrating web of shifting alliances, of rivalry and obligation. A disturbance at any node sent shivers racing along its silken strands. At the center of this particular web sat Diocles of the Golden Throat.

Pliny knew him, of course, by reputation. Diocles' oratorical powers were famous throughout the civilized world, his circle of friends reached even to Rome. Diocles wasn't a big man physically, he was shorter than Pliny, but he seemed somehow to swell, to grow as he addressed the citizens, councilors, and magistrates of his city. Tossing his leonine head with its mane of silver hair swept back, thrusting out his chest like a bantam cock's, sculpting the air with gestures precisely choreographed to accompany every shifting inflection, he sent his voice up to the highest tier of seats in the vast, open-air theater. To Pliny's trained eye it was a performance not to be missed.

A pity that the surroundings failed to equal the grandeur of the sentiments. The theater, at close hand, was a near ruin. After an expenditure of three million sesterces to repair it, it was subsiding with huge cracks and holes. The colonnade behind the stage was littered with column drums lying where they had been abandoned a year or more ago, and beyond it a giant crane rose up against the sky, its ropes slack, the circular cage of its treadmill, where slaves had once labored, now empty. And this same dismal scene, Pliny knew, was replicated in every city in the province. Huge sums had been raised to beautify the cities, to provide baths, aqueducts, gymnasia and every other amenity of civilized life, only to vanish—into whose pockets?—with the work still undone. And meanwhile anti-Roman sentiment and factional violence grew with every passing day.

It was for this that Pliny had been sent here. And today he would tell them plainly what he intended to do. He was by instinct a modest man but this morning he had proceded to the theater with all the majesty that a Roman governor could command. He rode in an open litter preceded by trumpeters and a dozen *lictors*, bearing the *fasces* on their shoulders and bawling at the crowd to make way. Behind him marched his senior staff, all in brilliant white togas, and following them a long tail of supernumeraries and assorted "friends." Unseen in the crowd, soldiers in civilian dress stood ready to pounce on anyone with an angry face or a stone in his hand. Meanwhile, Balbus, not to be outshone, led his own procession with nearly equal pomp from his headquarters in the treasury building. Here, then, was the might of Rome assembled—palpable, undeniable, inescapable.

Diocles, who was a former *archon* of Nicomedia and a member of the city council, was introducing Pliny now, his honeyed voice full of words like concord, harmony, honor, friendship, order. His faction cheered him wildly, as they were paid to do, but from here and there in the audience came catcalls from other factions.

Then Pliny took the rostrum and waited for silence. When he spoke it was in the careful, measured tones of the professional lawyer. His oratorical training was impeccable but he wasn't the showman that Diocles was. His speech, carefully written and memorized, was short and to the point. Rome depended on the wealthy men in every city to make the wheels of empire turn. But if they abused their position, squandered their money, punishment would be swift. He was embarking at once on a tour of every city in the province where he would examine accounts and hold hearings. He asked for their loyalty and cooperation.

The silence, when he sat down, was deafening. Which was about what he had expected.

Diocles swept toward him, followed by his retinue: all of them prosperous, well-fed, sleek; men whom Pliny must win over if he was to accomplish anything here.

"Splendid words, Governor, inspiring! Of course, my friends and I are all behind you." He indicated them with a jutting chin. The friends nodded and made noises of agreement. "What a relief to have things put to rights at last." *You arrogant barbarian. You spawn of a city that was founded by wild men and robbers. You pillager of all the world, you enemy of civilization. What mischief will you make among us now?* "I look forward to entertaining you at my estate one day soon for an exchange of views. Leaving at once, are you? For Prusa? Are things there as bad as that? Yes, I quite understand. Like Atlas, you must shoulder your burden, like Hercules, you have your labors, like Theseus—well, you know what I mean. Another time, then. In the meantime what can I do to make your stay pleasanter? Nothing? Oh, surely. What? A Greek tutor for your wife? Admirable!" *Another Roman whore, who prances around the city unveiled and reclines at table with men, actually talks to them like an equal! Oh, certainly, she wants to improve her Greek the better to abuse us in our own tongue.* "Yes, I think I know just the man."

Balbus had stood by silently during this exchange. Now he struck in. "Diocles, you should know that the governor comes with a special mandate from our emperor, overriding even my authority in fiscal matters." The tone was surly, the Greek rough and heavily accented. "We must all look sharp, mustn't we?"

"Oh, indeed so, Procurator," Diocles smiled. "But honest men have nothing to fear."

The two men held each other's gaze for a brief moment.

"You know, I envy the Greeklings in a way." Pliny said to Suetonius as they made their way back to the palace. "The fire, the excitement, the struggles for power in their little world. Like Rome was in Cicero's day, when oratory *mattered*, when lives were at stake."

"I suppose so," his friend replied carefully. "But, of course, one wouldn't wish those dangerous days back again. We're much better off without assemblies, elections, all that— "

"Oh, quite, I didn't mean…"

This was dangerous ground; they let it drop.

"What did you think of my speech?" Pliny asked after a moment's pause.

"At least they didn't throw cushions at you." A smile, as usual, hovered on Suetonius' lips. He found the world a source of constant amusement.

◇◇◇

From the Sun-Runner to the Father, greetings.

The Lion has asked me privately to nominate his son to be initiated into the rank of Raven. Ordinarily, I would not consider it, but I fear that the Lion—especially at this critical time—must be given what he wants. You understand my meaning.

Until the day of the Sun, nama Mithras

Chapter Five

That evening

"Daddy, mommy, look at me, I'm a chariot driver!" Rufus, red-haired, fat-cheeked and sturdy, his mouth and fingers sticky with honey cake, stood up in his goat-cart, and waved his whip. His words were a jumble of Latin and Greek, he hadn't sorted the two languages out yet. This birthday present, from uncle Pliny, carefully hidden in the palace stable until the moment of its presentation, was the best one of all. His other new toys—a hobby horse from Suetonius, a wooden sword from old Nymphidius, a kite from Caelianus, knucklebones, a top, a hoop, carved animals, a stuffed ball, a boat—all momentarily forgotten. The goat, which had stood motionless for some time, made a sudden jump, nearly tumbling the little boy out. Ione, his mother, ran to grab him, while Zosimus, his father, fumbled with the goat's halter.

"Gaius, he's too young for it," Calpurnia protested, though she was laughing.

"No, auntie 'Purnia, I'm big! I'm four! Daddy, make the goat go." Zosimus shot a worried look at his master and mistress. His own gifts, a writing set and an alphabet book—what else would a secretary give his son?—lay unnoticed where they had been instantly dropped.

"Rufus, give the other children a turn now," Ione said.

Caelianus' twelve- year- old boy and Nymphidius' eight-year-old granddaughter were looking envious. Pliny swept the boy up in his arms, swung him around, and set him down. "You know what that goat wants? I'll bet he wants an apple. Let's feed him, shall we?" Pliny was enjoying himself as much as little Rufus; more, if that were possible.

Suetonius, reclining at the adults' table, surveyed this picture of domestic joy and was puzzled. Rufus was a bright and engaging little boy but he was, after all, only the son of two freed slaves. Pliny had a reputation for generosity to his slaves and freedmen, but even so, to make such a fuss over the child, putting on this party with gifts from every member of the staff as if Rufus were his own—and that was the point, wasn't it? Pliny and Calpurnia were childless. Suetonius was childless too, but that was by choice; and he had left his wife—by their mutual consent—back in Rome. Pliny and Calpurnia were different. You only had to watch them around little Rufus. They seemed determined to be as much the boy's parents as Zosimus and Ione.

And there was an odd pair, when you thought about it—not that Suetonius thought about it much, but you couldn't help wondering. Zosimus was a precise, serious man of about thirty, a talented reader and musician, a more than competent secretary, who had been born a slave in the household and later freed. He was deeply loyal to Pliny, his former master, now his patron. But as a father he was ill at ease, awkward with the boy, as if he hardly knew what to do with him.

How different was Ione! She was a minx. Pretty, vivacious. Just beginning to show signs of a new pregnancy that rounded her features becomingly. She had been purchased as a girl, Suetonius gathered, and trained as a lady's maid. It wasn't known where she came from, probably sold by her starving parents, but Greek, of an uneducated variety, was her native tongue. She and Calpurnia were very close, more so perhaps than was proper for a mistress and her servant; always whispering together, sharing secrets like a pair of sisters. About five years ago, Pliny had freed Ione and married her to Zosimus. All rather sudden, one would have thought. And that young man couldn't believe his good fortune. He was devoted to her—you only had to see how he gazed at her. But Ione seemed—to Suetonius' observant eye—perhaps a little less in love with him.

No question, though, that she loved her son. Rufus had been lured away from the goat with more honey cake and now Ione was hugging him and dabbing at his face with a napkin while he squirmed. Meanwhile, the older children had usurped Rufus' hoop and his hobby horse and were racing up and down the marbled hall with shrieks of laughter.

In the midst of this merriment, a slave appeared to announce a stranger at the door. Pliny ordered him shown in and greeted him with a smile. Which was not returned.

"And you are—?"

"Timotheus, sir. The tutor. Diocles asked me to present myself to you and your, ah, wife." He pronounced the last words—*he gyne sou*—as if a wife were some fantastic beast in whose existence he only half believed. In Timotheus' world wives were rarely seen, still less heard. He was a sour-faced man, fifty-ish, with sharp features and watery eyes. He clutched a satchel filled with scrolls, the tools of his trade. A tired man sent to do a distasteful job.

"Yes, yes, of course! Remarkably prompt of our friend, I hadn't expected you so soon. Do come in. My wife will be delighted to meet you. I'm sure you two will get on—yes, well—'Purnia, come here, my dear…your new tutor."

She regarded the newcomer doubtfully with her large, dark eyes. "Delighted to meet you, sir," she said in halting Greek. Timotheus winced at her accent.

"Sit down, Timotheus, have something to eat." Pliny burbled. "Happy occasion this. After dinner we can discuss your fee, show you to your room. Perhaps you'll recite something for us this evening? Some light verse? I dabble myself, you know. Here, let me introduce you to everyone—" The tutor looked as if he had just tasted something unpleasant. But Pliny seemed not to notice, he loved playing host.

Soon enough Rufus developed a stomach ache from too many honey cakes and Ione carried him off to bed. Pliny followed them with his eyes until they passed through the door. Timotheus was prevailed on to recite something from a comedy and, though he did it not nearly so well as Zosimus, Pliny was effusive in his praise. Pliny's dinners never lasted long after sundown. The dining room emptied as families drifted off to their living quarters throughout the palace.

Pliny and Calpurnia lay in bed, wrapped in each other's arms, warm with love-making, the covers a tangle at the foot of the bed. Pliny inhaled her hair; he loved the smell of it.

"I wish you didn't have to go away so soon," she said.

"Can't be helped. So much to do."

"I could come with you."

"Out of the question, my dear. We'll be on the road day after day for a month or more. No place for a woman. Besides, I need you here."

"Do you, really?"

"You're the governor's lady. I'm leaving Suetonius behind to run the office but you will represent us socially. Meet people, entertain them, just like at home. You're wonderful at that sort of thing. You'll do us proud, as always."

And she would, but he never knew what it cost her. She was a matron of twenty-eight, beautiful, clever, accomplished—everyone said so—and yet the frightened fourteen-year-old bride that she had once been still trembled within her. She was a country girl, raised amid the mountains and lakes of northern Italy, who had suddenly found herself married to a man more than twice her age, a Roman senator, a lawyer, the nephew of a famous uncle, a man with important friends, the emperor's confidante. Her mother had died giving birth to her and her father had died not long afterward, fighting on the Danube frontier. Her grandfather had raised her—how she missed that dear man!

Pliny came from their part of the country; the two families had known each other for ages. His first wife had died and he wanted another. He was a kindly, gentle man, though not quite the husband of her girlish dreams. He seemed to her, in fact, more a father than a husband. The courtship, the wedding, the move to Rome, that vast and dizzying metropolis—all so fast. She had felt as though she were moving in a dream where one scene melted into another without sense or logic. She hadn't loved him then—how could she have? And, anyway, marriage wasn't about love, as her grandfather admonished her; that was only in poetry. Yet, Pliny's love for her was an extraordinary thing. When they were apart, he wrote her love letters that made her blush. And in time she grew to admire his generosity, his patience, his good humor; to take pride in his triumphs; to feel tenderly toward him. And yes, finally, to love him as a woman should love a man.

It had been hard at first. Though hardly more than a child, she was suddenly the mistress of an elegant town house on the Esquiline, surrounded by slaves whom she was expected to manage, while playing the hostess to clever, powerful men and their sharp-eyed wives. Somehow she had managed. She had made her husband proud of her. She had run his house, entertained his friends with her singing and skill with the lyre, would have borne his children, if—no, she wouldn't think of that now. Yet always that little girl that she had been, the one who cried into her pillow during those first nights while her husband slept placidly beside her—that little girl was still *her*.

"Of course," she said. "I'll be fine. There's plenty to keep me busy—the redecorating, my Greek lessons, and I have Ione for company. We'll console each other while you men are off putting the world to rights. And I think I want to start painting again."

"Do you? Splendid!" Her eccentric hobby delighted him, precisely because no other Roman woman would do such a thing—and she had a real talent.

"I want to paint Rufus, capture him at this age. They change so fast."

"Ah."

They were silent then for a while.

"And you," she poked him playfully, "you mustn't skip meals, and don't overtire yourself, and remember to keep your chest warm."

Pliny gave her a tender kiss. "Hush now, go to sleep. It'll soon be dawn and then I'm off."

But dawn came with a sickening lurch of the floor that threw them both out of bed. The floor buckled and a water jug on the bedside table fell to the floor and smashed. The shaking lasted only moments but when it stopped the bedroom wall was crazed with cracks and plaster dust hung in the air. Pliny lay on top of his wife, shielding her with his body, his heart hammering. From distant parts of the palace he heard shouts and cries for help. Then there was the sound of running footsteps and Zosimus and Ione burst through the door—their bedroom was close by—Ione holding Rufus to her, the child screaming.

"Patrone!"

"We're all right. Give us a minute. I want everyone outside in the courtyard, at once. See to it."

Zosimus dashed off. Ione helped Calpurnia to her feet and together they tried to comfort the child.

Damage to the palace, it turned out, was slight, only one roof had fallen in and no one was badly hurt. But from the top of the wall Pliny looked out over the city and saw, through an ochre haze, smoke rising in half a dozen places. The sight brought with it a sudden overpowering memory of the explosion of Vesuvius—the buried towns, the flaming countryside, the refugees stunned by disaster. He had been seventeen years old and barely escaped with his life. It still haunted his dreams.

With an effort, he shook off the memory. Fire and looting were their twin enemies now. He ordered his soldiers into the streets to protect the treasury and the temples. He had only two cohorts of auxiliaries, a pitifully small force; they would have to do their best. With his *lictors* and a gang of public slaves he raced through the rubble-strewn streets to the marketplace where several shops were ablaze, the air filled with flying cinders. To his amazement, he found the citizens simply standing and staring, doing nothing to extinguish the flames. Trajan had taken the extraordinary step of banning every kind of private association in the province—burial societies, workers' clubs, trade guilds, cult associations, even something as innocent as a volunteer fire department—on the grounds that they always turned into political cabals. Pliny and his men, with much yelling and shoving, got bucket brigades organized. By nightfall the worst was over. He left the scene only when Marinus, his physician, seconded by Calpurnia, insisted that he return to the palace and rest. He was already composing in his head a letter to the emperor begging him to authorize a fire brigade, which he would guarantee to supervise closely. But he knew what the answer would be.

Pliny delayed his departure until some degree of order was restored. Within a week, rubble was carted off and weakened walls were shored up, shops reopened, the taverns and brothels of the harbor returned to bustling life. Yet a sense of dread persisted. Street corner soothsayers harangued the crowds with dire warnings, you could see fear in the eyes of ordinary citizens and even within his own household. Little Rufus wouldn't let his mother out of his sight. Calpurnia looked tense.

An earthquake is a sign from the gods. Why had Poseidon the Earth-Shaker chosen this particular moment to strike the ground beneath their feet? Was it because a new governor had arrived who would shake them and squeeze them and bend them to his will? Or was it a warning to the Roman to tread lightly? Pliny was not a man who believed in omens. Most of the time. He ordered sacrifices to Poseidon at his temple near the harbor and led the procession himself. What more could he do? Finally, his departure could not be put off any longer. But as he set out at last on the road to Prusa he sent up a silent prayer that all would be well.

Chapter Six

A week later
The 5th day before the Kalends of October

"Got herself pregnant by her slave? What a little fool!"

"I can hardly believe it of her, the mousey thing."

"It's true. Why else did Fabricius send her back to Rome?"

"That man! No wonder she played around."

"Well, ladies, be honest. How many of us have tried it on with a slave—thought about it anyway?"

"These wretched Bithynians? I'd rather do it with a donkey!"

"Now, Nubians. When we were stationed in Alexandria I had six Nubian litter bearers."

"They carried you by day and you carried them by night?"

"Ask me no questions."

"Faustilla, you're terrible!"

"I wish I were in Alexandria. Or Antioch, or anyplace but here!"

"My husband goes to Antioch on business twice a year, never takes me, though."

"Well, my astrologer assures me I'm going to travel someplace exciting."

"He probably means Dacia. That's exciting, you can dodge arrows."

"Oops! Sorry."

"Memmia, you're soused already. You there, whatever your name is, come here and mop this up and pour us more wine. Why do you stand there like a post?"

"Well, what else is there to do but drink? Where is Calpurnia, anyway? I'm starving. Late to her own party, what manners!"

"She's an odd one, no mistake. Too quiet."

"Stuck up, I say. The way she looks at you, you don't know what she's thinking."

"I like him, though. Sense of humor, anyway. Not like mine."

"I don't know. My husband says he's all talk and no action."

"Can I ask, does anyone know a doctor they can trust? I'm at my wit's end."

"What, is your youngest sick again?"

"The poor thing. Children! We go through torture to bring them into the world just to worry ourselves sick over them. I swear by Juno I think I'd rather be childl—"

"Ssh! She's coming!"

"Please forgive me, ladies. I've been all morning with my tutor, we lost track of the time." Calpurnia, out of breath from racing up the stairs, settled herself on her couch in the small upstairs dining room."

"You're taking it quite seriously, Greek." This was Faustilla, the wife of Pliny's staff officer Nymphidius, a ribald old lady who had been born in Claudius' reign. She gave Calpurnia an indulgent smile. "I mean we all speak it enough to talk to the cook but why on earth do you want to go reading Homer, or whatever he's set you to."

In fact, Timotheus was dragging her through the *Odyssey's* archaic Greek line by line, which was not what she wanted at all, but she couldn't persuade the man to simply talk to her. She wouldn't admit this to Faustilla, though. "It keeps my mind occupied for one thing. Haven't you ever wondered why Latin and Greek have exactly the same words for father and mother but quite different ones for son and daughter?"

This was met by blank stares. Clearly, they hadn't.

"Timon, you can start serving the fish course," Calpurnia said in painfully correct Greek to her head waiter. She had taken a lesson from her husband and made it her first task to learn the name of every servant in the household.

Such airs! Fannia smiled to her couch-mate, Cassia, behind her hand. Conversation subsided while plates were passed and the women settled down to eat. Calpurnia and Pliny had brought their own chef with them from Rome but he had fallen ill en route and they had been forced to leave him behind in Athens. She had had to find a local replacement when they arrived. The man came with good references, probably forged. The roast hares were underdone, the grilled smelts were burnt black. Everyone tried not to notice.

Fabia, Balbus' wife, belched and spoke around a mouthful of food: "Poor you, Calpurnia, living in this shambles. Can't the governor requisition better quarters?" She gestured with a thick arm at the peeling fresco on the wall. It was unkind, and meant to be. Malice glittered in her eyes.

Calpurnia would not allow this woman to make her angry. She forced a smile. "Soon to be repaired. I've made my own sketches for a mythical landscape, children riding on the backs of centaurs, a temple in the distance. I'll paint some of it myself, workmen will do the rest."

Silence. The women were dumbfounded. Cassia, an engineer's wife, wrinkled her small nose and giggled. "The smell of that hot wax, the mess, really!" Embarrassed laughter around the table. An arch, knowing look from Fabia that said *What do you expect?*

The luncheon was on the verge of being a disaster. How Calpurnia loathed these gatherings, and yet she felt compelled to go through with them. She had endured many such occasions in Rome too, but there she was one senator's wife among many, not required to play a role that felt too big for her. This was different. She felt their resentment, their envy. And she was all alone, without her husband's boundless good humor and sociability to give her cover.

"We've heard that you and your husband are on intimate terms with our emperor and his wife," said Cassia brightly. What's she like?"

"Yes, tell us about Plotina," the others chorused.

"She's very nice," said Calpurnia.

"And...?"

"A very kind and sensible woman."

The wives couldn't conceal their disappointment.

"Well, what about *him*, Trajan?" Cassia pressed on. "People say he drinks too much and is too fond of little boys."

"People say a great many things they know nothing about," Calpurnia replied. She knew she was handling this wrong, could see the resentment in their faces. *Give them what they want*, she told herself, *be one of them, unbend.* But she could not.

Then Fannia, the wife of Caelianus, Pliny's chief clerk, gave a little cough. "And how is your husband, dear? Have you heard anything from him?" Fannia was the closest Calpurnia had to an ally among this nest of bewigged and bejeweled vipers. Unfortunately, her husband's status was lower than the other husbands represented here, and status, among them, was everything.

"I've had one letter from him, a short one. He's terribly busy." Gods, how she missed him! She had written him four letters in the past week.

"Enjoy it while you can," said Faustilla, sucking her fingers. "Nymphidius hasn't written me a single word. See if I care. He can stay away as long as he likes." Her husband was traveling with Pliny.

"You mean to say you don't miss him at night?" This was Memmia, who had managed in the meantime to spill another glass of wine on herself. Her tongue darted out over her lips wickedly.

"Why, the old man hasn't had it up in years. And I've got my 'pacifier', if you know what I mean."

"Hush, Faustilla, you're awful!"

Faustilla was not to be deterred. Her old, pouched eyes twinkled. "Had it made for me years ago by a shoemaker. This long, thick as your wrist, stuffed with wool, leather as smooth as a baby's bottom. Borrow it any time you like."

"Calpurnia, dear, excuse us, some of us aren't fit company," Atilia interrupted hastily. "And now, my dear, I'm going to presume on our short acquaintance." She gestured for silence, turned to the others, and explained, "Calpurnia and I met quite by chance in front of the temple of Asclepius the day Pancrates returned and then again a few nights ago at Fabia's. Well, ladies, I have a surprise for all of you—remember, Calpurnia dear, I told you I could arrange it. I daresay you didn't believe me. I've asked Pancrates to join us here today. Oh, my husband and I know him well. He's truly a marvel. And he's so anxious to meet you, Calpurnia. He's in the foyer now."

Before she could be stopped, Atilia was up and out the door. She returned a moment later with her prize. Calpurnia half rose from her couch in anger. How dare the stupid woman bring this charlatan into her home! But the wives gathered around him, all talking at once in happy wonderment. He ignored them all but, striding across the room to Calpurnia's couch, he stood before her and inclined his head. She had had barely a glimpse of him that day when he entered the temple to the wild cheers of his devotees. She only remembered the snake with its glittering scales that enveloped his shoulders like some obscene garment.

Now, at close range—and without the snake, the gods be thanked!—she saw him entire, and felt the force of the man. He was tall and dressed in a long-sleeved, unbelted tunic of some delicate white stuff that hung straight from his shoulder to his ankle. His black hair spilled in ringlets down his back, he had a hooked nose that curved toward his chin, his matted beard was streaked with gray. His complexion was swarthy like one of the southern barbarians (he accomplished this by staining himself with the juice of almonds) and, like them, his feet were bare. His bright, black eyes, sunk in sockets like twin caves, moved constantly as though seeing things hidden from others. He fixed them on her. "Lady, I will speak to you alone." It was a voice that presumed, that commanded.

Calpurnia's mind raced. Should she order the servants to throw him out? But plainly this man was not just some street corner diviner; he had an enormous following in the town. What might they do if she treated their oracle with disrespect? Then, too, Atilia, insufferable as she was, must not be slighted. Her husband was a pillar of the expatriate business community, a group they needed to conciliate. What would Pliny do? No matter, she was in charge, she must decide. He looked at her unblinking, waiting for her answer. And, in spite of herself, she was curious. Even if he was a howling madman, she thought, an interview with him was preferable to prolonging this gruesome lunch.

"Come this way," she said, standing up. Seven pairs of envious eyes followed them out of the room.

She led him to her studio, which was just down the hall; a room fragrant with wax and oil, cluttered with jars of pigments, braziers, easels, a table littered with brushes and spatulas, a pair of stools. They stood and faced each other. His dark eyes searched her face. "You don't like them, do you, those women? You shouldn't. You are more intelligent than they are, you have a purer spirit. I feel it."

Calpurnia laughed nervously. "Is this your stock in trade, flattery? I imagine no one quarrels with you if you tell them only pleasant things. You know nothing about me, sir."

Pancrates ignored this. He let his eyes wander around the little room, examining the pictures, in various states of completion, that sat on easels and hung from the walls. "Why do you paint? A painting is nothing but the shadow of a shadow."

She said nothing. She wasn't going to argue with this man about her art.

"And why do you paint only children? As I was coming in, I met a little boy racing down the corridor on his hobbyhorse. You've painted his face here, and here on these Cupids. Now that I look, I see him everywhere. But he isn't you son, is he?"

How could he know this? "Who are you?" she demanded. "Where do you come from?"

"I see I've angered you. Forgive me, lady." For the first time he smiled, showing a wide space between his front teeth. "Where I come from is no matter, but where I have been. I have travelled in India. I have seen the *martichora* with its human head and its long tail that shoots arrows. And I have seen the pygmies and the men who stand on their heads and shade themselves with their feet. I have lived with the Brahmans on top of their sacred hill and watched them rise into the air when they pray to the Sun. And I have seen the giant bearded serpents that live in that land and I have brought one home with me. With the aid of its spirit, I have advised kings and princes in every region of the world."

His long, brown fingers wove patterns in the air as he spoke; she could hardly tear her eyes from them. His voice was deep, thrilling. If Calpurnia's Greek had been better she would have caught a whiff of the wharf, the alley in his accent.

"So," he said," I have told you something about myself. Now I will tell you about *your*self. I sense sorrow in you—sorrow connected with a physical ailment." He touched his hands to his forehead. "Here? No." Keeping his eyes on her face, he lowered his hands to his chest. "Here?" The hands slid down his chest. "The stomach? No." They slid lower, level with his hips. Suddenly she could not breathe.

"Ah! I thought so. You lost your baby and now you are barren."

Stunned, she started to turn away but he held her chin and made her look at him. She felt herself trembling.

"Tell me." His voice like the voice of a god.

"I was fourteen…just a girl." Her breath came in sobs. "I didn't know what was the matter. And then the pain, the blood…I nearly died. And since then…we've tried everything. Doctors, spells, potions, I've slept in temples for healing dreams, sacrificed to Juno and Diana, Isis. And all the time, my husband, so kind, so patient. He has never reproached me, but I know, I know what he feels. We don't talk about it." Her shoulders worked with grief.

While she spoke he kept his eyes on her, his head tilted slightly to the left. They had begun by standing an arm's length apart.

She realized now that they were sitting, facing each other, almost knee to knee. She didn't remember how that happened. And she was speaking in her own language now—Greek abandoned—but he understood her. Finally, she swallowed hard and wiped her face with the fold of her *palla*. She felt naked in front of him. What sorcery had he used to make her tell him what she had never told any stranger?

"There are cures for your condition that the Brahmans know."

"No! Stop it! There is no cure. I'm not a child anymore to believe such things."

He smiled and shrugged. "We'll speak of it another time. I will leave you with a happy thought. Someone new will soon come into your life."

She laughed harshly—angry at herself and him. "Is that all your wisdom? We've only been here a week, someone new comes into my life every day."

He stood up abruptly. "Thank you, lady. I'll see myself out. If you wish to see me again, I am at your service."

"Wait—"

But he was gone.

She sat a long time with her head in her hands, feeling—what? Shaken, violated, hopeful? Had she just met someone extraordinary or only a clever fraud? She could not face going back to the dining room, to those hens who would peck at her, who would quiz her. As if in answer to her unspoken command, Ione appeared in the doorway. "Tell them I'm not feeling well. They may leave whenever they wish. Then come back to me." The freedwoman nodded and went out.

As Pancrates left the palace there was a smile on his lips. *No knowledge is ever wasted.*

The big covered wagon swayed and jolted, axles screeching, harness creaking as the mule team hauled it to the top of the long ridge that lay across the road from Prusa to Nicaea. Pliny tapped the driver's shoulder. "Hold up. Let the animals rest. Let us all rest a bit. Help me down." Even on a good Roman road like this, travel was exhausting. The driver jumped down from his seat, propped the stepladder against the front wheel and reached out to take the governor's hand. Behind them a train of a dozen wagons—an entire household on wheels—and a flanking squadron of cavalry sent up a cloud of dust into the brilliant blue sky.

Pliny stretched, flexed his shoulders, stamped his feet to get the blood flowing. They had been on the road since dawn and the sun was now high in the sky. "You know, this country reminds me of home," he said to Zosimus, who had climbed down beside him. "Mountains, gorges, pine forests, the bracing air," he inhaled deeply through his nostrils, "just like Comum. How I wish I were there! It's been too long."

Nymphidius trotted up on his horse. "We'll be lucky to reach the city by nightfall, sir. Up one blasted hill and down the next." The scenery had no charms for him.

"Nevertheless, call a half hour halt. And Zosimus, fetch me down my folder and a camp stool."

He spread his papers out on his knees, meticulous notes that described the unfolding disaster of the province's economy: everywhere new theaters, public baths, colonnades, aqueducts, all badly planned, unfinished, and left in ruins, leaving nothing behind but a welter of accusations and indictments for corruption which he, sitting on his *tribunal* hour after weary hour had to adjudicate. He was already sick to death of it, and he had only just started. After a few moments, he pushed it all away in disgust. "No. Zosimus, get me my writing kit and ask a messenger to come here. I owe Calpurnia a letter."

And Pliny drifted into pleasant contemplation of his happy and capable partner, safe at home.

Chapter Seven

The 4th day before the Kalends of October
The sixth hour of the night

That night she could not sleep. Finally, she gave up and went to wake Ione who slept in the bedroom next to hers.

"What should I think? Am I being a fool? Everything he claimed to *sense* about me he could have guessed or heard somewhere. Atilia and the others gossip about everyone, surely about me too. But if you'd seen his eyes…"

"And he said he could cure you, 'Purnia?"

She nodded, looked away.

Whenever they were alone together Ione called her by her pet name; only in the presence of others did she call her *matrona*, lady. Although most Roman matrons did not consider themselves properly cared for with any fewer than a dozen maid servants, Calpurnia was content to have Ione alone. They had become almost like sisters, especially now in this strange place where she had no one else to turn to. She had had a younger sister once, a lovely girl who had died of a long wasting illness when Calpurnia was ten. Her death had left a hole in her life. Ione was about the age her sister would have been and somehow this ex-slave—pretty, saucy, barely literate, with no family, no past—was able to fill it in spite of the barrier of rank that divided them.

"Then you must believe him. Who can doubt an oracle?" As simple as that. "Will you see him again?"

"I don't know. My husband won't allow him under our roof, I know that."

Ione winked. "Things can always be arranged."

As they talked, the sun came up. Rufus woke up and while they fed him breakfast and played with him Calpurnia's mood improved. Around the third hour of the morning the idea suddenly took her to visit the art gallery in the temple of Zeus. Diocles had recently made a gift to his fellow citizens of sculptures and paintings, some of them priceless originals. It was the talk of the town. She and Ione would go together and she would bring her easel, too, and sketch.

The gallery, which occupied a portico in the temple precinct, was crowded when they got there. The exhibition was everything she expected and more. Among the statues of bronze and painted marble she thought she recognized Praxiteles' *Artemis* and a *Heracles* by Lysippus—copies, of course, though good ones. But it was the paintings that took her breath away— portraits, landscapes, mythological scenes by the great names—Apelles, Zeuxis, Polygnotos. After surveying them all, she ordered her slave to set up her easel in front of a large *Niobe Mourning Her Dead Children* by Parrhasios; and what instinct drew her to that she would not acknowledge even to herself. She tacked a parchment to the easel, seated herself on her stool, and began to sketch in charcoal.

As she worked, onlookers came and went but she became gradually aware of a young man who stood beside her, resting his weight on one muscular leg, his hip thrust out, his arms folded, his eyes moving up and down from the original to her copy.

He saw that she had noticed him. "The eyes," he said. "Niobe's eyes. The despair in them. The film of tears. How do you think he did that? Thin washes of wax layered on ever so carefully, don't you think? Armenium, malachite for his pigments, but just a hint. Too much would spoil it. That's how I'd do it, anyway. But, of course, I'd make a hash of it." He smiled, showing a crooked front tooth.

She didn't quite catch all of this, he spoke so rapidly. But it sounded impressive. Politeness required her to say something. "Are you a painter by profession, then?"

He made a wry face. "Me? I have no profession. My family owns land, quite a lot of it."

She looked at him more closely now. How stupid to think he was a common artisan. His purple-bordered cloak and his rings were expensive. He was young, twenty perhaps, if that; clean shaven; oiled hair, black as ink and smelling of crocus, curling over his ears; nose and chin so finely sculpted that he might have modeled for Praxiteles himself; dark eyes under heavy black brows—they watched her with amusement.

He made her a small bow. "I'm Agathon, son of Protarchus, grandson of Neocles, great grandson of—I could go on but I won't. You've probably heard of us."

"I'm afraid not."

"Well," he laughed, "that's to my advantage." There was a pause. "And what shall I call you?"

"She glanced up at the painting. "Call me Niobe."

"An ill-omened name for such a pretty woman."

"You're very bold."

"It saves time." His smile, mischievous, slightly mocking.

What presumption! It was time to put an end to this. "I expect your mother will be looking for you."

"You see!" He snapped his fingers. "We've only just met and we're already fighting like old friends."

She wanted to escape but couldn't see how to. She searched for something to say. "Diocles has made the city a wonderful gift—all this."

"He can afford it." This was said with knowing familiarity, one aristocrat of another. "You're Roman, aren't you? The accent. Your husband's stationed here?" He had noticed her wedding ring.

And this was the moment at which she should have said, *I am the wife of Gaius Plinius Secundus, governor of the province.*

But she didn't.

"We've only just arrived. You must excuse my Greek."

"No one could excuse your Greek, but I can help you improve it, if you like."

"Do you talk like this to every strange woman you meet?"

"No. Where did you learn to draw so well?"

And, to her surprise, she found herself explaining how she had loved to draw as a little girl. And then had seen some paintings in a little temple of Ceres near their estate and pestered her grandfather to buy her materials and an instruction book until he finally gave in. "And then, when I moved to Rome with my husband, oh! I went everywhere, saw everything. Myron's *Zeus* on the Capitoline, Phidias' *Athena* in the temple of Fortuna, paintings by Apelles in the temple of Diana…"

His mouth set in a thin line. The eyes were no longer laughing. She stopped, mortified. "Oh, I'm sorry. I shouldn't have—"

"Those pieces belong in Greek temples, lady, not Roman ones. To the victors belong the spoils. You looted them and took them back to Italy by the boatload, not because you care anything for art but only because they are worth money. Money is what you Romans understand. At least, you have the grace to blush." The insolent boy was gone; instead an angry young man stood before her.

"You don't—like us," was all she could think of to say. A governor's wife at a loss for words.

"You call us *Graeculi*—Greeklings."

"I don't."

"But your husband and his friends do, don't they?"

"They don't mean anything by it."

"No?"

"I'm sorry, I have to go." She stood up, looking desperately around the hall for Ione and saw her some distance away. Her maid was out of earshot but she was staring at them with a quizzical arched eyebrow.

"No wait." He reached out and touched her arm and a shock ran through her and suddenly she was overpoweringly aware of his scent and the heat of his body. "I'm behaving like a boor," he said. "I find the one Roman in the world who cares for art and I attack her. I should be whipped."

"Yes, well, no need for that. Look, I really must go, it's gotten late, I have things—"

"Come again tomorrow."

"What?"

"Well, look here, in your drawing. The hands aren't quite right. Hands are tricky. Maybe we can fix them."

"I really don't think so. Goodbye, Agamemnon."

"Agathon. Let my slave carry your things for you."

"No, thank you, mine can manage." He mustn't find out where she lived.

"I mean it. Tomorrow."

She fled.

In her room, Ione helped her unpin the top-heavy mass of curls from her forehead and unwind the chignon at the back. Calpurnia shook out her long, auburn hair. She breathed deeply, smiled.

"A glass of wine?" Ione held out the flagon.

"Please. And pour yourself one." The misery that had seemed to crush her heart that morning was gone like the fading memory of a bad dream.

"He's very good-looking."

"He's a boy. He made me feel like an old woman."

"You look like anything but an old woman," Ione laughed.

"And can you imagine, he invited me to go there again tomorrow."

"And will you?"

"Of course not."

But she did.

◇◇◇

Two weeks later
The 5th day before the Ides of October
The tenth hour of the day

"If you keep fidgeting I'll never get it right."

"My neck is stiff."

"Bah! I give up, I haven't the talent. It would take a master to capture your beauty and I, alas, am only an amateur."

"Let me see it."

The slanting rays of the afternoon sun sifted through the branches of the plane tree in the garden of Agathon's town house. Water plashed softly in the fountain, somewhere a bird sang. He turned the drawing board toward her and she saw herself staring back, as though she were looking at her reflection in a pool—the large eyes, the strong nose (*too big!* she always thought), the wide mouth and rounded chin. The long neck.

"You have more skill than you give yourself credit for. If someone were to recognize me in this…You won't show it to anyone will you?"

"I promise. Only I will gaze at it when you're away from me. I love you."

"Liar." But she was smiling. This handsome boy did love her and the knowledge of it excited her more than she wanted to admit.

"And I will call it 'A Portrait of Callirhoe'." This was his love name for her. "You deserve a name of your own," he had said on the second day they spent together. "A name that means something. What does *Calpurnia* mean except that you belong to your father's clan." Callirhoe—*beautifully flowing.* It was the name of the heroine in a romantic novel that everyone was talking about that summer. He had given her a copy, which she was working at in spare moments, though the Greek was hard.

"Say my name again," she said.

"Callirhoe." It did flow beautifully.

"Drink some more wine." He filled her cup.

"You'll make me drunk. I never get pissed at home." She used the low, slang word.

He laughed. "Your Greek's improving."

"Thanks to you, my dear, I can curse like a sailor. I said something to my tutor the other day, I thought the poor man would have apoplexy."

"You want to be careful about that. Sour old men like him carry tales."

"Oh, I told him I'd learned it from Ione."

"Ione! What a treasure she is! How would we manage without her?"

And this was true. Ione went everywhere with them, at a discreet distance, scouting to see if the coast was clear, inventing alibis to tell the other slaves, who anyway were convinced that all Roman women paraded wantonly around town whenever it pleased them. He had taken her to the Odeon to hear music, to the theater, to the race course; even for a picnic up in the wooded hills from where they saw the whole city spread out beneath them.

She loved the woods. They reminded her of her home in the foothills of the Alps, where she used to walk and climb as a girl among rocky precipices and rushing streams and ice cold lakes and pine trees that reached up to the sky. They had spent the day sketching, talking of this and that, walking under the brow of a mountain ridge that was said to resemble a woman's profile—he said it looked like her, she said it looked like a cow's hind end.

Of course, he knew by now who she was, who her husband was. She had feared he might run away when she told him, but he didn't. Too cocksure of himself to be frightened. He was full of questions about Rome—the great amphitheater, the baths, the palaces and gardens. How many villas did her husband own, how many slaves? How did she spend her time at home? Was it true that Roman women dined in mixed company and went wherever they pleased? All of which she was happy to answer until his questions veered too close to her personal life, her marriage. Then she would change the subject. She was determined not to betray any confidences.

Wherever she went with him she wore Greek clothing and a blonde wig that she never wore at home. Still, there had been a terrifying moment at the theater. They were finding their seats when Atilia and Faustilla passed right by her in the aisle, close enough to touch. Her heart stopped. What could she have said if they'd recognized her? When the play was over she had told Agathon that it was finished. What was she thinking? She must be out of her mind. She couldn't go on like this—glancing around to see who might be looking at them, pricking up her ears at the sound of every footstep, hearing suspicion in every voice. For two days she refused to see him. But then she thought she was being silly. What had she done, after all? Nothing compared to what some of the other wives got up to, she was sure of that. She let him hold her hand, kiss her cheek, and he hadn't demanded more. And soon Pliny would be home and she wouldn't be bored and lonely anymore and it would be all over—no more than a pleasant memory. Where was the harm, really? And so she had sent Ione to him with a message.

"I have a present for you," she said. She liked giving him presents. She unwrapped a little silver statuette of Artemis, no bigger than her hand. "My husband and I broke our journey at Ephesus and visited her temple. They sell them there."

"Thank you. I will pray to her every day."

"Who else do you pray to?"

"Tyche, Fortuna you call her. She rules our lives. She brought us together."

"No, Fate brought us together. You were foretold to me."

"Was I really?" He wanted to know how. She lied and said it was a dream. Not for his ears her meeting with Pancrates.

The sun went behind a cloud and suddenly it was chilly. She shivered.

"You're cold. Shall we go inside?"

"No, I love it here, the view of the bay from up here." The house was built on a hill, overlooking the sea. "And all this is yours?"

"The family owns it but my parents and brothers seldom come into town. My father's devoted to farming. I'm not. I'm a great disappointment to him. The estate's dull and so I live here unless I'm commanded home, which isn't often."

"And you aren't lonely."

He smiled, showing the crooked tooth that made his too perfect features just human after all. "I'm never lonely. Here—" He took a coverlet from the bench and wrapped it around her shoulders, folding his arms around her, lightly touching her breasts. Suddenly, he buried his face in the angle of her neck and kissed her. She lifted her face and he kissed her eyes, her lips. And she knew she should stop him but she couldn't. Pale fire ran beneath her skin—some poet had said that, and it was true. And she wanted him, this laughing Greek boy, as she had never wanted any man before. Finally, she broke away. They looked at each other, lips parted, breathing hard. Not knowing what to say.

◇◇◇

The following morning Suetonius came to see her while she was painting Rufus, who sat on Ione's lap. His expression was grim. She shot Ione a terrified look. Oh gods! Does he know, does he suspect something?

"I say, sorry to bother you."

"Yes?" She fought to keep her voice steady.

"Has Fabia said anything to you recently? Balbus' wife?"

"What?—No."

"It seems the fiscal procurator has gone missing. No one's seen him in the past three days. We've searched the city for him, questioned his staff. Nobody knows where he is. Either he's had an accident or something worse. I just thought his wife might have said something to you."

"No, we haven't spoken."

"That does it, then. We need Pliny here to deal with this. I'm going to send a courier after him and ask him to return at once. According to his itinerary he should be near Nicaea. He can be here in a matter of days."

She felt as though the ground had been suddenly cut from under her feet.

Chapter Eight

Seven days later
The 14th day before the Kalends of November
The second hour of the day

Pliny had not visited Balbus' villa since the night of that disagreeable dinner party and the thought of returning there gave him no joy, but interviewing Fabia seemed the logical place to begin.

Though it was early morning, the coast road that skirted the wooded hills outside the city was already crowded with coaches, farm wagons, donkeys with panniers full of produce headed for market, and Pliny's light two-wheeled carriage was slowed to a walking pace. He had decided to travel with only his senior *lictor*, Galeo, and a shorthand writer. The immense retinue that typically followed a governor wherever he went would only encumber him today and he wanted to approach Fabia as a concerned friend, not an investigating magistrate.

He had left Zosimus at home for a well-deserved rest. *Mehercule*, he needed a rest himself, he was bone tired. He had returned from Nicaea at speed—a three-day journey accomplished in two—and, arriving before dawn, had taken time only for a hurried bath, a bite to eat, and a quick conversation with Suetonius, roused from his bed. The fiscal procurator was still missing, work at the treasury had come to a standstill, and rumors were turning ugly. What could have happened to the man?

A glowering *janitor* met them at the door. Pliny remembered him. The man was built like an ox, with massive shoulders, folds of fat around his neck, and a chin that jutted like a boulder. He had the look of a retired gladiator; Pliny imagined him with the *secutor's* head-enveloping helmet and mail-clad sword arm, stalking his opponent in the arena. He led them to the atrium. If Pliny had expected to find Fabia distraught, red-eyed from weeping, angry even, he was disappointed. Her face was a mask, the eyes opaque. He didn't know her well enough to know what to make of this. Did the woman ever show emotion?

She settled her bulk onto a slender-legged chair that looked too fragile to support her and dismissed the slave with a wave of her ring-heavy hand. He hesitated a moment as though he were reluctant to leave her alone.

"Do we need *them*?" She indicated Pliny's attendants. He sent Galeo outside but motioned to the shorthand writer to keep his seat.

"I assure you, lady, I will do everything possible to find your husband. I appreciate how difficult—"

"I've already told your man, Suetonius, everything I know." Sharp, almost offensive.

Pliny was reminded again of her odd accent. Her tone took him aback, but he pressed on. "Yes, well perhaps something has been overlooked. When did you realize that your husband was missing? Be as precise as you can."

"Ten days ago, the fourth day before the Ides, the Day of the Sun. I saw him off in the morning. He didn't return for dinner."

"The Day of the Sun? That's a Chaldean custom, I believe, to name the days after the seven planets. Was your husband interested in that sort of thing?"

"He had an interest."

"Did he show any signs of unusual behavior in the days before he disappeared?"

She hesitated a fraction. "What do you mean, *unusual*?"

"What sort of mood was he in—worried, irritable, distracted? Did he say anything that struck you as out of the ordinary? Was he in difficulties of some sort? Are any of his belongings missing, any money?"

"What are you suggesting? You think he's run off?"

"Let's be frank with each other. Such things happen. Has he done anything like this before?"

"Anything like *what*? My husband was a good man and a loyal servant of the government. I defy you to prove he wasn't."

The short hand writer scratched away furiously on his tablet.

"I notice you just spoke of him in the past tense. You believe he's dead, then?"

"Well, what else?" Her color darkened, she half rose out of her chair.

"Then I must ask you who his enemies are."

"I have no idea."

"Well, what do you think happened to him?"

"Murdered by bandits, obviously. None of us is safe in this wretched country. They're all itching to cut our throats. I told him so but he wouldn't listen, not him."

"And yet the coast road is a busy thoroughfare all the way from here to the city, I've just been on it. And we've had no reports of bandits in the area."

She glared at him in silence. He felt as though he were interrogating a hostile witness on the stand instead of a woman who wanted her husband found. Pliny was more than a lawyer; he was the servant of an autocratic regime—even if, at the moment, it wore a benevolent face. Survival in this world meant being sensitive to every look, every word—spoken and unspoken, from a rival, a palace official, even a slave. Pliny had survived and thrived. His thoughts turned back to the Verpa case—that senatorial informer whose murder he had investigated fourteen years ago. How naïve he had been then, how easily taken in by appearances. He had learned much in the years since then. He felt certain she was concealing something, but pressing her further now would accomplish nothing. Unsympathetic as she was, she was still the wife of a high-ranking official who, one hoped, was still alive somewhere. There was nothing to be gained by making an enemy of her.

"May I just have a look in the *tablinum*?"

She looked for a moment as if she would refuse, then shrugged, got heavily to her feet, and led him into Balbus' office. The procurator plainly did not share Pliny's tidy habits. The room was strewn with scrolls, *tabellae*, and heaps of loose sheets piled everywhere. While Fabia stood watching him, Pliny made an attempt to sort through the mess in the hope that something would catch his eye. And something did: a sheaf of star charts and, underneath these, what appeared to be a handbook of astrology.

"Your husband is a *mathematicus*? You mentioned he counts the days as the Chaldeans do. Frankly, I wouldn't have suspected it of him. He strikes me as too practical a man for this sort of thing." Pliny, like his idol Cicero, was not a believer in that arcane science.

"He tries. He says it makes his head hurt. I don't know why he bothers." Pliny noted that Fabia was now being careful to speak of her husband in the present tense.

"If you don't mind, I'd like to borrow this."

"Whatever for?"

"I'm not sure. There may just be something helpful in it."

She shrugged. "Take it then."

"Well, I think I've seen enough for the moment. Might I just go out to your stables before I leave and speak to the stable hands."

"Why?"

"You have some objection?"

"I'll come with you."

"If you like."

"Mother—!" Just then a figure darted into the room. Pliny, with only a moment to observe him, got the impression of a youth of about sixteen, tall and painfully thin, the muscles and tendons like knotted cords under his skin. When the boy saw Pliny, he stifled a cry, turned and fled. Almost without thinking, Pliny rose and started after him but Fabia blocked his way, looking as if she might fight him. He stepped back and spread his hands in a placating gesture.

"Your son?" He recalled the figure that he and Calpurnia had glimpsed on the night of the dinner party.

"He isn't well. You'll leave him alone."

"I meant him no harm. May I talk with him?"

"You wanted to see the stables. Come, then."

The stableman and three young grooms leapt to their feet as Pliny and Fabia and the shorthand writer appeared in the wide doorway. They had been playing knucklebones on the floor. Pliny loved horses and passed many happy hours in his own stables, trading advice with his grooms. The stableman, a swarthy, bewhiskered man of middle age, came forward and ducked his head in respect. Pliny gave him an encouraging smile.

"How did your master travel to the city? By carriage?" There was no carriage anywhere that he could see.

The stableman shook his head. "Horseback, your honor. He liked to ride, for the exercise. Always said the city streets were too crowded for a carriage anyways."

"And who would ride with him?"

The man's eyes flickered for a second. "He rode alone."

"Always?"

"Yes."

"Where is his horse?"

"Missing."

"Really. In my experience, a riderless horse will nearly always find its way home. Was there anything unusual about that particular day when he left for the last time?"

The stableman studied his feet.

Fabia struck in, "I've already told you there was nothing unusual. If you don't mind, Governor, these men have work to do."

"Of course, madam. I have no more questions for the moment." He looked at her levelly. "If anyone has done harm to an officer of the Roman State, I will not rest until I bring that person to book. Rely upon it."

Fabia stood in the doorway and watched Pliny and his men mount their carriage and drive off. The boy came up silently and stood beside her. She circled his thin shoulders with a vast, protecting arm. "It's all right, my baby," she said.

Chapter Nine

Suspicion was written across Silvanus' beaky face. Pliny and his two attendants had gone straight from interviewing Fabia to the treasury building in the precinct of the Temple of Rome and Augustus in the center of the city. Sentries at the door had jumped to attention and Pliny sent one of them to fetch the chief accountant.

He eyed Pliny warily. "This is no place for you, Governor."

"That is not for you to say," Pliny snapped. "I'm here to learn what's become of your procurator." They sat in the accountant's cramped office. There was no chair for the shorthand writer, who was forced to take his notes standing up. Towering bookcases, crammed with scrolls, lined every wall. Only a small window admitted any light. A fit habitation for a mole, perhaps; scarcely for a human. No wonder the man was so pasty-faced. "Did you see Balbus the day he disappeared?"

Silvanus' jaws ground as though he were masticating food. It was a disconcerting habit that Pliny had noticed that night at Balbus' dinner party. His words came slowly as though each one must be thoroughly chewed before it could be spat out. "He never arrived that day."

"And what did you do?"

"Nothing."

"What did you do the next day when he didn't arrive?"

"Nothing."

"Well, what did you *think*?"

"That he was ill. The next day I inquired of his wife. Then I sent someone to your office."

"To your knowledge has he ever disappeared like this before?"

"No."

"Where do you think he might be?"

Silvanus' eyes focused somewhere over Pliny's right shoulder. The jaws went on working. "I don't know."

Pliny tried a different tack. "Tell me about yourself, Silvanus. Have you a family? Where do you live?"

The eyes momentarily met Pliny's with a look of alarm. *Am I being accused?* "I live here. I have no family."

"And you've been with Balbus a long time?"

"Eleven years. I was his slave at first. He emancipated me before a magistrate, all legal, I can prove it. I'm a Roman citizen." The point was clear. *You can't torture me.*

"What kind of administrator was he?"

"I've no complaints."

"Right." Pliny got swiftly to his feet. This was getting him nowhere. "Until Balbus reappears, if he does, I am assuming control of the treasury. Don't bother asking if I have the authority. I do. Now, I want a thorough tour of the premises and a rundown of your procedures, omitting nothing. Lead the way."

The jaws—just for a moment—stopped grinding.

Pliny had served a term as head of the Treasury of Saturn—the Roman State treasury—and knew what to look for. What he saw did not please him. The building, which had once housed the royal treasure of the kings of Bithynia, was a warren of cluttered rooms and crooked corridors built around a wide courtyard. One whole side of it was the counting room. Here were long tables at which sat public slaves. They should have been hunched over ledgers, calculating with their fingers. Instead, they sprawled idly on their benches, talking, throwing knucklebones. They barely looked up when Silvanus and Pliny entered. It seemed pointless to ask why no one was working.

"Take me to the vault," Pliny commanded.

The chief accountant lifted a trap door that lay at one end of the counting room and they descended a flight of stone steps that ended at an oaken door, secured by a massive bronze padlock. Silvanus produced the key from a wallet that hung at his belt and, with a grunt of effort, swung the door open. He lit a lamp inside.

Pliny found himself in a brick-lined chamber whose walls were lost in shadow. The air was hot and stale. A pyramid of iron-bound chests reached nearly to the low ceiling. Each chest was fastened with a lock and from each hung a parchment tag imprinted with a signet.

"How many keys are there?"

"Two. One for the procurator, one for me."

"And where is his?"

"Hanging in his office. I'll show it to you, if you like."

The land tax in silver was, as Pliny knew, assessed by the procurator upon each city in the province. Local magistrates apportioned the tax among the landowners, collected it, and sent the required amount in chests like these under seal to Nicomedia. Some of it moved overland in cumbersome wagons guarded by soldiers, the rest, collected from the coastal cities, came on navy warships. Everything possible was done to secure these shipments. Was it enough? Probably not. And in Bithynia-Pontus where corruption ran so deep? The question answered itself. Suspicions—almost certainties—were starting to take shape in his mind.

"Is all of this year's collection in?"

"Yes."

"How do you know?"

"I count the chests as they come in."

"And if a chest went astray? Would you know?"

"If the total didn't add up to the assessment, of course I would know. But it does add up."

"But do you open each chest and actually count the coin?"

"Of course not. We open them when we need to make disbursements."

"Open that one—over there."

"Why?"

"Open it."

Silvanus drew another key from his pouch, a smaller one, and unlocked the chest. Pliny looked in. It was full to the top with silver drachmas—the lifeblood of the Roman Empire. The tag read *Three talents, eleven minas, fifty-three drachmas. Sent under my seal. Polemon, Treasurer of Heraclea Pontica.* At a glance, it looked about right.

"Are you satisfied, Governor?"

"I am far from satisfied. I want a count of every coin of this year's collection. Tomorrow I will send you my clerk, Caelianus, to supervise this. As of this moment, I am posting guards at this door. No one, including you, is to enter until I say so. Hand over your key."

"But we have disbursements to make. The garrison to be paid, the sailors of the Pontic fleet, road repairs, earthquake damage, and the amount we have to send to Rome."

Pliny left the chief accountant still protesting—the man seemed to have found his voice at last—and returned to the palace, suddenly overcome with a feeling of infinite weariness.

He found Calpurnia in the garden, reading in the slanting rays of the late afternoon sun. It was early October yet the weather continued unseasonably mild. Soon enough, though, they would be driven indoors by frigid winds blowing in off the sea. She put down her scroll when she saw him and offered her mouth to be kissed.

"I'm so glad you're home," she said, "why didn't you wake me this morning?" He sank down on the bench beside her. She took his hand. "You look tired."

"And you look more beautiful than I even remembered. You're thriving here, aren't you? I knew you would. What are you reading? Homer?" He picked up the *capsa* and read the label: "*Chaireas and Callirhoe by Chariton of Aphrodisias.* One of those romances the Greeklings are so fond of?" He put it down with an indulgent smile. "Is it any good?"

"It's silly. A girl who's captured by pirates on her wedding day. Husband goes searching for her."

"Where did you get it?"

"At a book stall."

How easy the lie. She had not premeditated it, yet there it was on her tongue as though only waiting to be spoken. "Gaius, tell me what's going on. Balbus is missing? I couldn't get much out of Suetonius."

"I'm calling the staff together now. We have to do something, though damn me if I know what. I'll leave you to your book. We'll talk at dinner."

Pliny paced up and down the room with his hands behind his back while the others followed him with their eyes. Nymphidius, the old soldier, scarred and lame, who had come out of retirement to serve with him; Postumius Marinus, his physician, always frowning through his tangle of gray beard; Caelianus, his clerk, a precise, observant little man; Aquila, his chief centurion, a hard-featured man, armored in greaves and a corselet of bronze scales; Suetonius, a shade too clever and rather too full of himself, the object of the others' jealousy; and Zosimus, the lowest in status but the closest to Pliny in affection.

Pliny had just finished the recitation of his interviews with Fabia and Silvanus.

"You're thinking he's embezzled tax money and run off?" said Caelianus. "Why?"

"Because if we assume that he's disappeared of his own volition, it has to be something at least that serious. And it will be your job to see if he has. I'm sending you over to the treasury tomorrow. I want it all counted down to the last *obol* and compared to the tallies. Take as many men as you need but work fast."

Suetonius adjusted the fold of a new cloak so that it hung just so. "And if he hasn't disappeared on purpose?"

"That is an alternative I would rather not contemplate. The assassination of a Roman official could set this province on fire."

"Still, I just don't see it. Balbus has been in public service for twenty-some years and no one's ever accused him of anything, so far as we know. The emperor appointed him, after all, and Trajan is scrupulous about these things. And does he strike you as a runner? Running is a last resort. Surely he'd try other ways to protect himself first—trying to bribe *you*, for example. He hasn't has he?"

Pliny gave him a wry smile. "I like to think my reputation for probity has preceded me."

"Oh, quite." Only Suetonius could banter with him like this.

"Still," said Zosimus. He was careful to raise his hand and wait to be called on like a bashful schoolboy, conscious that the others wondered why Pliny included him in these meetings at all. "Still, that villa, all that art? Could he afford all that on a procurator's salary?"

"Excellent point, my boy," said Pliny. Zosimus, at thirty-four, was far from being a boy, but to Pliny he was still "my boy" and probably would be until he sprouted grey hairs. "But not conclusive. No one doubts that a procurator squeezes people, accepts *presents*, maybe persuades his *friends* to sell him things at knockdown prices. You know how it goes. It's a fine line, and I'm sure Balbus knows how to walk it carefully. Helping himself to the taxes, however, is another thing."

Nymphidius massaged his swollen knee; he suffered cruelly from arthritis. "I agree with Suetonius, I don't think he's run. And if he hasn't, then someone's done away with him. Not bandits, you're right about that, Governor. The coast road's busy in the morning, someone would have seen, and he disappeared before he ever reached the treasury—that is if we believe Silvanus."

"But can we believe him?" said Pliny, throwing himself into his chair. He pinched the bridge of his nose between his thumb and forefinger. "They could be in it together. I don't like the looks of that man."

"And we can't tickle this fellow Silvanus, just a little?" Aquila growled, flexing his fingers as though in anticipation of having a go at the chief accountant.

"A Roman citizen? You know better than that, Centurion. Trajan would be furious if he found out. *Not in keeping with the spirit of our reign.* No. If I find prima facie evidence of guilt, I can send him to Rome for trial, but that's all I can do."

"On the other hand," Suetonius put in, "you remember them at the dinner. The way Balbus humiliated him, called him ugly and stupid in front of all of us. I should think if anyone would like to put a knife between Balbus' ribs it's our friend Silvanus."

"*If* we find him with a knife in his ribs I will give that serious consideration."

"So, then, Governor," said Marinus, "we wait until the money's counted?"

"I have no better idea at the moment. We simply have nothing to go on."

"And in the meantime, will you continue your circuit of the province?"

There was a long silence while Pliny sat with his chin in his hand. "I'll give it a few more days here," he said at last, "and hope that something turns up. Then I must go back. Damn the man, he couldn't have picked a worse time to disappear! What I'm uncovering at Prusa, Nicaea, Caesarea—the rot goes much deeper than I thought. Rich men are lining their pockets while the province is on the brink of rebellion. And meanwhile our procurator is—where? He tried to conjure some mental image of Balbus—Balbus on a ship, sailing for a distant port; Balbus in a coach, racing for the Persian frontier; Balbus lying dead and unrecognized in a gutter somewhere; even Balbus hiding in his own house right under their noses. He couldn't make any of it seem real. He stood up. "Enough for this evening, gentlemen. Thank you. I'll let you go to dinner. Perhaps tomorrow our minds will be sharper, I hope mine will."

Ione tucked Rufus in and kissed him. The little boy clutched the front of her dress with his small hands. "It's all right, darling, we're right next door, I'll leave the lamp on. If you have bad dreams again you can come and get in our bed." He had been like this ever since the earthquake.

Zosimus was already undressed and in bed. "You can't imagine what it's been like," he said. "I don't know how the master keeps going. I've seen him stopping on stairs sometimes to catch his breath. I'm worried about him. His uncle had a weak chest too, it's what killed him. Marinus wants to bleed him but he keeps putting him off. And now this other business. Anyway, how are you? What's my girl been up to?"

"Oh, it's been quite dull around here. Must you go back soon?"

"Who knows?" He reached up and drew her down to him. "I love you."

She purred, "Are you sure you're not too tired?"

"Not a bit."

She took his *mentula* in her hand. "Has it missed me?"

"Terribly."

"It hasn't been anywhere else, has it?"

"Promise."

She pulled her *tunica* up over her head and tossed it across the room. She straddled his hips as he lay on his back and he rose up to meet her.

"'Purnia, I've missed you terribly," Pliny said. They had shared a light meal together in their chambers and were now undressing for bed, though it was still early. "I brought you a present. Here, unwrap it."

"Oh, Gaius, it's beautiful!" It was a necklace strung with pearls and little gold oak leaves. "I'll wear it tomorrow."

He lay down on the bed, closed his eyes, stretched, and sighed. She lay down beside him. "Have you been keeping busy, my dear?" he asked. "Tell me what you've been doing."

And she might have said, *I've met a charming young Greek, a local landowner's son. And guess what, he knows about painting, he's actually taught me a few things. Of course, he thinks he's in love with me—an old matron like me! You must ask him to dinner one night soon, you'll like him.*

But the words would not come.

Tomorrow, she thought, I'll tell him tomorrow. In fourteen years of marriage she had never kept a secret from her husband. Her dear husband, so good, so loving—although, she thought, he had never really been a boy, not an impertinent, winking, charming boy like Agathon. No, don't think of Agathon. That was over, a brief fantasy, like a waking dream, and now her life would flow again in its accustomed channel. As she wanted it to. Truly she did.

Pliny's eyes were closed and he snored softly. She suddenly felt a great tenderness for him. She pressed her body against his and slid her hand between his legs. He stirred but did not wake. *The poor man, let him sleep.*

But there was no sleep for her.

Chapter Ten

The 13th day before the Kalends of November
The first hour of the day

The next morning Caelianus was ushered into the dining room just as Pliny was finishing his breakfast. The clerk looked worried.

"I've just been to the treasury, sir, to start the counting. Silvanus isn't there. No one's seem him since yesterday."

Pliny was gripped by a sudden premonition. He threw down his napkin, called for his bearers, and the two men set off at once.

"Where are the chief clerk's living quarters?" he demanded of the door slave who admitted them.

It was a bare, cold room—almost a cell—that Silvanus called home: the furnishings Spartan, the floor bare stone, the walls unadorned save for a threadbare tapestry that covered the wall behind his narrow cot.

"Look over here, sir," said Caelianus. "Scuff marks on the floor, like something might have been dragged over it."

"Leading to or from his bed, no, more likely from the wall behind it. Here, help me move the bed."

Pliny tore aside the tapestry and ran his fingers over the plastered wall. "Look here, there's a crack. He thumped the wall, producing a hollow sound. In an instant he and Caelianus, on hands and knees, had pulled away a low door cut into the false wall and exposed Silvanus' secret. The compartment was just large enough to hold three or four of the regulation treasury chests. Only two were still there.

"He got away with as much as he could carry, Caelianus. It must have hurt to leave the rest. Damn the man! How did he get out of the building without being seen? How did he carry it at all? The strength of desperation, I suppose."

Pliny confronted the clerks, the door slaves, the sentries, every last inhabitant of the building, all herded together in the big counting room.

"None of you saw anything, heard anything last night?"

They looked at one another and shook their heads.

"The chief accountant has been stealing, probably for a long time. Did any of you suspect? Speak up, I promise you won't be punished."

Now there were knowing looks on a few faces and muttered words quickly exchanged. Then one of the junior clerks, a fat-bellied youth, stepped forward. "We knew, your honor. He let us get away with a bit too."

"Thank you," said Pliny. "And now I will ask you a very important question and I want a careful answer. Did Vibius Balbus know that Silvanus was stealing?"

The fat young man looked around at his comrades; two or three of them nodded encouragement. "He asked some of us if we thought so. Not long ago. Said there was a new governor now, meaning yourself, sir. That you were going to poke your nose in where it didn't belong and things had better smell like roses, or else. Well, I didn't like to snitch on Silvanus but the procurator was that angry I was afraid not to tell the truth in case it came out some other way and I was caught lying. So I told him 'yes.' He turned so red in the face I feared he'd have an apoplexy then and there."

"And what happened after that?"

"Don't know, sir. If he had it out with Silvanus it wasn't in our hearing. And that man always looks so sorrowful you don't rightly know what he's thinking."

Within the hour, Pliny had men at the harbor and at every stable in the city that rented coaches. But no one answering Silvanus' description had been seen. The man might be anywhere.

And so might Balbus—if he was still alive.

That night Pancrates, as always, toiled with his assistants over the day's haul of queries.

"Have a look at this one, Master."

He took the tablet from his oracle writer, held it near the lamp, and squinted at it: *Will I be punished for slaying the lion? Glaucon, son of Phormio.*

"A lion? Is the man a *venator*?"

"Hardly. We know who Glaucon is. Comes from a wealthy family, big local landowner. What do you think he means?"

Pancrates chewed on the end of his moustache. "Let's put a scare into him and see what happens. Tell him he's angered Hercules, who slew the Nemean lion and resents competition, something like that, you know what to say. We will keep an eye on this Glaucon."

Chapter Eleven

Nothing was said publicly about Silvanus' disappearance. Pliny put Caelianus in charge of the treasury with orders to carry on counting the money. The clerks were confined to the building day and night. But Balbus' disappearance was the only topic of conversation in the Roman community. According to Calpurnia, the wives were in a state of near panic, and it wasn't long before word spread among the Greeks as well. Wild rumors circulated, and reported sightings of the procurator came in daily. He was seen in a harborside tavern, or lurking around the temple of Zeus, or on the road to Prusa, or in a dozen other places, all equally improbable. Nevertheless, Pliny sent his men to investigate each report. Meanwhile, Fabia kept to herself.

With a confidence he did not feel, Pliny sought to reassure the local grandees. Diocles, whose network of connections reached everywhere, was the obvious choice to receive this message. Pliny had asked him to come in the morning, unobtrusively, for a private meeting with himself and his staff. Instead, he had arrived with a small army of his cronies, including most of the city magistrates and his colleagues on the council, and trailed by a crowd of idle and curious citizens, who milled outside the palace gates. Typical of this little man with his outthrust chest and swept back hair and booming voice, who seemed never to overlook an opportunity to tweak their Roman noses. Pliny was forced to move the proceedings from his office to the audience hall and scare up refreshments for forty people.

"Of course, Governor, we loyal citizens of Nicomedia will do everything in our power to assist you in this crisis." Diocles seemed to linger over the word *crisis*. And his voice, Pliny feared, could probably be heard out in the street—the man never merely spoke, he orated. "And you have *no* idea where he might be? With your permission, my people will begin a thorough search for the procurator. It is, after all, our city, you will grant that we know it better than you do."

Pliny murmured his thanks. The last thing he wanted was for the Greeks to find Balbus before he did. "Diocles, you can help me best," he said, "by telling me everything you know about the procurator. You've known him, I gather, since he took up his post here some two years ago."

"Indeed I have, Governor, and found him an excellent man, too. Fair and honest, which, I may say, has not always been the case with our Roman masters." The arms spread wide in a gesture of confiding frankness, the voice so well-modulated that just the merest note of resentment fell on Pliny's sensitive ear. *Did the man think he was living in Pericles' Athens? The Bithynians had had one master or another for three centuries.*

"But how well did you know him personally," Suetonius asked, "his habits, his foibles, weaknesses?"

"I'm afraid I can be of no help to you there." The bland expression never wavered. "We did not socialize."

"Really," said Pliny. "I would have thought he was a man worth your while to cultivate."

"And why would you think that?"

There were more questions to Diocles and his friends, all of them artfully evaded. Finally, Pliny stood up. "Thank you all for coming." There was no point in prolonging this charade. If they knew anything, they were not going to share it with him, and Diocles was too powerful a man to be pushed. "Whatever has happened to Vibius Balbus," Pliny assured them, "the administration of the province is unaffected. I am in full control here. It would be unfortunate if this were a cause for civic unrest." Just a little emphasis on *unfortunate*, which Diocles surely did not miss.

"Oh, to be sure," the orator agreed. "But you will—keep us apprised?"

"Of course."

As the delegation filed out of the audience hall, Diocles turned back. "And your lovely wife, Governor, how is she progressing in the mastery of our language? I hope Timotheus has proved a satisfactory tutor?"

"What? Oh, yes, quite. I think she told me they've just started book two of the *Odyssey*." He had no idea where she was in the poem or if she was reading it at all. He must remember to ask her.

"Ah, Homer, the fountainhead of our civilization. *Emos d'erigeneia phane rhododaktylos Eos, orunt' ar' ex eunephin Odysseos philos uios heimata essamenos…*"

Pliny held up his hands. He was sure that Diocles was capable of reciting the entire book from memory given half a chance. Homer was always in the man's mouth.

Once Diocles and his band had departed the hours passed slowly. Pliny paced and fretted. Arranged and rearranged the objects on his desk. Bathed. Took his midday meal with Calpurnia, who looked pinched and pale and barely touched her food, although she laughed when he questioned her and said it was nothing. After lunch, he called yet another meeting of his staff.

"You think Silvanus killed Balbus?" Suetonius asked.

"Or maybe they're in it together," Nymphidius offered, "Balbus slipping away first, Silvanus afterwards, and all the rest of it just play-acting."

"Either way I simply can't imagine how it was done" said Pliny. "Two men vanished without a trace."

They looked at each other in glum silence and he was about to send them all away when they heard voices raised in the corridor outside his office. He went out to investigate.

The doorkeepers—who considered it a part of their job to prevent him from ever talking to anyone who did not have an appointment—were struggling with a man, red in the face and clearly angry, who was demanding to see the governor. Another crank probably, but the man's clothes were expensive and his accent not the worst. Pliny had nothing but time on his hands, he could spare this fellow a little of it. He ushered him into the office.

The man straightened his clothes, took a breath to calm himself, and introduced himself as Isidorus, a dealer in fine silks and brocades. He had gone yesterday to the Street of the Leather Workers, he explained, to shop for a saddle and bridle, not your ordinary stuff but something expensive, a birthday present for his son-in-law, who was quite a gentleman and owned a horse. And he was in one shop, examining what was on offer, and quite a respectable place, the owner was known to him and not a dealer in stolen goods either, no certainly not. But there was a very handsome saddle for sale with matching bridle, all ornamented with turquoises and onyxes, and an embroidered saddle cloth with it, top quality, make no mistake, he knew quality when he saw it, and the thing of it was, you see, that it looked familiar, he knew he had seen that saddle somewhere before, and then it came to him—just like that!—perhaps some god whispered it in his ear, who could say? But he was dead certain that it was the procurator's saddle, no question about it, that gentleman rode down his street every day on his way to the treasury, which is just past the Street of the Cloth Merchants, don't you see?

Isidorus stopped and looked around him in alarm. They were all on their feet, Nymphidius' fingers dug into his shoulder.

"Here now," he squeaked, "no call for that!"

"Where," Pliny brought his face close and spoke softly, "did this merchant get the saddle?"

"Well, that's what I'm trying to tell your honors. A couple of peasants sold him the stuff. His wife is from their village, don't you see, so they thought he'd give 'em a good price."

"And where is this village?"

"He can tell you. He's just outside. He doesn't want any trouble."

Chapter Twelve

The mounted column, with Pliny at its head, left the city at the ninth hour of the day, taking the road, at a walking pace, northeast up into the foothills. According to the leather merchant, who now guided them, the village lay about eighty *stades*—ten Roman miles—away. With luck they should reach it by nightfall. Suetonius and Zosimus had urged him to wait until tomorrow before setting out, but Pliny would not be delayed any longer than it took to gather supplies for an overnight journey and bid a hasty farewell to Calpurnia. A dozen cavalry troopers, commanded by Aquila, and a lumbering wagon for their tents went with them.

The sky had been overcast all day and now the wind rose, thunder rumbled in the mountains, and a slanting rain drove in their faces. Shrunk inside their traveling cloaks, they urged their horses on. The ground rose steadily. Soon the paved, poplar-lined road dwindled to a dirt track and then to a barely visible forest path, dark with the shade of overhanging trees. In these dense woods of fir and oak and beech, branches shuddered in the wind and whipped at their faces, dripping ferns and bracken soaked their knees. The horses' hooves sank fetlock deep in a wet carpet of fallen leaves. Their nostrils steamed in the watery air.

The temperature dropped steadily as the day waned. Pliny shivered and felt the breath congeal in his lungs. His uncle had died from a weakness of the lungs. It was a deadly family infirmity that he had inherited. Maybe he should listen to the others and turn back, the weather might clear tomorrow. But then the leather merchant's wife might have time to warn her kinsmen. No. Press on.

Calpurnia stood in the middle of the dining room, supervising the fresco painters who were reproducing her sketches on the wall panels. The shutters shook as gusts of wind hurled the rain against them. Ione, at her side as always, studied her with an appraising eye.

"'Purnia, this is your chance."

Calpurnia pushed back a tendril of hair. "I don't know what you're talking about. Add more cinnabar, Lysias, I want a deeper red there."

"It's been nearly two weeks since you've seen Agathon. Four days since his slave brought you the letter begging to see you. Have pity on the boy. You could go to him today."

Calpurnia turned on her savagely. "Stop this! I should have you whipped for talking like this."

Ione regarded her steadily. "If it makes you feel better."

"I threw the letter away and that's the end of it."

"If you say so."

"Ione, please. I can't. I can't. Lysias, go away, take the others with you, we'll start again tomorrow. Ione, you're like Nemesis luring me to my doom."

"I don't know about that, I'm not an educated woman, but I know something about love."

"Love! Don't be ridiculous."

"I see you pining away before my eyes. My husband notices. So does yours."

"By the gods, what would you have me do?"

"Only what you did before. Drink wine, laugh together, draw your pictures, maybe a small *philema* or two." The Greek word for 'kiss' sounded somehow more innocent. "Nothing wrong in that."

Calpurnia groped for a chair and sank into it with her face in her hands. She drew in a long breath through her nostrils and let it out slowly. "Could I? Could I, really?"

Ione pulled her mistress' hands away and looked in her eyes, luminous with tears. "Poor 'Purnia. How long will you punish yourself like this? Come with me, now. I'll bathe you and fix your hair and dress you—your saffron gown and the silver sandals, your amethyst earrings. I'll make you so beautiful for him."

The palace in which they lived was an ancient pile that sprawled over half an acre and much of it was empty and unguarded. At dusk they slipped out a door in an unused wing. Wrapped in their cloaks, the two women ran through the dark, rain-lashed streets. Calpurnia felt herself moving as in a dream, helpless as though some other will than her own were animating her.

"Hey, you there, stop!" A figure lurched out from the shadow of a doorway and blocked their path. "Come on, ladies, I pay you good. I like two at a time." Dressed in dripping rags, the figure staggered toward them. They rushed past him, spilling him into the gutter. "Filthy whores!" he shouted after them. "Filthy whores!" They hurried on, missing a turn in the dark, groping their way back, coming at last to the steps that led up the hillside to the town house, treacherous in the dark and wet. Calpurnia slipped, bruising her knee. But the pain was nothing, she was at his door now. His door! Moments passed while she pounded on it. At last the housekeeper answered her knock and recognized her.

Leaving Ione in the entrance hall, Calpurnia followed the old woman into the *megaron*.

"Callirhoe!" Agathon turned in surprise and opened his arms wide. "I never hoped to see you again! You nearly missed me, I was just—"

"Going out?" She recognized his best cloak and tunic, smelled the scent in his oiled hair. "To spend the night drinking with your friends? I'm sorry, this was a mistake, I'll go." She heard the shrill accusation in her voice—like some shrewish wife. Of course, he had his own life. What did she think?

He stood back and smiled his crooked smile. "You've saved me from an evening of dissipation with dull companions, for which I thank you. Don't be angry. It's you who have avoided me, you know. What has changed your mind?"

What could she say? That she was a desperate, foolish woman? That her own maid had persuaded her to do what she knew she mustn't? That she loved him to distraction and was past caring what happened? All she could do was look at him with pleading eyes.

Agathon saw her confusion. He took her hand and drew her down onto a chair and sat beside her. "It doesn't matter. You're here. Baucis," he turned to his housekeeper, "bring us wine and something to eat. Give the excellent Ione something too. I see her lurking there in the doorway."

Calpurnia drank off her cup in one draught and poured another. She needed it for courage. She had made up her mind.

"Steady now," Agathon laughed. "I don't want to have to carry you home tonight."

"I needn't go home tonight." It was the merest whisper.

He raised an eyebrow. "Your husband's away again?"

She nodded.

"For how long this time?"

"I don't know."

"And so you…?" He drew closer to her. "Are you sure, my love? Are you quite sure?"

She filled her hands with his hair and kissed him with a passion that was close to anger.

And now he had picked her up, and now he was carrying her up the stairs to his bed chamber, and now his breath was on her cheek, his weight pressing on her, his hands under her gown…

"May as well finish off this wine, then." Baucis eased her old bones down onto Agathon's chair and motioned Ione to the other one. "Not a wise woman, your mistress. She's laying up a store of misery with that one. I've known him since he was a baby."

"We women are never wise," Ione smiled over her wine cup.

"And you're playing a risky game too, my girl. This could all come crashing down on your head."

"I'm only a servant, I do what I'm told."

The old woman leaned close and gave her a searching look. "I've been a house slave all my life and I've seen more than one pretty young thing like you come to grief. They meddle in their masters' affairs for many reasons—idleness, wantonness, ambition, jealousy, vengeance. I wonder which is yours."

Ione met her gaze with a face like a mask, revealing nothing. "You think too much, old woman."

They descended on the village at nightfall like an attacking army. Pliny was no soldier, he left such things to Aquila, who only knew one way to deal with barbarians. The village was a haphazard sprawl of thatched huts, huddled around a muddy clearing and surrounded by a flimsy palisade of wattles. The troopers burst through, yelling and brandishing torches, kicking in doors and dragging people out. Amid the screams of women and children, the bleating of goats, and the honking of geese, they shouted commands in Latin to frightened, uncomprehending faces.

Eventually, they identified the village headman, a skeletal old man who looked ready to fall down with fright. The leather merchant, who was looking unhappier by the minute, pointed out the two men, a father and son, who had brought him the saddle. They were hanging back in the crowd, trying not to be noticed: it was obvious why the Romans were there. Pliny and his officers crowded into the headman's hut to be out of the rain while the troopers stationed themselves around the palisade. The headman understood a few words of Greek and the leather merchant spoke a little of the country people's dialect. In this way Pliny interrogated the two.

While out hunting, they said, they had found two tethered horses in a wooded clearing. They saw no sign of the riders, they hadn't killed them, they swore it by all their gods. When they saw the horses, they couldn't believe their good fortune—these were fine animals, especially the grey with the beautiful saddle. Yes, the horses were here, with the one saddle which wasn't so fancy. They were sorry. They begged for their lives.

Chapter Thirteen

The 11th day before the Kalends of November
The fifth hour of the day

Pliny rubbed his chin, which now bore a two-day stubble, and tried to think philosophical thoughts of patience and self-control. But the waiting was hard. He and Postumius Marinus, sat on camp stools in an army tent pitched outside the village, listening to Zosimus recite something to pass the time. Pliny only half paid attention; his mind was out in the deep woods with his troopers and the young men from the village as they searched in widening circles from the spot where the horses had been found. The men could move faster through this rough country without an old man like him slowing them down. He had sent back to Nicomedia yesterday to requisition Balbus' hounds, who knew their master's scent, and to ask his physician, Marinus, to ride up and join him. The search had gone on until nightfall yesterday and resumed at dawn. If they had no success today he was resolved to return to the city.

"Sir!" A breathless trooper ducked under the tent flap. "We've found something."

"Stir your old bones, Marinus, mount up!" Pliny shouted, feeling suddenly no longer old.

Their way led upwards, farther into the hills. The rain had stopped overnight and now sunlight sifted through the branches. Overhead, squadrons of migrating storks filled the sky. Looking up, Pliny noticed for the first time that distant ridge that was said to resemble a woman's profile. It had been shrouded in mist when they first arrived. As they rode, the forest gave way to towering outcroppings of rock cut by deep crevasses and they were forced to dismount and proceed on foot, just as Balbus and his nameless companion must have done.

If it was Balbus.

They had traveled a good half hour when they heard the baying of the dogs and smelled the sweet, pungent, gagging stench of putrefaction.

"Over here, sir. Cover your nose, it's pretty bad."

Suetonius held out a hand to steady him as Pliny half slid down the steep side of a bramble-choked gully. There, two soldiers leaned on their shovels, their neck cloths tied around their faces like highwaymen. The dogs jumped and strained at their leashes, scratching the ground and nearly pulling their handlers into the pit. Marinus followed him down. The body lay in a shallow grave, bloated and blackened and crawling with maggots, an obscene intrusion in that pleasant autumnal setting—but, unmistakably, Balbus.

"How long do you think he's been here?" Pliny asked.

The physician shrugged. "He's been missing, what, twelve days or so? Still plenty of flesh left. But it's cooler up here in the hills and the body was covered, that makes a difference. The question is, *What* killed him. Get these damned dogs out of my way." Marinus squatted beside the corpse and studied it silently while Pliny stood back, trying not to breathe.

"Hard to be sure, of course, the state he's in, but I don't see a wound anywhere, and I've looked at plenty of wounds in my time." Marinus had begun his career as physician in the *Ludus Magnus*, invaluable training for a doctor. "Let's roll him over."

No one moved.

"Come, come," he snapped. "It's a body. You call yourselves soldiers?"

They turned the corpse, using their spades and Marinus bent to his work again. "Ah!" he murmured after a moment. "Come and look, Governor." This vertebra is crushed." He touched it with a finger where the flesh had come away. "Our friend the procurator has had his neck broken."

Pliny led his staff away to a spot where the smell was bearable. They sat on the damp ground and talked.

"Not robbers, that's plain," Nymphidius said. "He's still got his clothes and rings."

"Then why?" demanded Pliny. "And what on earth was he doing out here in the middle of nowhere? And who rode the other horse?"

Suetonius shook his head. "Balbus was a big man, an ex-soldier. There won't be many who could have broken his neck like that."

"Well, it was no riding accident," said Marinus. "The body's a good half mile from where they left the horses. And why would his companion, whoever it was, just bury him and leave him?"

"They must have been out here looking for something," Pliny mused. "Your men have been all over here, Aquila, is there anything?"

"There's a bit of a path that runs along nearby. Easy to miss. The lads followed it up that way." He pointed toward a stony hillside above them. "It just petered out. They poked around, didn't find anything. According to the villagers, no one lives out this way."

"Right." Pliny stood up. "Aquila, get the body wrapped up and loaded on the wagon, we're taking Balbus home. I particularly want to see Fabia's face when I deliver it. And for the time being, all of you, it *was* a riding accident, you understand. There must be no word of murder. Aquila, I want no loose talk from the men about what they've seen. I hold you responsible."

Pancrates bent his hawk-faced head over Calpurnia's hand and brushed it with his lips. His dark ringlets spilled over his shoulders. "Your maid brought me your message this morning, *matrona*. It's been too long since we spoke. How can I help you? You do not look well. Have you been sick?"

She pulled him down on the couch beside her. "Sick? Yes, I am sick. Here." She touched her hand to her breast. Her voice sounded to her own ears faint and far away.

"Ah. The heart. That is the cruelest sickness of all. Tell me." He took her hand in both of his and squeezed it.

"You told me I would meet someone new. I didn't believe you, but I have. A man. And I love him." Her chin trembled. "I fight against it but I'm too weak. Ione only encourages me. I have no one else to turn to. And then last night…"

"Last night you took a step that you cannot take back. I see it in your eyes."

"And it felt—I can't tell you. But now…"

"You've never done something like this before?"

She shook her head.

"You're a woman of rare virtue."

"I thought I was. I always imagined that one day they would inscribe *univira* on my tombstone as they did my mother's. But no more."

"And now what? Do you imagine a future with this man?"

"That is madness."

"But love is a kind of madness, as the poets tell us. I see a handsome man. Older perhaps…?"

"No, young. So very young."

"Just as I thought."

"And he looks like a young god, and he's an artist and sweet-natured and he makes me laugh and…" She looked away.

"But what could be more natural? A beautiful woman like yourself deserves to be loved passionately. You have no reason to reproach yourself. Of course, you honor your husband, but he's preoccupied with high affairs of state, is he not? Look how he has dragged you from your home, your friends, and family to this alien place and then he neglects you. You have a right to feel as you do. We are all creatures of temptation. And your husband suspects nothing?"

"He sees only what he wants to see. He's so clever in some ways and so innocent in others. Sometimes I'm furious at him for being so blind." She began to cry. "What am I to do? It can't live like this. You are a seer—what do you see?"

"Spit in your hand."

"What?"

"Do as I say."

She spat and Pancrates touched her palm with his finger and put it on his tongue. He frowned. "I see what has been done to you. You are the victim of magic, lady."

"What, you mean a love potion? No, he would never—"

"The signs are unmistakable. Do you doubt such things exist?"

"No, but—"

"And do you want to be restored to your senses, to the love of your husband, that good man?"

"Yes," she whispered.

"Louder. You must mean it."

"Yes!"

"I can devise a spell against it. But I must know your lover's name."

"His name? No, I couldn't..." She snatched her hand away from his.

"If you're going to keep secrets from me, lady..." He made to stand up.

"No, don't, please. Don't go. His name is Agathon."

"There are many with that name."

"Son of Protarchus, grandson of Neocles."

"Well, well. I don't know the young man but I know the family. Very prominent, very rich." He reached for her hand again. "Now calm yourself, Calpurnia. I tell you again, you've done nothing wrong. I can cure you, and your husband need never know a thing. I gather he is away at the moment?"

She nodded. "First it was the assizes and now this business with the procurator. They're out in the countryside now looking for him."

Pancrates black eyebrows shot up. "Are they indeed? And does your husband confide in you about his business when you're together?"

"He always has."

"And quite right too. You're a woman of good sense." He leaned closer, his deep-sunk eyes seemed to bore into her. "If he tells you about this missing procurator I want you to tell me, you understand? We must have no secrets if I am to help you. You have already trusted me with your lover's name. I wonder how the father would react to knowing of his son's adventures."

She recoiled from him. "What do you mean? You wouldn't…"

"Well, of course, I wouldn't like to."

Her eyes widened in sudden fear. "Why do you care about the procurator? It doesn't concern you."

"Everything concerns me." The voice was like silk and like steel all at once.

She leapt up, her bruised knee nearly buckling under her. He tried to hold her back but she tore away from him. She saw the chasm opening at her feet. "Filthy Greek spy! Get out!"

He stood slowly and smoothed his spotless white gown with his long-fingered hands. "As you wish. We'll talk again."

"We will not!" she screamed at his back. Then she fell weeping on the couch.

In an instant Ione was beside her. "I saw him leave, 'Purnia. He looked at me with a murderer's eyes! What happened?"

"Ione, I've done a terrible thing. I've put myself in that man's power. And Agathon, and my husband too. I want to die!"

"Darling, don't say that."

"I mean it. But first I will tell Gaius everything, everything, the minute he returns. I swear I will."

Ione turned a stricken face to her. Old Baucis' words came back to her in a rush. *This could all come crashing down on your head.* She sank to the floor and grasped Calpurnia's knees, a suppliant. "Everything? And what about me? Your husband may forgive you but he won't forgive me."

"But I won't—"

"He'll get it out of you. He'll know you couldn't have done it alone. He'll throw me into the street to starve, and Zosimus too, and the child. He *must*. Everything I did, I did for your happiness, mistress. Will you betray me too?"

"*Mehercule*, it feels good to be home again. I was never one for camping out."

They reclined at dinner: Pliny and Calpurnia, Suetonius, Nymphidius, Marinus, and Zosimus. The meal was finished and the wives, except for Calpurnia, had been excused. Pliny would keep no secrets from her. He grimaced. "What a business this is!"

"Have you written to the emperor yet?" Suetonius asked.

"As soon as we got back. One copy to go by sea, the other overland. It could be a month before he gets either one of them, if then. Rough seas in the Aegean, an early snow in the mountain passes of Illyricum—I've often thought that our empire effectively ceases to exist between October and May. I've written him four times since we arrived and haven't had a reply yet. We're on our own here, my friend, and must make the best of it."

"And the body?" Calpurnia asked.

"Is here in the palace. An army carpenter's knocking together a box for it and tomorrow I'm taking it to Fabia."

"Gaius, I'm frightened for you. You must wear a cuirass under your tunic and carry a dagger."

"'Purnia, I'll do nothing of the sort. We can't go around looking like we fear for our lives here. You know what will leap to people's minds."

Every Roman schoolboy knew. The slaughter of eighty thousand Romans, most of them hated tax farmers, together with their families in a single night in all the cities of Bithynia and Asia by order King Mithridates of Pontus. It had taken twenty years of war to avenge that atrocity. And two centuries had not dimmed the memory of it; the natives still named their children after that monster.

"And that's why we must maintain that Balbus' death was an accident until we get to the bottom this. So, not a word about this to the wives, my dear. I can trust you can't I?"

"What?" She felt the blood drain from her face.

"I said, can I trust you, my dear."

"Oh. Yes, yes, Gaius, of course you can trust me."

He moved closer to her on the dining couch and covered her hand with his. "Quite enough gloomy talk for one night. I noticed you limping, have you hurt yourself?"

"It's nothing. I slipped in the bath."

He stretched and stifled a yawn. "I've spent three nights sleeping on the cold ground, missing you, my dear. And I see you haven't slept well either—such dark circles under your eyes. Oh, I know I've neglected you. I'm truly sorry. But with all this…I will make it up to you, I promise. Gentlemen, if you'll excuse us. We're off to bed." He gave her a wink.

Zosimus put his arm around his wife and fumbled for a kiss. She turned away.

"What's the matter? You haven't been yourself all evening."

"It's nothing."

"Tell me."

"Leave me alone, can't you? Go to sleep."

And the poor young man lay awake in the dark, wondering what he had done.

Chapter Fourteen

The next morning
The 10th day before the Kalends of November

Aulus crouches behind the curtain of the little storeroom, hardly breathing. A ray of dusty light falls through the small, high window, but it doesn't find him in his corner. If he looks, he sees each single dust mote drifting in it like an atom in the void—his senses are keyed up to that pitch. His nerves vibrate like harp strings. He clutches his body, shaken by seismic shudders, his thin shoulders working up and down. His spine is taut, bent like an archer's bow, ready to break. He wrings his hands. Did he groan? Did he make a sound? He clenches his jaw until his teeth hurt. He has been in an agony of fear since *that day*, knowing they would come for him. And now they have, that man who was here before, who saw him—the governor. *He knows.*

"My condolences, lady," the governor is saying. "There's no doubt it's him, I have his signet ring here. I shouldn't want to view the corpse if I were you, it's, well, not a pleasant sight. We discovered him in the woods, miles from the city, near the spot where a couple of villagers found his horse. No, I do not intend to crucify them! It seems he fell from his horse and broke his neck. A tragic accident."

An accident. Aulus lets his breath out slowly. *Is it possible?*

The governor is sitting in their atrium, his face composed in a somber expression, the corners of his mouth pulled down, but the eyes alert, moving here and there, fixing again on his mother, who stands before him immovable as a statue. Aulus, in the little side-chamber, can almost reach out and touch them.

And now the governor is puzzled, he shakes his head and pulls at his chin. "What was your husband doing out there?" he asks. "You don't know? Come now, that's not good enough. You must have some idea, he must have said something, some word. A man doesn't ride out in the middle of nowhere for no reason. And he wasn't alone. There was another horse, a chestnut. I've brought the horses along, if you'd care to look. None of yours are missing? You're quite sure? It would be pointless, I suppose, to question your stableman again." The governor sighs in exasperation.

Oh, mother, thank the gods for your strength!

And now the governor is saying, "You may have heard something about the disappearance of Silvanus, your husband's chief accountant. We're keeping it quiet but these things have a way of getting out. He was stealing from the treasury and he's gotten away clean. Did Balbus ever mention a problem with him? Had his suspicions, you say? Talked about sacking him? Indeed he was a sullen, ill-favored character. And a sneak and a liar to boot? Well, very interesting." The governor stands up now. "Back to the sad matter at hand. A private funeral would be best, don't you think? No need to make too large an occasion of it. Eulogies, of course, from his colleagues and any close friends. I'll handle the arrangements. Of course, I've notified the emperor. Well, then, I'll just have them bring the casket in."

And now four men are carrying in the box. It drops to the floor, making a noise in Aulus' over-stretched ears as loud as a thunderclap, as reverberant as an earthquake. *Breathe, breathe!* he tells himself. But he *sees* the horror inside as though his eyes could pierce those wooden planks. The box sits like a huge, brutal, accusing *fact*. If it had a tongue what would it say? And now a kaleidoscope of images whirls through Aulus' brain—jagged sparks and fiery red circles. There is a roaring in his ears, his throat constricts, saliva runs down his chin, his bowels unloose.

He wants to run away but there is no place to run. His muscles jerk and contract until he thinks his bones will break. *Don't fall, don't fall!* But he feels himself rolling over on his side, limp as a bag of stones, his head poking through the curtain. And the last thing he sees is the governor's shocked face hovering over him.

The Sun-Runner to the Father, greetings:

This is a catastrophe. The Lion is dead. The Romans have found the body and, though they claim it was an accident, I fear the worst. We may all be in danger. With your consent, Father, we must suspend our gatherings until such time as we know more. The risk is too great. Nama Mithras.

Chapter Fifteen

That afternoon, Pliny convened his staff again. They ate a light lunch while they discussed the case.

Suetonius, carefully peeling a hardboiled egg, asked, "Are we keeping the murder a secret from Diocles?"

"Especially from him," Pliny answered firmly. "But I don't delude myself that our story will hold up long. Someone, a trooper or one of the dog handlers, will talk. And when it becomes known that the second highest Roman official in the province has been murdered we *must* be seen to take decisive action. This is a disaster, gentlemen, and we must deal with it swiftly. And we can't do it by just sitting here. The tip about the saddle was a gift from the gods, but we can't expect more like that. The answer to this puzzle is not going to walk in through the front door. We must go out and find it, and we haven't much time."

"And just how do we do that, Sir?" Aquila growled.

"We're in a better place than we were before, Centurion. When Balbus had simply vanished we had nothing to go on. Now we do. We know that *someone* hated him enough or feared him enough to kill him. Either Silvanus out of fear or someone else for reasons we can't even guess. And, mind you, the motive must have been irresistible to take such a risk. Every crime has a logic to it, if we can discover it. It is always the final act in a long train of events."

"Like following the clew."

"What's that, my boy?"

Zosimus, aware of his humble station, seldom spoke at these meetings. When he did, it was to the point. "Theseus and the Minotaur, Patrone. You know the story. How Theseus had to follow a clew of thread that led him back from the Minotaur's lair through the Labyrinth? It's like that. We have hold of one end of the thread and we must walk it back to the other end. Following the clew."

"Or clews," Pliny laughed for the first time, it seemed, in a long time. "I thank you for that image, my boy, it's very apt." Zosimus blushed to the roots of his hair. "But I suspect what we have here is a tangle of many threads, and each one must be followed to its end."

"One of them being embezzlement—unless we've abandoned that theory?" asked Caelianus. He had come over from the treasury building to confer with them. "All we know for certain is that Silvanus was stealing. Whether Balbus was also, who can say? The counting is going slowly; the clerks are mutinous, they stop working every time I take my eye off them."

"No theory has been abandoned," Pliny answered.

"Silvanus is our murderer," Suetonius said firmly. "I can't forget the way Balbus humiliated him at dinner. Even apart from being caught with his hands in the money chest, he had, reason to hate Balbus."

Pliny shook his head. "You were imagining a knife in the ribs, as I recall. But breaking Balbus' thick neck? I doubt the chief clerk's physically capable of it. Not single-handedly anyway."

"And then there's Fabia," Marinus suggested. "In my experience, there's always a woman at the bottom of these things."

Suetonius cocked an eyebrow. "Your experience of women being precisely what?"

"Is that bald spot of yours getting bigger, my literary friend?" Marinus leered at him. "I've read somewhere that pigeon droppings rubbed briskly into the scalp does wonders."

These two had been having at each other lately. All of them were on edge.

"Yes, there's Fabia." Pliny swallowed a sip of watered wine and dabbed at his lips with his napkin. "And there is a slave in that household, too, who I'll wager could break a neck. Worth thinking about. If there's a mistress in the picture, for instance, I would not like to be the man who crossed Fabia."

"Tattooed Thracian, they say," Suetonius pulled a comical fierce face.

"Such is the rumor. When I spoke with her this morning and mentioned Silvanus she was more than happy to blacken his character. I got the distinct feeling that she'd like us to think he murdered her husband."

"But you didn't actually say he'd been murdered?"

"Oh, no, I told her it was an accident. If she does have something to do with his death, I don't want her to know how much we know. Not until we have a motive."

"Right, then," Suetonius said, "now we're getting into my line of country. Did Balbus have a woman on the side? Did he visit the brothels? Did he have gambling debts? I assign myself the task of discovering these things."

"Thank you, my friend, your expertise in these matters is well known."

Suetonius bowed his head modestly. Marinus snorted in his beard.

"And," added Pliny, "I have a job for Zosimus here, too. I want you to go out into the streets, my boy. Oh, not to the brothels and gambling dens, I wouldn't want to get you in trouble with Ione! But hang about in the *agora*, in the *palaestra*, the baths, the cook shops, and talk to people. I want to know what's being said out there, not just about Balbus but all of us. You're the only Greek I absolutely trust. Will you do this?"

The young man's eyes lit up. "I will start this morning, Patrone!"

"Good riddance to 'im, say I. They should set up a statue to the 'orse that broke 'is fucking neck for 'im. One less Roman leech sucking our blood, ain't I right, sir? You're not from here are you? So maybe you 'aven't 'eard."

The fact of the procurator's death and the alleged cause of it had, with almost magical rapidity, made its way to the farthest corners of the city.

The blowzy proprietress rested a fat elbow on the bar and refilled Zosimus' cup with a thin and vinegary red. The secretary had no head for wine and was beginning to feel the worse for it. Soon, he promised himself, he would return to the palace and have Ione put a cold cloth on his forehead. It had been a long, and not very fruitful, day. The things he had heard, he could hardly bring himself to repeat to his patrone. He had set out that morning full of enthusiasm to carry out his commission to "catch tongues," proud to be called the one Greek that a Roman could trust. And the young man had no difficulty striking up conversations with strangers. It was his face, he supposed. A broad, open face with a nose like a dumpling and innocent brown eyes; the face of one who was, perhaps, just a little simple. No one suspected that such a face concealed the well-stocked mind of one who had been trained from boyhood to recite all the comedies of Menander and Terrence from memory. His parents had been slaves of the old master, Pliny's learned uncle, who had noticed the child's quickness and cultivated it. When the uncle died in the smoke of Vesuvius, Zosimus had passed to the nephew. And the younger Pliny had treated him with the greatest affection and intimacy, even sending him for a rest cure once when he was sick, then manumitting him without requiring him to buy his freedom, and finally marrying him to his darling Ione. Zosimus would gladly give his life for Gaius Plinius.

He had begun the day at the *palaestra* among idlers watching the wrestlers and runners at their sweaty practice. As the sun rose higher, he had drifted with the crowd to the *agora*, to the welcome coolness of the portico that ran along one side, stopping along the way to buy a piece of grilled squid from a street vendor. The courts had been in session all morning and now the jurors spilled out of the courthouse, buzzing like Aristophanes' wasps.

Everywhere, knots of men stood nose to nose, gesticulating and shouting, the way Greeks always did. Zosimus pretended to read the public inscriptions on their marble slabs, and listened. Not all the conversation was about the Roman procurator's unexpected demise, but much of it was, and none of it was complimentary. His fine estate, his handsome horse, his entourage of lackeys worthy of some Persian king—and all of it paid for by their taxes. And he would be replaced by another barbarian from that race of plunderers, equally brutal and grasping. Would there ever come an end to their slavery?

With his ears ringing, Zosimus sought solace in the baths. But Nicomedia's bathhouse was shockingly dilapidated and dirty, the water coated with a greasy scum. He didn't stay long.

He browsed for a while along the street of the potters, the street of the carpenters, and the street of the bronzesmiths, lined with cramped workshops where men bent over bowls and lamps, tapping with little hammers. He strolled along narrow, zigzagging lanes where old women sat in their doorways, shelling peas and cackling to each other, and sturdy, straight-backed young women trudged from the public well, balancing water jugs on their shoulders; where school children chanted their lessons in a sidewalk classroom and dogs ran along, sniffing hopefully at piles of refuse.

He turned a corner and found himself in the midst of a noisy procession of Isis worshippers—shaven-headed men carrying tall palm fronds and priestesses jangling their rattles. They passed by, leaving a trail of flower petals.

He came down at last to the harbor. The fishermen had come in with their catch and were spreading their nets out on the quays to dry. The water in the bay was grey and choppy. The fishing boats stayed close to shore now and soon would not go out at all. The big merchantmen were already berthed. The city was preparing itself for winter. The walls of the big warehouses bore a load of scrawlings: prostitutes advertisements (*I'm yours for two obols*), election slogans (*Elpenor for archon)*, the faded announcement for a gladiatorial show in which men had died and were, by now, forgotten. And among them the occasional *So-and-so kisses Roman ass*. And worse. Zosimus was not beyond blushing.

And finally he had stopped into this sailor's grog shop that smelled of seaweed, and sedition. He'd heard enough for one day. He threw some coins on the counter and left. The sun was sloping down to late afternoon as he mounted the street of the leather workers up toward the treasury and the great temple of Rome and Augustus that overlooked a wide plaza: the soaring Corinthian columns and painted architrave, the vast gilded bronze doors, and within, the gold and ivory statue of the Deified Augustus. It dwarfed the buildings around it. It breathed Roman power, Roman pride.

There was a crowd gathered in front—fifty, or maybe a hundred, men surrounding a speaker who stood on the lowest step of the temple podium. Over the hubbub of voices, Zosimus could not make out the man's words, but there was no mistaking the shrill and angry tone. Sighing resignedly—for this was certainly what Pliny had sent him out to look for—Zosimus worked his way to the front. It was one of those ragged street corner ranters of the Cynic sect, troublemakers of the worst sort, who spewed out their hatred of all lawful authority. The crowd was cheering him on.

Suddenly, Zosimus had a premonition and turned to look for a way out. And, at that instant, with a clatter of hooves on the cobblestones, a score of Roman cavalrymen galloped into the square and charged the crowd, swinging their long-bladed swords. Some fled in panic, but others stood their ground. Stones flew through the air, a trooper was dragged from his horse. The blades flashed up and down. A trumpet blast rang out and then more soldiers appeared, infantrymen with their shields locked together and spears thrusting. Zosimus was lifted off his feet in the press of bodies, forced up against the flank of a horse. He never saw the blow that caught the side of his head and sent him sinking down unconscious amid a tangle of legs.

Chapter Sixteen

The 7th day before the Kalends of November
The ninth hour of the day

A blustery wind bent the branches of the poplars that lined the path leading from the house to the riding paddock. A sudden gust made a whirlpool of leaves along the ground and pressed their grey mourning clothes against their legs. An ideal day for the business at hand, Pliny reflected. The wind would fan the flames of the pyre and dissipate the greasy smoke: all that would soon remain of Fiscal Procurator Marcus Vibius Balbus.

Pliny and Calpurnia, his staff and their wives stood together in a show of solidarity. The Greeks—Diocles and his entourage with a few others whom Pliny did not recognize—formed their own little knot some distance away. Each ignored the other. Pliny understood why. Since the riot of three days earlier the city was seething. Pliny had had sharp words for Aquila and the other centurions. He was surprised the Greeks had come at all: perhaps only to enjoy the spectacle of Balbus' death.

Pliny was on the point of expressing this thought to Calpurnia when a shriek, long and ululating, pierced the air and all eyes turned toward the house. The doors swung open and the hired mourners emerged—a procession of women, led by flute players and trumpeters, their hair unbound, beating their breasts and wailing. Pliny had hired the best undertaker in Nicomedia and spared no expense.

Behind them came the catafalque swaying on the shoulders of eight pallbearers. As it drew near, Pliny recognized one of them: the bulging muscles, the hands like hams—but a slave no longer. The man now wore a liberty cap; clearly he had been manumitted in Balbus' will. An inducement, perhaps, to break his master's neck?

And last of all came Fabia, walking with her head high, her hair and grey clothing loose. Pliny looked closely as she passed by: her eyes were dry. And the son who should have walked at her side? Nowhere to be seen.

While the wailing of the women continued, the pallbearers wrestled the casket up onto the stack of pine logs that occupied the middle of the paddock. Given the condition of Balbus' corpse, the casket remained closed. For Balbus there would be no toga, no laurel wreath, no coin in the mouth. Charon, the boatman of Hades, must go unpaid.

A makeshift podium had been set up beside the pyre for the eulogists. And now here was Diocles mounting it and commanding silence. Did the man ever miss an opportunity to exercise his golden throat? It was a bravura performance, Pliny was forced to admit. Praise for the deceased mingled with veiled condemnation of Roman arrogance and insinuations of divine wrath—but all so carefully dressed up with allusions to Agamemnon and Xerxes and other ancient tyrants who met unhappy ends that it fell just short of treason. One remark struck Pliny as odd. Diocles had spoken of the dead man's loyalty to his friends. Friends? As far as Pliny knew, Balbus didn't have any.

After Diocles, a couple of others spoke, straining to find something nice to say about the procurator. And finally Pliny delivered a few words—honest public servant, dutiful husband and father, sadly struck down in the prime of life by a cruel twist of Fate—that sounded hollow even to himself. Then the pyre was lit, the flames crackled and leapt up, and they called the dead man's name one last time, as custom required.

Afterwards, the guests milled around in the atrium, the only space large enough to accommodate the funeral meal.

Fabia was encircled by the wives, including Calpurnia, making consolotary noises. With Suetonius in tow, Pliny joined them; he had every intention of confronting the widow head on. "Once again, my deepest sympathies, lady. And may I say I'm sorry not to see your son here. Surely he wanted to bid his father farewell?"

"He is unwell, confined to his bed."

"I am sorry to hear it. In fact, I mentioned your son to my physician, Marinus, and he would very much like to examine the boy. Possibly something can be done—"

"No." She backed away, nearly upsetting an end table. "Thank you, no."

Seeing her distress, Calpurnia stepped between them and drew her husband away. The wives closed in again.

"What was that about?"

"I'll explain later. Somehow," he said under his breath, "I will get that woman to crack."

"There you are, Gaius Plinius!" Diocles pushed through the crowd with his bantam strut, several cronies in tow. "And Suetonius Tranquillus too. Here's someone I'd like you to meet, he's a pillar of our community though I can seldom persuade him away from his country place. Protarchus, may I present the governor and his lady. And this, I believe, is his youngest son—I'm sorry, what is the young man's name? Ah, yes, Agathon."

"An honor." Protarchus nodded a shaggy head. "Sad occasion and all that." He was a shy man who found words difficult.

"I've wanted to meet you for the longest time, sir." Agathon stepped forward and spoke with an easy smile. "You know, I've never been inside the palace. I've heard it has some interesting old mosaics. It happens I'm quite interested in art."

"Well—," the young man's enthusiasm was nearly overwhelming. "You don't say. You must pay us a visit then. You know my wife's an artist. She's fixing the place up. You and she should have a lot to talk about. She's—well where has she gone? She was here a moment ago. 'Purnia?"

◇◇◇

A long train of carriages wound its way back to the city. The evening was damp and cool. Pliny and Calpurnia huddled together under a rug in their covered coach. The driver, in his box, hunched over the reins.

"Well, that's over with," Pliny sighed.

"I feel for Fabia."

"Do you? I never met a less sympathetic woman. It's clear she doesn't want me to talk to her son, and without her permission I don't see how I can. There's a mystery there—they know something. But how to get it out of them? She's a woman of wealth and rank, I can't treat her like a common suspect."

"You'll find a way." She squeezed his arm affectionately.

And he knew that he would. He didn't cut a dashing figure, he knew; he wasn't as quick-witted as some, not as brave, or as brilliant. But he was tenacious and determined: not exciting virtues, perhaps, but good Roman ones. It wasn't brilliance, after all, that had made Rome great, it was steadiness and determination.

"What's wrong with the son?" she asked.

"What? Oh. Marinus thinks it's probably the Sacred Disease. And in that case their secretiveness is understandable. Ignorant people, that is to say most people, regard it with dread."

They were quiet for a while, rolling and bouncing with the motion of the coach. Pliny squeezed her hand. "'Purnia dear, something I've been meaning to ask you, all this business with Balbus drove it out of my mind. Zosimus tells me that he saw that charlatan, the one they call Pancrates, leaving your apartment some days ago. I dislike the man. He's a troublemaker, this oracle of his is nothing but a swindle and bad for public order. I can't imagine what business you would have with him, you're too sensible a woman to fall for his line of talk. Anyway, I don't want him in the palace again. I must insist. In fact, the more I think about it, the more I believe I ought to expel the fellow from the province."

"Yes," she answered. *Could he feel her skin go cold? She was being spied on! What else did Timotheus see?* "Yes, get rid of the man. He forced himself into my apartment, wanting to tell my future, so he said. I had to order him out."

"Outrageous! It's that damned woman Atilia and the others who encourage people like that. I'll deal with him in short order." But then a thought occurred to him. "On the other hand, my dear, distasteful as he is, these sort of people sometimes have their uses. I'll wager there's many a household he's wormed his way into and many a secret he's learned. It's just possible he knows something that might help me with the Balbus case. I think perhaps I ought to have a little talk with this Pancrates."

"Oh, surely not."

"Why not? Of course, I'll make it plain that he must have nothing more to do with you. I've upset you, I'm sorry."

Did he hear the panic that clawed at her throat? She was terrified that her thoughts would betray her.

"Well here's something that might amuse you." He gave her hand another squeeze. "Back at the funeral dinner. I thought you were beside me but you'd slipped off somewhere just as a young man was introduced to me. What was the name, Agathocles? Something like that. Nice manners, good family, good-looking too, if you like the effete, moist-eyed sort of youth. Practically invited himself up to the palace. Claims he's interested in art. Well, I thought you might like his company. Take your mind off things. We must have him over the next time we entertain."

Silvanus ground his jaws and listened with deep satisfaction to the woman. He paid her more money than she'd ever seen in her life to go out and buy his food for him, and to keep her mouth shut and her ears open. Now she was rattling on about the procurator's funeral—the whole city was abuzz with it. If only he could have been there, invisible, to see the ugly, bloated corpse blacken and shrivel in the flames! He would have to be content with imagining it. If ever a man deserved death it was Balbus. How he loathed him.

Silvanus told the woman to leave him. He sat at his rickety table and fell hungrily on the bread and sausage she had brought him. What a clever fellow he was. Hiding practically in plain sight. Long ago he'd prepared this bolt hole, a hovel, indistinguishable from its neighbors, in a sprawl of shacks and market gardens along the city's ragged edge, and he could stay in it as long as necessary while they ran here and there, looking for him. Only one other person knew where he was and she wouldn't tell. She had too much to lose. And, when the time was right, he would steal away with his two chests of silver and live like a prince in Persia maybe, or Arabia.

Chapter Seventeen

The 6th day before the Kalends of November
The eighth hour of the night

She slipped out of bed silently, careful not to wake him. She had lain awake for hours, writing and rewriting the thing in her head. She still didn't know what she should say, only that she must say something. Taking a lamp, she crept out into the antechamber of their bedroom, sat down at the small table and opened the *tabellae* that lay on it, the waxed leaves smooth and ready for use. She bent her head low, twisting a lock of her hair in her fist, and made deep, almost savage strokes with the stylus. Finally, when she had filled up both leaves, she threw the stylus down. She tied the leaves tightly together and, moving noiselessly, barefoot on the cold marble floor, felt her way down the corridor to the room where Zosimus and Ione slept. She scratched at the door. Nothing. She knocked as loudly as she dared and finally heard a stirring within. The door opened and Zosimus' bandaged head looked out.

"*Matrona*, what is wrong?"

"Fetch Ione, please."

"But she's sleeping."

"Fetch her!"

A moment later, Ione appeared in the doorway, rubbing her eyes. Calpurnia pulled her out into the dark corridor.

"Take this." She thrust the *tabellae* into her hand. "As soon as it's light you'll carry it to Agathon's house. "

"'Purnia, no! With your husband right here in the house? Have you lost your mind!"

"Do as I tell you."

"Oh gods! I wish this had never started. It's me who'll suffer for it, Baucis was right." She tried to push the *tabellae* back on her mistress.

"Obey me!" Calpurnia slapped her hard across her face.

The *tabellae* fell to the floor with a sharp *clack* that echoed in the silence. The two women stood face to face, panting, not speaking, Ione's eyes wide with shock.

"I'm sorry, oh, I'm sorry." Calpurnia threw her arms around her and buried her face in her neck. "But you'll do it, Ione, you must. Here, hide it in your bosom, Zosimus mustn't see."

Ione closed the door and sank onto the edge of the bed.

"What did mistress want?" Zosimus asked. "Why, what's the matter with you, you're white as a ghost. What did she say to you? Tell me. I'm your husband, Ione, I insist." He tried to put his arm around her but she shrank away.

"My *husband*. You poor man. It's a poisoned gift you got when you were given me."

It was as well that he couldn't see the look in her eyes.

...what are you doing to me? Seven nights since I let you have every-thing you wanted from me and not a word from you. And then you dare to play that charade with my husband! What sort of man are you? No, forgive me. I love you too much. Have you poisoned me with a love philter? I won't let myself believe that. I must see you. But if my husband invites you to the palace, I beg you not to come. I haven't got your nerve, I couldn't bear it. I'll arrange something. Write back and say you love me. If you don't, I'm afraid what I might do. Have pity on me.

Agathon finished reading and tossed the tablets aside. What had he gotten himself into? This was no longer amusing. He enjoyed taking risks, life was dull otherwise. Yes, talking to her husband was foolish but he couldn't resist. If only she could be like him—enjoy a little something on the side now and then and let it go at that. But, of course, she was a woman, and women always take these things too seriously. Love potions, what nonsense! If he had a potion that would make her fall *out* of love with him, he'd pour a flagon of it down her throat. And what did she mean at the end? Was she threatening him? It was time to put a stop to this before he got himself into serious trouble.

Chapter Eighteen

Suetonius pushed the hooded figure ahead of him through the door, then shut and bolted it. "He came meek as a lamb."

"Sit down." Pliny indicated a rough stool.

A single lamp lit the little room. Three stools and a table were its only furniture. Huge amphorae of wine stood in racks around the walls. The voices of drinkers and dicers came faintly from the room beyond.

The figure sat as commanded and threw off his hood, uncovering the oiled ringlets of his hair, the flowing beard. "You surprise me, Governor. And the reason for this kidnapping?"

"No one has kidnapped you. I find it convenient to meet here; the palace has too many eyes and ears."

Suetonius had chosen the tavern and paid the owner generously for the use of his back room and his silence. He and Pliny wore plain tunics and Greek cloaks, and Pancrates had been hooded to disguise his unmistakable appearance if anyone should pass them in the street. They had entered unseen from a back alley.

"Your charming wife has perhaps said something. She quite misunderstood—"

"This has nothing to do with my wife, whom you will never see again. I warn you."

"As you like." Pancrates smiled easily. "But then I'm afraid I don't understand—"

"Understand this. You're a fraud. I can prove it, and I will run you out of this province unless you do as I tell you."

"My, my. Hard words. You don't believe in divination, Governor? The Pythia at Delphi? Your own Sibylline Books?"

"The day before yesterday a servant of mine submitted two sealed questions to one of your assistants. He was instructed to say that one question asked for a cure for lung trouble and the other asked what was the safest route to Italy. In fact, both of them asked, *What was Homer's birthplace?* Needless to say, the answers we got were quite wide of the mark. If I should decide to make this public—"

"Not a thing would change. Do you think others haven't played your little trick? We're careless sometimes, but it doesn't matter. Fools will always believe what they want to." The prophet spread his hands. "But I don't want you for an enemy, Gaius Plinius. I am properly afraid of the power of a Roman governor. All right, you've exposed me, you may as well hear it all. I was born in the slums of Sinope. I was a wharf rat, a thief, I sold stolen goods in the marketplace. My name was Cerzula. I never knew my mother or father. I lived by my wits. And I discovered at an early age that I had a talent for listening to the unspoken word, for reading the unconscious language of the face, and for speaking fair. At the age of twelve, I was taken under the wing of an old fortune teller who taught me to read and write and trained me in his profession. He gave me the name Pancrates, *Omnipotens* as you would say in Latin. But it was my idea, my stroke of genius, twenty years ago in a village in Paphlagonia, to bury a blown goose egg with a baby snake inside it, then to run into the market place wearing a gold-spangled loin cloth and waving a scimitar and proclaiming that Asclepius, god of healing, had arrived amongst them in the form of a serpent. I dug up the egg and produced the divine serpent, which at once inspired me to offer remedies for their ills. Needless to say, they were all agog. As the serpent grew, so did its reputation, until people were flocking from all over Asia to consult it. It has been, if I may say so, very profitable. And whom have I harmed? For the price of a drachma, I offer hope, consolation, reassurance—which is all any physician does, and they charge a good deal more than I do. And it matters not a bit how many people you denounce me to, there will always be more with their coins in their hands, begging me to give them peace of mind."

"That's all very well," said Pliny, "but, in fact, you do more than offer medical advice to the ignorant crowd. Other people, people of wealth and standing, ask you questions about decisions they have to make, about what their enemies may be plotting against them, or so I've heard."

"Sometimes."

"And your answers must be plausible, must have the ring of authenticity. How do you manage that?"

Pancrates set his lips. *I've said all I intend to.*

"Speak up, man, or you'll leave this room in shackles. Those are my *lictors* sitting out in the tavern. You've already admitted enough for me to throw you in prison and have your serpent sliced up for hors d'oeuvres."

He gave Pliny a long appraising look, in the end he shrugged. "I have informants."

"Where?"

"In places that would surprise you."

"Would one of those places be Vibius Balbus' house? Did he or his associates ever consult your oracle?"

"Ah, now I see what this is about!" Pancrates smiled. "You don't want to put me out of business, you want to use me. Well, I have no objection to that. Balbus, Balbus, what do I know about Balbus?" He lifted his gaze to the ceiling as though seeking inspiration. "I know he had a mistress—" Suetonius slapped his fist into his hand with a sound that made the prophet startle, "—quite a beautiful widow, and rich too. Her name is Sophronia. Have you heard of her?"

"Not the brothel-keeper?" said Suetonius, who for some time had been acquainting himself with the city's lower depths in the interests of research.

"The same. And not just any brothel. *Elysium*, as it's known, is a veritable palace of delights. She trains her *hetaeras* herself in all the arts of Aphrodite. In addition, the woman has investments in a dye works, a brick yard, several tenements, and a merchant ship. She and the fiscal procurator were lovers for more than a year. There was even talk of him divorcing his wife and marrying her."

"And you know this how?" Pliny demanded.

"Please, Governor, allow me to keep a few secrets. In return for certain favors, I did not tell his wife about their affair."

"Blackmail."

"If you like."

"Is it possible that Fabia found out anyway?" Suetonius said.

"That I don't know. The lady has never consulted me."

"What else do you know about Balbus?" Pliny asked.

"Nothing comes to mind. But I will, of course, keep my ears open. Now that he's gone, I am more than happy to exchange information in return for *your* favor. Do we have an understanding? Don't look so pained, Gaius Plinius, you're the one who invited me here."

Pliny scowled. "I will contact you from time to time through an intermediary. And, Pancrates, never, *never* set foot in the palace again unless I send for you."

The prophet bowed his way out.

"This could be it!" Pliny jumped off his stool and began pacing. "We have the motive."

"But only if Fabia knew," his friend replied. "She'll deny it, of course."

"For the moment, let's work at it from the other end. I want you to find out everything you can about this Sophronia. Imagine it, Balbus planning to marry a whore!"

"But a rich and independent one. I wonder, what he could offer her that she couldn't buy herself?"

"Maybe it wasn't about money."

"What are you suggesting, true love?"

"Roman citizenship. Worth more to these provincials than anything."

"Makes sense," Suetonius conceded. "Here's another thought, though, for what it's worth. Pancrates was blackmailing Balbus. Blackmail often leads to murder. Pancrates is no weakling, and he grew up rough by his own account. They quarreled, fought, things went too far."

"Out in the woods?"

"Well, by any theory of the case we don't know why he was out in the woods."

"Hmpf, I suppose. But no, the man's a swindler, not a killer. No, Sophronia's the key to this. You've got your work cut out for you, my friend. Introduce yourself to her. That monograph on famous whores you're always talking about writing—perhaps she'll be flattered."

"You'd be surprised how many are," Suetonius grinned.

Chapter Nineteen

The third hour of the night

"Come on, Agathon, don't hold out on your friends. What's she like, this Roman bitch of yours?" The girl, naked to the waist, laughed and leaned across to refill his wine cup, brushing his face with her breasts.

The three young men and their *hetaeras* reclined around a table strewn with the wreckage of an expensive meal. They had been there all evening and were quite drunk.

"You're a naughty boy, Agathon." One of the youths, whose flowered wreath had slipped over one eye, punched his shoulder. "You'd best take care. Trifling with their women? You could end up food for the lions."

"Come on, then," the girl insisted. "Don't be mysterious, what's she like? Has she got a pair like these?" She pushed her breasts in his face again. "How is she in bed, or haven't you got that far?"

Agathon put his finger to his lips. "Locked behin' th' hedge of my teeth, as th' poet says." His tongue was thick with drink. "Said too much already. Anyway, 's all over. Over an' done with. But since you asked, darling"—he held his cupped hands to his chest—"they're *this* big!" A laugh started in his throat and then died. With a sudden lunge he grabbed the girl and buried his face against her. "Don't wan' him to see me!" he mumbled into her shoulder.

All around the room conversation died.

How is it, Suetonius reflected, as he stepped through the door and handed his outdoor cloak to a boy, *that they recognize a Roman before I even open my mouth? Something noble in the visage, no doubt.* He was dressed elegantly in the Greek fashion, a short pleated tunic of lime green and a purple *chlamys* of fine linen draped over one shoulder; a wreath strategically placed to cover his bald spot, as Julius Caesar used to do. His working clothes, as he like to think of them.

Suetonius paused to take in his surroundings; he was impressed. *Elysium's* exterior, the blank wall it turned to the street, gave no hint of what lay within. The air was heavy with perfume. The flickering light of lamps on ornate stands, artfully placed and trimmed, gave just enough, but not too much, illumination. In the center of the spacious interior a fountain splashed—a gilded Triton pouring water from his conch into the mouths of dolphins. Around the walls, paintings depicted the amours of the gods: Leda opening her luscious pink thighs to a Zeus-embodied swan, Aphrodite admiring Ares' heroic cock, painted an angry red. Others illustrated all the positions and techniques of love which could be had for a price. At a score of gilded tables groups of revelers reclined on silk-draped couches: the men of all sorts—young, old, thin, fat, bearded, bald; the *hetaeras* who shared their couches, all of one sort—young and beautiful. In one corner, a pair of musicians played on the drum and double flute as a lithe African girl, clad only in a golden belt around her hips, her skin black and lustrous as jet, performed sinuous turns and pirouettes, holding saucers of flame in the palms of her hands, bending backwards until her head touched the floor. Some in the audience threw coins at her feet.

A young slave wearing Persian tunic and trousers approached and gestured that Suetonius should follow him. He had sent word ahead asking for an appointment with Sophronia.

He felt the eyes that followed him as they mounted the stairway to the mezzanine of private rooms. Behind him, laughter and conversation resumed.

She sat behind a desk in a small, bare office; on a stool beside her, a watery-eyed little man bent over an abacus. The desk top was covered with papers. She waved Suetonius to a chair. "Thank you, Byzus. We'll finish later." The accountant gathered his scrolls and crept out of the room, ducking his head at the Roman guest.

"Wine?"

"Thank you."

The wine service, heavy chased silver and rose crystal, sat on a sideboard. Suetonius estimated it was worth half a million at least. She filled his goblet but took nothing for herself. He rolled the wine in his mouth—an excellent Chian.

She fixed him with a level gaze. "To what do I owe the attention of a Roman official? I can spare you a quarter of an hour, no more."

Her skin was a rich olive, her hair, pulled back and coiled on the nape of her neck, was thick and black. She was in her forties, he supposed, still beautiful, though the corners of her mouth were beginning to set in hard lines. She wore a simple white gown, belted under the bosom. Gold bracelets set with rubies circled her wrists. Suetonius, who had made some inquiries about her, had been told of her exotic beauty. He wasn't prepared for how tiny she was; not even five feet, he guessed. What an incongruous pair she and Balbus must have made! He inhaled her scent—myrrh and roses, he thought, and hints of other things he couldn't put a name to.

He had joked with Pliny about interviewing her for his monograph on famous whores but one minute in her presence told him that she would not be amused. She was a whore with the bearing of an empress. And the empresses of his acquaintance were not noted for their sense of humor.

He found himself uncharacteristically stammering. "I, ah, understand that you were a particular friend of the late procurator."

"You come here to pry into my private affairs? So like a Roman, you nation of moralists!"

Once as a boy he had surprised a mother lynx and her brood in their den when hiking in hills near his home. The animal was smaller than his dog, but he sensed that if he took another step forward she would slash him to ribbons. He felt that same premonitory chill now.

"Whoever told you that is lying." She thrust out her chin, challenging him.

"According to our source"—*speak softly, don't threaten*—"Balbus was going to leave his wife and marry you. His death must have been a shock and a deep disappointment. My sympathies."

Her dark eyes searched his face. *Would the lynx pounce?* Finally, she gave a small shrug. "What difference can that possibly make now?"

"Because, lady, his death was no accident."

She was a woman who knew how to control herself. Still, the eyes narrowed just perceptibly. A muscle twitched in her cheek.

"Murdered? And you don't know by whom? And you think I do?"

"We're hoping you might be able to help us." Suetonius leaned forward in his chair and gave her his most confiding look; this was the moment where he would win her cooperation or fail. "Is it likely that Fabia knew about your affair with her husband?"

"I have not admitted to any affair."

"Could she have known?" he repeated.

"That stupid cow!" Her voice rose a pitch. "If she did she's a better actress than I give her credit for!"

Ah, the mask has dropped! And there's real feeling there. Use it. He leaned back, giving her space. "How did you two meet?" *A sympathetic friend.*

She allowed herself a smile. "He was a customer. He would come in the daytime, never at night, so his wife wouldn't suspect. He would go through three or four girls in an afternoon. Most of the girls sleep during the day. I had to keep a few on call just for him. At first it was the girls, then it was me."

"You won his heart?"

"I'm not such an old woman yet." She lowered her eyes.

"Indeed not." *She wasn't above fishing for a compliment.*

"He hated his wife and talked about divorcing her and making me his concubine. He said he could obtain Roman citizenship for me and my son, said he had friends who were close to the emperor. And then he promised to marry me."

Exactly as we'd thought! Suetonius reflected with deep satisfaction. *Now try a different tack, circle around.* "Tell me something about yourself, Sophronia. How do you come by—all this? His gesture took in the room and what lay beyond.

She went to the sideboard now and poured herself a goblet of wine, then poured more for him. "My father was a successful merchant. My late husband, not so successful. He went down with his ship in a storm five years ago, leaving me with a load of debts and a young son, who is now twelve years old and wants to be a Roman legionary when he grows up! Can you believe it?"

"And you found it necessary to go into this particular line of business?"

"Whoring? It's a good deal less risky than shipping. Respectability doesn't interest me, profit does. I discovered I had a talent for business. I've taken something sordid and made it elegant. It isn't about sex, you know, it's about theater. Sex is only the last act. If you don't approve you can leave."

Angry again, I've touched a sore spot. "On the contrary, lady, I'm filled with admiration. Anyone who commands a fortune like yours—"

"If only I *did* command it." She set her goblet down hard, splashing some of the wine. "I have a brother, a half brother actually, Argyrus. My father's first wife was a Greek woman. After her death, he married again, this time a Persian—you may know there is a sizeable Persian enclave here—she was my mother."

Half barbarian, Suetonius thought, *I could almost have guessed.* "And so Argyrus is older than you are and pure Greek and—"

"And my oldest living male relative, yes. Your Roman women enjoy an enviable freedom. It's not the same with us. He controls my fortune and does nothing but waste it, sucks my blood like a leech."

"But if you had married Balbus, Argyrus would have lost control over your money."

She didn't say anything. She didn't need to.

"And where might I find this brother of yours?"

"Here, as often as not, helping himself to the merchandize free of charge."

"Would you object if I interviewed him?"

"Why should I?" she murmured.

"Thank you, Sophronia, you've been very helpful. The governor and I appreciate it."

Perhaps it was the wine; the frown lines were softening, there was almost a wistfulness in her gaze. "I hope you catch whoever did it," she said. "Balbus was not—not an easy man to like. What can I say, he was a Roman. But he meant something to me."

"I'm sure he did."

She squared her shoulders. "So. Have I answered all your questions? Then let me ask *you* some."

For the next few minutes he opened himself to her—not everything, naturally, but more than he had planned; perhaps more than was wise. He had no children, he told her. His wife was in Italy. It was a marriage of convenience. He talked about his boyhood in North Africa, about his ambition to make his mark in literature. Finally, he even told her about his monograph. She laughed and made him promise to send her a copy when it was done.

They had far exceeded the quarter of an hour she had said she would allow him.

"I've taken enough of your time, Sophronia," he said at last. He made to get up. "Thank you again for seeing me. I can find my way out."

She looked at him under her heavy lashes. "You needn't go," she said.

Chapter Twenty

The day before the Kalends of November

The following morning, Suetonius located Pliny several miles beyond the city. With an architect and surveyor at his heels, the governor was inspecting the ruined arches of an abandoned aqueduct. It was a cold, clear day. Suetonius had ridden out on horseback and found that the sharp air revived him a little. He hadn't had much sleep.

"Five million sesterces gone to waste!" Pliny was scowling. "And into whose purse did it disappear? I aim to find out. Meanwhile the city is starved for water. As long as the Balbus case keeps me in Nicomedia, there's plenty to do here. We're trying to see how much of the old brickwork is salvageable." He signaled to his companions to take themselves out of earshot. "I expected to hear from you last night. You spoke with Sophronia?"

"The conversation went on, ah, a little longer than I had planned. You'd gone to bed by the time I got back."

"Really." Pliny raised an eyebrow. "You found her company agreeable?"

"Yes, well, I mean—"

"But not too agreeable, I hope." He gave his friend a penetrating look.

"No. We discussed my monograph. She was most informative."

"I can imagine. You know we need to be impartial dealing with these people. No entanglements. You do understand that."

"Yes, absolutely. Yes."

"Well, and what did you learn?"

Suetonius recounted their conversation.

Pliny's eyes lit up. "Extraordinary! We guessed right on every count! Argyrus just might be our man." He clapped Suetonius on the back. "I'll be the rest of the morning here. You ride back and tell my *lictor* Galeo to bring Argyrus in. Where will he be, at the brothel?"

"Possibly, but I advise against arresting him there. Cause too much of a stir. Best we pick him up at home even if we have to wait. Sophronia can tell me where he lives."

"Right you are."

"Where do you want to question him? We can use the tavern again, keep things hush-hush."

"Hmm. I see your point, but no. Have the *lictors* take him down to the dungeon and leave him there for a few hours. I want this man thoroughly frightened."

◇◇◇

Afternoon

The ancient kings of Bithynia had equipped their palace with a warren of airless underground cells, where generations of nameless and forgotten prisoners had dragged out the last years of their lives. The walls were covered with their desperate scribblings. A larger area served as guardroom and torture chamber. It was a place to unman even the bravest.

"Is this how honest citizens are treated now? Hauled out of bed by Roman bullies? My wife's not well, they left her in hysterics. I have important friends, this won't go unnoticed, I promise you."

Though it was cold in the dungeon, Argyrus was sweating and his color was high. He was a ferret-faced man of about fifty, with a pointed nose, a receding hairline and a mouth full of bad teeth. He mopped his face with his sleeve.

"An honest citizen," said Pliny, looking at him severely, "has nothing to fear."

The stone walls of the chamber were damp and encrusted with niter. Outside the iron-bound door, two brawny guards, took up their post. A shorthand writer sat in a corner of the room, his stylus poised.

"And just what does that mean?" Argyrus was more angry than frightened.

"Vibius Balbus, the procurator, was last seen alive the morning of the fourth day before the Ides of October. Where were you during that day and the following night?"

"Balbus! What does he have to do with me?"

"Answer the question, please."

"I don't understand your Roman dates."

After a moment's calculation, Suetonius offered the equivalent in the local calendar.

"What, twenty days ago?" Argyrus protested. "Don't be absurd! How do I know where I was? D'you know where you were?"

"I advise you to think."

Argyrus retreated into a sulky silence that lasted some moments. "Well, at *Elysium*, I suppose, my sister's place. Like I said, my wife's practically an invalid, we don't often—"

"Never mind that," Pliny snapped. "Who saw you there? Did you spend the night with a girl?"

"Philaenis, yes, she's my favorite."

"And she'll vouch for you?"

Argyrus' color deepened to a dangerous shade of purple. He struck his thigh with his fist. "It's Sophronia! She's put you onto me. Balbus and her. I see what this is all about. She wants you to think I did something to him? Killed him?"

"What will Philaenis say if we question her?"

Argyrus' eyes darted around the room. He was frightened now. "Philaenis will say whatever my sister tells her to say, damn her. I give her gifts but Sophronia *owns* her, the barbarian slut!"

"Watch your tongue!" Suetonius shot back, half rising out of his chair.

Pliny gave him a warning look. "Calm down, your sister hasn't accused you of anything."

"Then why am I here?"

"To clarify a few things for us. You would, of course, lose control of her money if she were to marry Balbus."

"Marry him! Don't make me laugh. She doesn't want a husband. She poisoned her last one, you know. Oh, yes. Poor man developed a flux, turned yellow, and shriveled up and died screaming with pain. She hates men. Can't stand to be controlled by anyone."

Suetonius glowered at him. "Her husband drowned at sea."

Argyrus attempted a laugh. "Is that what she told you?"

"Let us come back to the matter at hand," said Pliny. "You can't deny you had reason to resent Balbus' attentions to her."

"Doesn't mean I killed him! Look at me. Do I look like I'd be a match for that man in a fight? Do I look like someone who skulks around in the woods in the middle of the night?"

Pliny looked at him sharply. "Who said anything about the woods?"

"Well—I mean, that's what they said, isn't it? Riding accident in the woods."

"We said it was a riding accident, we didn't say where."

"You did—I mean, well it's obvious, isn't it?—" Panic flickered in his eyes. His head swiveled from Pliny to Suetonius and back. "What are you going to do to me? Don't torture me, I couldn't stand it, I'm not strong. Please. I'll—I'll swear an oath on the altar of Zeus—anything!"

"What's an oath to you?" Suetonius sneered.

Argyrus puddled the floor around his feet.

"No," Pliny held up a hand, "no. I'm not going to torture you. Or keep you here." Indeed, he couldn't imagine this pathetic figure overpowering Balbus. "But I warn you not to leave the city and not to talk to anyone about this interview. You understand me? You can go."

"And stay away from Sophronia," Suetonius growled.

◇◇◇

"All right but he could have hired assassins," Suetonius argued. "I wouldn't have let him go so easily."

"And you, my friend," Pliny replied, "are letting your emotions rule your head. Argyrus is a miserable character, but a murderer? Now that I've seen the man, I don't know."

They sat once again in Pliny's office together with Nymphidius, Marinus, Aquila, and Zosimus. Servants had brought in their lunch on trays.

"You say he knew about the woods," said Marinus.

"Yes, but it is a reasonable guess, isn't it? Look, as far as motive goes, he's the likeliest suspect we have, but as for means and opportunity?" Pliny shook his head.

"But then that applies to any suspect," said Nymphidius. "We've been through this before. Who might have known where Balbus was and who was the other horseman?"

"The likeliest person to know where he was is someone who followed him from his home that morning," Pliny replied. "And that brings us back to Fabia."

"But only if she knew about his affair," Suetonius reminded him. "Sophronia was pretty sure she didn't."

"And, of course, she'll deny it if I ask her," said Pliny wearily. "I've been remarkably unsuccessful in getting that woman to admit anything. I honestly don't think I have the stomach to go back there again."

"Well, where do we go from here then?" said Aquila.

Pliny looked around the table, hoping to see inspiration in some face. And found none. "There is still too much we don't know. *Why* was he where he was? Where was he going? Someone, somewhere knows the answer. We need to dig deeper. Zosimus, my boy—" he smiled at the young man whose forehead still bore the mark of his recent wound, "our clew of thread has so far led us up against a blank wall. We need another clew."

They talked a while longer to no purpose. Then, as the others got up to leave, Zosimus begged a moment to speak to Pliny privately.

"Patrone, I'm sorry to bother you with a personal matter when you have so much else on your mind, but it's Ione."

Pliny looked a question.

"I mean, well, she's not herself these days. Irritable, cross with me and little Rufus, like something's preying on her mind, and when I ask her she just turns away and won't say anything. So I was thinking perhaps if you spoke to her?"

Pliny squeezed his shoulder affectionately. He was still feeling guilty about what had happened to his favorite freedman, though the wound luckily wasn't as serious as it had looked when the soldiers carried him home that day covered in blood.

"I'm sorry to hear it," he said. "She's always been such a cheerful soul. But really wouldn't it be better if Calpurnia spoke to her? Women tell each other things, you know, they don't share with us men."

"But they talk all the time, Patrone. Once even in the middle of the night, the mistress woke us up to talk to her. I don't know what they said but when Ione came back to bed she was in a terrible state."

"Really? In the middle of the night, you say? Well, I don't know what I can do but I'll have a word with 'Purnia about it."

"Thank you, Patrone."

That night

Pliny thrashes and struggles. His toga, wet and clinging, envelops him like a burial shroud, pinning his arms to his sides. No matter how hard he tries, he can't break free. He is suffocating. He cries for help but they ignore him—Calpurnia and Ione, talking in low tones. What are they saying? He can't make it out. Why don't they hear him? Won't someone help him? His heart is near bursting—

"Gaius, Gaius, wake up!"

With a wrenching effort he tore himself free of the dream. He was tangled in the damp sheet. It was moments before he could catch his breath and still his heart.

"Are you all right? I couldn't wake you." Calpurnia bent over him. "You're soaking wet, shall I call Marinus?"

"No, no, I'm all right now. I was dreaming. What hour is it?"

"I don't know—not yet dawn. There's someone at the door with a message for you. He says it's urgent."

Chapter Twenty-one

The Kalends of November

An elderly man was waiting for him in the antechamber, flanked by two sleepy-eyed door-slaves, who eyed him with resentment. He was one of the Night Watch, he said, whose job was to patrol the streets on the lookout for fires. He ducked his head to Pliny. "They're dead, sir, all of 'em. The whole family, slaughtered like. The husband, the wife, the little—"

"Whose family, man?" Pliny peered into the Night Watchman's frightened face.

"Glaucon, your honor. One of his servants come running out of the house as I was passing by. I went into the house with him and looked. Then I come here, not knowing where else—"

"Take me there." Pliny called for his cloak and shoes and sent someone to rouse his chair bearers and Galeo, his senior *lictor*.

Glaucon's was a large, handsome town house near the temple of Artemis, a short walk from the palace. The servants who met them at the door were gibbering with fear. They had been wakened in the middle of the night, they said, by groans and the sound of retching coming from the master's bedroom. When they burst in, they found him dying; he took his last rattling breath as they watched. His wife was already beyond help. They ran to the children's rooms—Glaucon had two young sons and a daughter—and found them dead as well; and Glaucon's old mother, not dead, but unconscious and barely breathing.

Pliny sent Galeo back for Marinus and when the physician arrived they inspected the bodies together. The stink of vomit was everywhere. In the master bedroom, Glaucon lay on the floor in a puddle of it. He had kicked over a bedside table in his death struggle and the pieces of a smashed water jug lay beside it. His wife was half on, half off the bed, her mouth open as though in mid-scream, her lips blue, her shift rucked up around her waist, exposing her nakedness. They went to the children's rooms. In one, two boys of about eight or nine—they looked like twins—lay clutching each other. In the adjoining chamber, a pretty girl of about thirteen had gotten as far as the doorway before she collapsed. Glaucon's old mother lay in her bed, eyes closed and soaked with sweat. A servant girl sat beside her, bathing her face with a cloth.

Pliny realized his legs were trembling. His stomach rebelled and acid rose in his throat. Marinus, who was inured to death, saw how pale he looked and put out a hand to steady him.

"Who could have done this, Marinus?"

"Mustn't leap to conclusions. Could be nothing more than a case of bad shellfish. What did they dine on?"

"I've already asked," replied Pliny. "Roast lamb and vegetables. No oysters, nothing like that. Have we got a murder on our hands?"

Marinus looked thoughtful. "Poison? Not something I know much about. I've heard that *sandraca*, some call it *arsenikon*, can be ingested in food or drink and kill you a few hours later, depending on the dose. Makes sense that the man died last. He's a big fellow, isn't he? You saw the shoulders on him. Took longer for the poison to work its way through him."

"But the old woman?"

"Old women don't eat much. I'll stay with her, if you like. If she pulls through, we may have an answer."

"Please." Pliny shook his head wearily. "The city's on the verge of panic already, and now this. We must do whatever we can. I'll leave you in charge, then. Send for me at once if she revives." He paused in the doorway. "Is this *arsenikon* hard to get hold of?"

"I wouldn't think so. It has various uses. I believe painters use it for a red pigment."

As he left the house, the sun was just rising over the housetops and already a curious crowd of early-risers had gathered outside in the street. In another hour the whole city would be abuzz with news of the atrocity.

Pliny returned to the palace to find Pancrates waiting for him outside his office.

"I told you never to come here unasked," Pliny glowered at him. "I warn you I'm in no mood—"

"Please, Governor," the prophet looked pained. "I only want to prove my usefulness. I came as soon as I heard."

"About?"

"Why, Glaucon, of course. What else?"

Pliny took him inside and shut the door. "What do you know about this?"

"About his death, nothing. The family is well-to-do. They have crop land and orchards and do a bit of trading on the side—Glaucon's brother, that is—he's the brains of the family. Glaucon, himself, I fear, was a bit slow-witted. But what a wrestler in his day! Oh, he was famous. In the all-out he would break arms and legs. Nobody could stand up to him."

"Is that all you have to say? I could have learned this from anyone."

"Tch, tch, such a temper, Governor. Well, you're under a lot of strain, aren't you? As a matter of fact, that isn't all. What I was about to say, is that poor Glaucon consulted us not too long ago. Whenever the prophet said 'us', he meant himself and the god. '*Will I be punished for slaying the lion?*' was his question. Well, we couldn't imagine what he meant, there haven't been lions in these parts for a hundred years."

"'Slaying the lion.' And when did he consult you?"

"A few days after the procurator's disappearance."

"And what answer did you give him?"

"We told him 'yes' to see what would happen."

"And what happened is that he was murdered."

"So it would seem."

Calpurnia had seen him enter. She was waiting for him out of sight. As Pancrates trotted down the palace steps, she rushed at him and seized his hand. "Please! I wrote Agathon a letter. He hasn't answered! What shall I do?"

He pushed her away roughly. "I thought I was the filthy, Greek spy," he snarled. "I've been warned away from you, madam. Your husband and I have an understanding. I can do nothing for you."

◇◇◇

Late the next day, word came from Marinus that Glaucon's mother was conscious and able to speak. Pliny went there at once. He was met at the door by none other than Diocles.

"A terrible business," murmured the orator. "I'm a friend of the family, you know. They appreciate your concern, don't you, Theron?"—he nodded toward a man whom Pliny assumed was the brother—"but this is a matter for the civic authorities, not your office."

Did anything happen in this city, Pliny wondered, *that Diocles did not instantly involve himself in?*

"If it's a question of adulterated food," Diocles hurried on, "the magistrates will see to it that the merchant is found and punished."

"And if it's poison?" said Pliny.

"Great gods! Why would you suspect such a thing?" The orator adopted an expression of horror.

"*If* it's poison," Pliny continued, "that affects the public order. My business. If you'll excuse me, I'm going to question the mother."

"Only family members are permitted in the *gynekeion*—"

But Pliny had already pushed past him. Marinus met him at her bedroom door. "They ordered me to leave," the physician said. "I politely refused."

"Probably not so politely," Pliny smiled ruefully. Postumius Marinus did not suffer fools lightly.

"She is very weak, though. Don't tire her. Her name's Berenice, by the way. And she doesn't know yet that the others are dead."

Berenice lay in bed, a veined and fragile dry leaf of a woman, her white hair spread out on the pillow, a coverlet pulled up to her chin.

"Berenice," Pliny leaned over her and spoke softly in her ear, "I am the governor. Can you tell me what happened to you?"

"She looked up with watery, unfocused eyes. "Who are you?"

"The governor. I'm here to help. Tell me about dinner last night. Did you eat anything out of the ordinary? Anything not made in your own kitchen?"

She was quiet for so long he was afraid she was past understanding. Then she whispered, "Yes." Her story came out in wheezing phrases, broken by pauses when her eyes fluttered and her mind seemed to wander. Pliny put his ear to her lips to catch her words. They had just finished dinner when someone came to the door carrying a covered tray of dates stuffed with pine nuts. The man handed the tray to her son and she heard what he said: *A gift from the Persian to the bridegroom.* Pliny made her repeat this. She was certain those were the words: *Perses* and *nymphios.* She asked her son what the man had meant, but he wouldn't answer her and he seemed suddenly in a bad mood. Nevertheless, they passed the dates around, they were very large and sweet, and everyone had some. Glaucon ate the most. She only had one, though, not being very hungry.

"Did you recognize the man who brought the dates?"

"No."

"A Persian, he said? Did—does your son know any Persians?"

"I don't know, I don't think so."

"And he isn't a bridegroom is he? He's been married for years."

"No. No. He'll tell you himself." Suddenly her eyes widened and she tried to raise her head. "Where is he? Where is my son, my daughter-in-law? Why aren't they here? Who are you?"

Pliny told her as gently as he could. She turned her face to the wall and began to weep soundlessly.

"I'd give her a sleeping draught," said Marinus, "but in her condition it could kill her."

"That might be a mercy," Pliny answered.

The two men stole quietly out of the room and returned to the *megaron* where Diocles and Theron were waiting.

"Well—?" Diocles began.

Pliny ignored him and turned to the brother. The man appeared to be deep in shock, sitting speechless with his head in his hands. "Theron, your brother and his family were murdered. I'm sorry, I know it's a heavy blow, I don't say it lightly. I will do everything in my power to find out who did this—"

"*We* will find out who did it!" Diocles was on his feet, the blood rising in his face. "I insist you accept our help, Governor."

Finally, Pliny had had enough of this pompous nuisance. "Sit down!"

The two men glared at each other until Diocles snorted and turned away.

Then Theron spoke, mumbling to himself. "We were invited for dinner, my wife and I. Had another party to go to first—never got here."

"Theron." Pliny put a hand on his shoulder. "Kindly show me to your brother's office or wherever he kept his papers. There may be something there."

Diocles opened his mouth.

"Don't!" said Pliny

The office was a small room at the back of the house. There wasn't much in it. Glaucon, it seemed, had not been much of a reader or a writer. A few scrolls, a few wax tablets. Pliny scooped them up and handed them to Galeo. Then one item on the desk caught his eye. A handbook of astrology.

He had seen its twin before.

◇◇◇

The Sun-Runner to the Father, greetings:

You have heard by now that the Bridegroom is dead—surely murdered. The conclusion is inescapable that one of our number is the killer. I say this although I know it pains you to hear it. I am doing everything I can to learn more. I pray we find him before the Romans do. This governor is no fool. Guard yourself well, Father. Nama Mithras.

◇◇◇

"'Purnia, we've been here too long, give it up for today. People will start to wonder. We'll try again tomorrow."

Calpurnia did not answer but gripped Ione's hand tighter and pulled her along. They had already visited the temples of Artemis and Asclepius that morning and now were circling the exhibition space in the temple of Zeus, where she and Agathon had first met. For five days now, since she had sent Agathon the letter, she had stolen every moment she could to slip away from the palace and visit all the temples where art works were displayed—not with her easel and paints; she didn't even pretend to be studying the masterpieces—but only with the desperate hope of seeing *him* again.

She didn't know what else to do. The fever in her blood gave her no rest.

And what would she say if she saw him? She couldn't think that far ahead. Every day, in the privacy of her studio, she sketched his face over and over, trying to capture his glancing eye, the half-smile on his lips, every curl of his hair. And feeling the image dissolve as she tried to grasp it. And throwing her charcoal down in despair. Why hadn't he answered her letter? Why was he so cruel? And surely Gaius guessed something. How could he not? But she was past caring about that.

She circled the gallery again, looking with unseeing eyes at the paintings and statues that had once given her such pleasure. Never taking one eye from the pillared entryway. The gallery wasn't crowded; no more than a dozen or so visitors. The minutes crept by—half an hour, an hour.

"'Purnia, my feet hurt," Ione complained. "There must be a better way than this to meet him. Where else does he like to go?"

"Yes, all right," Calpurnia sighed. "You're right. I'm not thinking. Let's…"

And then there he was! Coming through the door, alone. He paused and looked around. Was he looking for her? Suddenly she couldn't breathe. In the center of the gallery was a large statuary group, a copy of Laocoon and the sea serpent. She ran behind it, pulling Ione with her. Unseen, she watched him as he moved around the gallery.

She would talk to him. Now. She would step out from her hiding place. Walk toward him with an easy smile. And Aphrodite, whose little image she prayed to nightly, would put the right words in her mouth. She didn't know what they would be, but the goddess wouldn't fail, *couldn't* fail her.

She swallowed. Drew a deep breath. Closed her eyes for a moment and sent up a prayer to the love goddess.

"Calpurnia! How nice to see you, dear."

Faustilla, Nymphidius' formidable wife, swooped down upon her, her voice like a trumpet, her red gash of a mouth stretched in a grimace of feigned delight. Behind her came Fannia, the meek, bird-like little wife of Caelianus.

"Well, of course, you are the artist, aren't you?" Faustilla blared. "So of course you'd be here, wouldn't you? We thought we'd just pop in for a look, didn't we, Fannia?"

Fannia offered a hesitant smile.

"Well, I haven't seen so many naked men"—Faustilla leered at the nude statuary—"since I was a girl and sneaked into the men's baths. Speaking of baths, we're on our way there now, it's the ladies' hour you know. Come with us. Haven't you had enough of this musty old stuff?"

"I—I'm sorry, Faustilla," Calpurnia stammered, "I really can't—that is, I'm waiting for someone."

"Nonsense. Waiting for whom—your lover?"

"What?"

"Great gods, look at your face! Can't you take a joke? Well, we're all so serious these days with what's been going on."

"Going on?"

"Some family of Greeklings got themselves murdered yesterday. Doesn't the governor tell you anything? My husband doesn't tell me anything either. All very hush hush. It's enough to give one palpitations. I remember when emperor Claudius was murdered. I was just a child, of course—"

"Excuse me, Faustilla, please!"

He was gone! She looked around wildly. One moment he had been standing in front of the statue of a laughing satyr and now he was nowhere.

"I have to go!" She seized Ione's hand and dragged her away.

Faustilla watched Calpurnia's disappearing back and shook her bewigged head. "Fannia, something's not right with that woman."

Fannia nodded vigorously. "You're right, of course, Faustilla. The way she and her maid carry on like a pair of conspirators. Spends more time with her than with any of us. T'isn't proper."

"Ione! That stuck up little bit of stuff. She needs a good whipping is what she needs. Teach her her place. Gaius Plinius ought to control his womenfolk better. I have a mind to say something to him."

"But, of course, the men are so busy." Fannia was afraid she might have gone too far.

"We'll see."

Chapter Twenty-two

Pliny thumped the table. "We have hold of a new clew, gentlemen, and this one may finally lead us out of the labyrinth!"

The staff was once again gathered in his office and this time their expressions were eager and engaged. Their chief's excitement was contagious.

"You think Glaucon killed Balbus, then?" Suetonius asked.

"Balbus' neck was crushed. Not many men have the strength to do that, but Glaucon, the ex-wrestler, did. And then, for some reason, he began to worry about what he'd done."

"And his question to the oracle provoked his murder," Marinus finished the thought.

"*Will I be punished for slaying the lion?* Those were his words?" said Aquila. But why 'lion'? It's a damned peculiar expression."

"Brave as a lion?" Suetonius offered. "Balbus was a tough ex-soldier; it could fit. Still, we really don't have anything concrete that connects Glaucon to Balbus."

"But we do," said Pliny triumphantly. From the jumble of scrolls that he had taken from Glaucon's house and which now covered his desk, he withdrew the little handbook of astrology and unrolled it. "This is identical to the one I took from Balbus' house. I've just been comparing them side by side, they're copies of the same text. Fabia told me that Balbus studied it diligently although it 'made his head hurt.' I'd guess that Glaucon, who by all accounts was no genius, suffered the same ache. The question is, why were both of them intent on studying this little book and how did they come to possess it?"

"Interesting," said Nymphidius. He massaged his knee "But that's only one piece of the puzzle. The poisoned dates were a gift 'from the Persian to the bridegroom.' But Glaucon had been married for years, and who is this Persian?"

"Just like a Persian," said Aquila angrily, "to slaughter a whole family. They haven't got human feelings like us."

"There are Persians in the city," said Suetonius. "A few hundred. They have their own quarter together with the Jews and Armenians." *According to Sophronia*, he was about to add, but suddenly felt reluctant to bring her name into the discussion.

"And this Persian who wanted Glaucon dead," said Marinus, "must therefore be complicit in the murder of Balbus. A Persian murdering a Roman official? A bad business—especially if it's the prelude to something worse."

"You don't mean—?" Zosimus blurted out, fear in his voice.

"A second Mithridates!" Aquila growled. "Another massacre!"

"None of that talk now!" said Pliny sharply. But he was more worried than he let on. Could Persian spies have somehow learned of Trajan's plans to launch an invasion of their empire from Bithynia-Pontus? Was Pacorus, King of Kings, planning to strike first?

"Anything in Glaucon's papers that mentions Persians?" Marinus asked.

"Not so far," Pliny admitted. "I haven't read everything yet."

There was an uncomfortable silence. Finally, Suetonius asked, "What do you propose, Gaius Plinius?"

"I will talk to these Persians."

They wore the baggy trousers and long-sleeved, embroidered tunics of their nation. Their long hair and beards were oiled and curled. They were shop-keepers and merchants, the leaders of their community. They stood, a dozen of them, in Pliny's antechamber, muttering in their beards. They were frightened. Persia and Rome had been enemies for generations. Roman legions had invaded their land once and been massacred. There had been wars over the possession of Armenia and the frontier was a scene of constant skirmishes. They had no reason to trust a Roman governor.

They pushed forward their spokesman, Arsames, an elderly, dignified man with grey in his beard, an importer of eastern spices and perfumes. He sank to his knees, stretched out his arms, and knocked his forehead on the floor.

"Stand up, man, I'm not one of your barbarian kings," Pliny said sharply.

With the help of two of his comrades, Arsames struggled to his feet. If he heard the snickers from the Romans in the room, he ignored them.

"Forgive me, master—our custom." He spoke passable Greek.

"Nor am I your master," said Pliny sharply. "What I require from you is information, not cringing obeisance." In a few words he told them that a prominent Greek and his family had been poisoned by a Persian. "I want that man, and I expect you to produce him."

Arsames translated for the others. With one voice they cried out their innocence, raising their hands to heaven. No Persian had done—would ever do—such a thing! Who was Glaucon? They did not know him. Why would they wish him dead?

Pliny held up his hands for silence. "Nevertheless, *nevertheless*," he said when he could make himself heard, "Glaucon is dead and we have a witness who swears that a Persian sent the poisoned dates."

"No!" Arsames shook his head. "This is a slander on us. An excuse to persecute us."

Now Pliny felt himself at a loss. He didn't want to draw a line from Glaucon's murder to Balbus', whose death was still officially an accident. "I'm not accusing all of you, Arsames. But one of your people *is* a murderer. I want you to help me find him. You would be wise to cooperate." Pliny put on his most severe expression and Arsames' eyes widened with fear and confusion.

Suddenly, from the rear of the chamber there was a commotion and a woman's voice was heard demanding shrilly to be let in. Her head didn't come up to their shoulders but she shoved her way through the press of men, a small whirlwind of indignation, until she stood before the astonished Pliny. Suetonius stepped forward smoothly. "Sophronia, what an unexpected pleasure, but really—"

"Why have you dragged these men here, Governor?"

While Pliny was searching for his voice, Suetonius went on quickly, "Really, this is no place for you, my dear."

"Why not? I'm a Persian. When they can be attacked, so can I."

Before he could reply, she turned to Arsames and spoke to him in rapid Persian. He looked hardly less confounded than the Romans by her presence. He knew who she was, of course, and did not approve of her. None of them did. But if, as it seemed, she knew these Romans and didn't fear them, he was ready to put aside his scruples.

She turned back to the Romans. "These men know nothing about this murder, nor do I. But if you want their help, you had best not threaten them. They are proud men. My mother's people live amongst them. If there is anything to be learned, we will learn it. From now on, I will be your go-between."

"I thank you, madam," said Pliny, finally collecting himself. "Whatever you learn you may communicate to Suetonius in your, ah, place of business."

"Oh quite," she said. "The gods forbid that a whore should sully your doorstep."

Pliny was again speechless. Worse, he was beginning to seriously wonder whether the Persians had anything to do with this.

That evening, under a lowering sky, five coffins were borne on the shoulders of pallbearers to the cemetery beyond the city wall. Flutes shrilled, mourners shrieked and tore their garments, but this was more than the imitation grief of hired professionals: the whole city had turned out for this sad event. An immense sea of people trailed the cortege and their outrage was genuine and palpable. And among the crowd, certain men circulated, who sometimes whispered and sometimes shouted that it was the Persians, the hated foreigner, the ancestral enemy, sly, grasping businessmen, deniers of the city's gods, who had slaughtered this noble Greek family and were only waiting for the opportunity to kill again, kill them in their beds, kill without mercy. Must they wait until more innocents were poisoned? Drive them out! Burn them out!

And, having done their work, they pocketed the coins they had been promised and slipped away.

That night a mob rampaged through the Persian quarter, looting shops, throwing torches into homes and dragging the terrified inhabitants out into the street to be beaten and raped; making no distinction between the Persians and the Jews and Armenians who were unlucky enough to live side by side with them. Flames leapt into the night sky, visible from the palace. Pliny sent every soldier he had into the quarter and they battled the mob all night long, chasing looters through dark alleys, putting out fires, forming a human shield around the houses that weren't burning.

Dawn broke lurid through a pall of smoke that overhung the city. Worse was the sullen miasma of hatred and fear that settled on it. Pliny crucified six looters, declared martial law, suspended meetings of the council and assembly, and ordered his men to break up street corner gatherings of more than three. He opened the palace grounds to the Persian families who had been burnt out of their homes, and Calpurnia—defying the muttered comments of the wives—took charge of caring for them. Pliny had never felt more proud of her.

But it wasn't only the Greeks he had to deal with. A delegation of Roman businessmen, not only from Nicomedia but from Prusa and Nicaea as well, demanded an audience. Why was Balbus' murder—for few now doubted that it was murder—still unsolved? Why had he brought the Persians in for questioning only to let them go? Was another Mithridates loose in their midst? Could he protect them? Because if he couldn't then, by the gods, they would protect themselves!

Time was running out. Pliny knew he was on the verge of losing control of the city and the province. It had been a mistake to summon the Persians in such a public way; he blamed himself for what had happened to them. But who *was* this Persian who had poisoned Glaucon and his family? Was it perhaps no Persian at all but someone else, some personal enemy of Glaucon's, who wanted to shift suspicion onto the foreigners? And what was the connection between Glaucon's death and Balbus'? That there was a connection he was convinced.

Once a semblance of order had been restored in the city, Pliny made inquiries as to where he might find Glaucon's brother and learned that he was still at the family's house, overseeing the rituals for purifying it from the pollution of death. He sent Galeo after him.

Theron was a handsome man in his early fifties, some five years older than his brother. He looked older than that now. Grief had aged him. His skin was grey, his eyes pouched and exhausted. And he plainly wanted nothing to do with Pliny.

"I apologize for invading your home, Theron. It was necessary to question your mother without delay."

"My mother died early this morning."

"Then all the more so. I am truly sorry. I want you to help me find their killer."

"It was the Persians, of course. Why are you protecting them?"

"Did your brother have any dealings with the Persians or a particular Persian?"

"Not to my knowledge."

"Did your brother have enemies that you know of?"

"None. Everyone who knew him liked him."

"Tell me about him. What sort of man was he?"

Theron looked at a loss for words. "Well he—I mean, a good husband, good father. Loved food. Loved sport. Horses and dogs. Lots of friends—even some Romans, though I don't know why."

"I'm told he was a tough competitor in the wrestling ring. Injured his opponents. Perhaps he killed someone? Could there be a grudge?"

"But that was years ago," Theron protested.

"Would you call him an intelligent man? I know this is painful but please be frank."

"You mean books and so forth? No, he wasn't much for that. When we were boys he would escape from our tutor every chance he got."

"Well then it's curious that I found this among his effects." Pliny produced the astrological handbook. "A bit abstruse, I would think, for the non-mathematical mind. I've spent a little time with it and I can't make much out of it myself."

Theron leaned over and peered at the scroll. "I've never seen this before. You say it was Glaucon's? He never said anything to me about stargazing."

"Well, we have a small mystery then." Pliny set the scroll aside. "Did your brother by any chance have dealings with Vibius Balbus?"

"What, the procurator? No. Why should he?"

"Did he interest himself in provincial affairs? Taxation, for instance?"

"I told you, he liked hunting and living well. He left politics and business to me."

Pliny was silent for a moment, considering how he would phrase his next question. "Would you say your brother was a man who could be easily led? I mean into doing something that he might have regretted later? Might even want to confess?"

"Confess? Confess what? I don't know what you're talking about. Look, my brother is a victim, not a culprit. I warn you—"

"Calm yourself, please. I know this is difficult for you."

"Do you?" Theron shot back. "Those children"—he swallowed hard—"were as dear to me as my own. His wife and mine were like sisters."

"Then help me avenge them. Somewhere there is a door waiting to be unlocked and a key that fits it."

Theron answered him with a bleak look. "I've no key."

"But we haven't begun to look. You say Glaucon left politics and business to you. What sort of business do you engage in?"

Theron shrugged, "We sell a part of our crop. We export dried fruits from our orchards. When we have spare cash we invest in construction, sometimes in trading ventures, or our banker does for us. We do well enough."

"Your banker. And who might he be? I only ask because in going through your brother's papers I noticed a receipt for the deposit of three minas of silver with a certain Didymus."

"That's him. A good man, reliable. Done business with him for years. But this deposit? It's news to me."

"Interesting."

"And what has this to do with my brother's death?"

"Probably nothing," Pliny sighed.

Chapter Twenty-three

Didymus was a small man of about forty with a round face and a round, protruding belly. His mouth was a red Cupid's bow, his eyes bright under springing brows, with something of the child in them. His clothes were good but not ostentatious. His most striking feature was his right arm, or, rather, the absence of it below the elbow. "Mauled by a dog when I was a tyke," he explained almost as soon as he had entered Pliny's office. "Mustn't complain, though. I do well enough with the one." He offered a shy smile. "And what did you want with me, sir? I must say I was flummoxed when your man came for me." Didymus sat upright in his chair, leaning slightly forward, an expectant look on his face.

Pliny let him talk. The man was nervous, anxious to please. But that was to be expected.

"Terrible, wasn't it, sir," Didymus rattled on. "I mean the riot. Bad for my business, I can tell you. When there's civil strife money goes into the ground—literally, I mean. People bury it."

"And do you do business with the Persians?" Pliny made a temple of his fingers and rested his chin on them.

"Me, sir. No. I mean they keep to themselves, don't they? I say, did they really poison Glaucon and his poor family like everyone says? Well, they are barbarians, aren't they?"

"I'm hoping you might shed some light on that. You knew Glaucon, I understand."

Consternation filled the banker's eyes. "I did, sir. But as to murder, well, I don't—"

"Tell me something about your business."

"Well, it's the usual. There are six banking houses in the city. I'm not the biggest of them, but I do all right. People deposit money with me, which I lend at interest, or invest, or transfer to a third party, however they instruct me. I charge a modest fee, of course."

"And where do you keep these deposits?"

"In my vault, sir. It's quite safe. You must come down and visit us some time, we're at the harbor."

"And Glaucon, I believe, had deposited a sum with you. When was that?"

"Yes, sir, three minas as I recall, to invest as I saw fit. He did that now and again. And that would have been, let me see, a month or so ago."

"And did you invest it?"

"No, sir, not yet. Waiting for something good to come along. Of course, now I'm going to return it to his brother."

"You're an honest banker, then." Pliny smiled.

"I am, sir." He smiled modestly.

"What about Vibius Balbus, were you acquainted with him?"

Didymus bowed his head. "That's a sad turn of events, isn't it, sir? Riding accident they say. And leaving behind a widow and a son, an unfortunate young fellow so I've heard."

Pliny was suddenly alert. "What have you heard?"

"Just the gossip of the marketplace. Not quite right in his head. Sees things that aren't there. Full of crazy notions."

"I had no idea he was such a subject of conversation. But I asked you if you knew Balbus. Did he ever transact business through you?"

"No, sir, he didn't."

Pliny was silent for a moment, considering how much he should give away. "I have some information that before his death Glaucon consulted the oracle of Pancrates as to whether he would be punished for killing a lion. Does that mean anything to you?"

The Cupid's bow formed itself into a tiny frown. "Pancrates, you say? I wouldn't put great stock in what he says if I were you. To tell you the truth, I once consulted him, well, my wife badgered me into it. She suffers something awful in her legs, poor woman. So I submitted a request for a cure, paid my drachma. We got back some nonsense about an ointment to rub in our dog's eyes. And we don't even have a dog! Well, I ask you."

Pliny suppressed a smile. "That's as may be. But the lion—does it mean anything to you?"

"No—no, I'm sure it doesn't. Was there anything else, then, sir? I'm afraid I've told you everything I know."

"And I'm grateful for your cooperation."

"Oh, not at all, sir. And may I say, sir, you're welcome to visit us anytime. Perhaps I can put you in the way of a good investment."

"Thank you. I will keep it in mind."

Winking and smiling, Didymus bowed himself out.

Chapter Twenty-four

The Nones of November

On the third day following the attack on the Persians, a delegation of the city council called on Pliny to beg permission to perform their customary procession and sacrifice to Zeus, the city's patron god. Pliny cautiously agreed to suspend martial law although he warned them that he would keep troops in the Persian quarter. If the festival went off without violence, he would allow things to go back to normal. It was Suetonius who suggested that they go a step further, join in the ceremony and make an offering to Zeus on behalf of the Roman community as a gesture to the Greeks.

"Excellent suggestion," Pliny had said, "and I'll go further still. These have been grim days and we could all do with a little diversion. I'll order up a banquet and we'll invite the Greeks."

"Even Diocles?" Suetonius grimaced.

"Even him."

"And Sophronia perhaps?" Suetonius looked hopeful.

"Absolutely not."

The festival went off smoothly. There were some catcalls when Pliny and his entourage appeared but, at least, nothing was thrown at them. Pliny had purchased a handsome bull and made a gift of it to the priests to sacrifice with prayers for goodwill among all the inhabitants of the province. It made an impression. The day was rounded off with, inevitably, an oration by Diocles.

◇◇◇

That night lamps blazed in every corner of the palace's newly-decorated dining room. The cooks had labored all day over complicated dishes that Pliny, abstemious creature that he was, never ordinarily ate. Troupes of acrobats, jugglers, and musicians had been recruited on short notice. At the head table, Pliny reclined with Calpurnia, his senior staff and their wives, and Diocles, sans wife. Like any respectable Greek woman, she did not dine with strangers. At other tables, were mixed groups of Greeks and Romans—Pliny had planned the seating carefully. At one of them, Zosimus reclined with Timotheus, Calpurnia's tutor, presumably deep in conversation about some nice point of Greek versification: Zosimus smiling, Timotheus not (the man had never been seen to smile since he had entered Pliny's household). Little Rufus, who had been allowed to stay up late for the occasion, ran here and there among the couches, every-where petted and fed.

Some were absent: Theron had declined the invitation, pleading that he was in mourning; Fabia made the same excuse.

By tacit agreement, no one spoke of Balbus or Glaucon or the Persians. Calpurnia complimented one wife on her gown, another on her tiara; spoke Greek to Diocles and accepted his effusive praise for her accent. There was a great deal of laugh-ter—but it was brittle and forced. Pliny sensed the effort behind his wife's gaiety. He now realized—though Calpurnia never complained of it—that the wives had united against her. He watched her out of the corner of his eye. She tasted everything, but ate little of it. But her wine glass seemed always empty and she called for more. He had never seen her drink so much. When had that started? When he spoke to her, he felt awkward, he hardly knew what to say to her anymore.

"My dear, I invited that young Greek, Agathon. Thought he might amuse. Sent his regrets, though."

"Who?"

"You remember, he was at the funeral, I told you—"

But she quickly looked away.

Suetonius' well-tuned antennae sensed the tension and he outdid himself to be amusing, regaling them with tidbits of backstairs gossip about the sexual escapades of Messalina and Agrippina. Pliny heard himself laughing too loudly at things that didn't really amuse him. He, too, was drinking deeper than usual.

And suddenly he wished that everyone would go away.

Calpurnia sat before her mirror, allowing Ione to unpin her complicated hairdo with her practiced hands. Pliny, who had seen off the last of the guests, entered their bedroom.

"You may leave us, Ione," he said.

"But I haven't finished—"

"I said leave us."

For a moment their eyes met, master and servant, and what passed between them in that look Calpurnia did not see.

"Of course, sir. Good night, mistress."

"I love your hair," Pliny said. He stood behind her, removed the last of the pins, and lifted it in his hands. "It's what I first noticed about you. You wore it so long then, when you were a girl. I gave you tortoise shell combs for it—do you remember?—when I came to ask your grandfather for your hand. You blushed and I was afraid you'd run away. That was the moment I knew I loved you."

"I remember. I still have them." Her voice flat, toneless.

"'Purnia, look at me. Turn around. Are you sick? Marinus thinks you are. I will tell him to bleed you tomorrow morning."

"I don't want to be bled."

"For your own good."

"I'm not sick. Why do you accuse me of being sick?"

"I'm not accusing you. *Mehercule*, 'Purnia, I only want you to be happy. I see now I shouldn't have brought you here, to this alien place. When the sailing season opens again I'll let you go home, if that's what you want."

"I haven't said so."

From the courtyard came the distant voices of the last tipsy guests calling for their chair bearers.

"You haven't said anything! Damn it, Calpurnia, what *is* the matter with you?"

"Don't shout at me."

"I'm not shouting. I—Look, Zosimus asked me the other day to talk to Ione, he's worried about her. And I did, or tried to. She wouldn't say anything. But why did you visit her in the middle of the night? It upset her, Zosimus says. What is going on between the two of you? I insist you tell me."

"Can't I talk to my maid when I want to?" She was on her feet. Two red spots burned in her cheeks. "Zosimus is imagining things. And you had no right to—"

"No right! I am the master here! What aren't you telling me?"

"You're hurting me!" He released her, leaving white marks on her upper arm where his fingers had sunk into her flesh.

"Forgive me, I'm sorry. 'Purnia, how have we come to this? I don't want to bully you. I wanted us to make love tonight."

"You have the right. You are the master."

She turned away from him, feeling more alone than ever. Because she knew now that she could no longer confide in Ione, not with Zosimus keeping his eye on her. Now she had no one.

Pliny saw her put her head in her hands, her shoulders working up and down. He could think of nothing to say. He went to her and put his arms around her. She buried her face in his chest and wept.

◇◇◇

The 7th day before the Ides of November

The morning found Pliny brooding in his office. He had fallen asleep only a little before dawn and then woken up with a start in the middle of a nightmare in which he was running from room to room in the palace, a windowless labyrinth of twisting corridors, searching for little Rufus, that precious child, whose pitiful cries for help eluded him no matter which way he turned.

Calpurnia was still asleep and he got out of bed carefully so as not to wake her. They had made love, he with passion and she with—what? Something less. And nothing was settled between them. There was still some mystery there. He massaged his neck and tried to focus his thoughts on the one mystery that he *must* solve: Balbus, Glaucon, and whatever it was that linked their deaths. The small bronze bust of Epicurus occupied its accustomed place on his desk. He touched its forehead and wished for the gift of that great man's wisdom, as though he could receive it through his fingertips. But the philosopher was mute.

A knock at the door. Zosimus probably, bringing him something to eat, fussing over him. The dear boy, more of a wife to him than his wife was these days.

"Come in," he spoke to the door without enthusiasm.

It swung open, revealing one of the *optios* with his hand on the collar of a very dirty little boy.

"Sir! Found this lad trying to climb the gate outside. Says he's run away from the procurator's estate. Begs not to be sent back there. Says he has something to tell you."

Chapter Twenty-five

"Shall I chuck him out, sir?"

The boy, who looked to be about ten years old, wiped his crusty nose with the back of his hand. He was on the verge of tears.

Pliny came around the desk and bent down. "Who are you?"

"Epam—Epaminondas."

"A big name for such a small person."

"They just calls me 'boy' around the stable."

"The stable? Vibius Balbus' stable?"

The boy nodded. "You ain't gonna send me back. They'll kill me for sure."

"And why would they do that?"

"I stoled a bite of food. They don't feed us hardly nothin', not since Master died. Cook beat me black and blue, said he'd cut off my hand if he caught me again." The boy's chin quivered.

"Well, we won't let him do that." Pliny patted his head and immediately regretted it: Epaminondas' hair was alive with lice. "Now, what is it you have to tell me?"

The boy frowned at his feet, unable to get the words out.

"Here, come and sit down. I expect you're hungry. I've some bread and cheese here. Will that suit you?"

Pliny waited while the boy crammed the food into his mouth with both hands and washed it down with large gulps of water.

"Now, then, what's this all about?"

"About the young master, sir. The one we're all scared of."

"Balbus' son? Why are you afraid of him?"

"Well, he has a curse on him, doesn't he? We all spit in our bosom whenever he comes around the stable. Which he did, sir. I mean the day Master disappeared. The young master rode out with him. 'Twasn't even daylight when they left. Roused us all up to saddle the horses."

"The horses. Was Aulus' horse a chestnut?"

The boy nodded vigorously. "The one you brought back, sir. Which Mistress said weren't ours, but it is. She said she'll sell us all to the quarries if we breathe a word to anyone. But I can't stick it there no more, and so I thought…" His voice trailed off. He gazed hopefully at Pliny.

Pliny let his breath out slowly. "Clever lad. Let no one ever discount the intelligence of a slave, even the humblest. You've a pretty good idea what this information is worth, don't you?"

"Will you buy me off the estate, sir? Otherwise—"

"You drive a hard bargain, Epaminondas," Pliny smiled. "All right, I'll pay for you. Do you like horses?"

"Yessir, I love 'em. Hope to ride my own someday."

"Well, perhaps you will."

Pliny summoned the *optio* and told him to have Epaminondas thoroughly scrubbed, fed, and handed over to his stable master with instructions to find him suitable duties.

He had not seen Fabia since the day of Balbus' funeral. The passage of time had taken a toll on her appearance—her hair was unkempt, her face unmade—while, if anything, it had increased her natural obduracy. Her feet were planted firmly in the doorway, her arms crossed, as though she really intended to physically bar them—Pliny, Suetonius, Marinus, and four *lictors*, led by Galeo—from entering. Behind her could be glimpsed her muscular freedman, a second bulwark.

"I *will* speak with your son," Pliny said again, making an effort to keep his voice low, "with your permission, madam, but, if necessary, without it."

"He isn't here."

"Really? And where would he go? He isn't well, is he?"

She said nothing but thrust out her chin at him.

"*Lictors!*"

Three of them moved her aside, pinning her arms behind her when she tried to wrestle with them. The freedman raised his fists and took a step forward, but hesitated when Galeo threatened him with his cudgel.

"Search the house and grounds," Pliny commanded.

"Tyrant! Bloody tyrant!" Fabia screamed, her voice hoarse with tears of rage.

Pliny went immediately to the little room off the atrium where he had found Aulus hiding before. It was empty now. "Marinus, go through the rooms on this floor. Suetonius, take two of the men and search the grounds. I'll look upstairs."

And it was Pliny who found him at last, cowering behind a clothes press in his mother's bedroom, doubled up with his arms over his head.

"It's all right, it's all right now. No one will hurt you." He spoke softly, as though gentling a frightened horse. "I'll call your mother now."

Fabia crouched beside her son, wrapping him in her arms, shielding him with her body, a lioness protecting a sick cub.

As Pliny and Marinus watched in silence, Aulus kicked out his legs and threw back his head. His eyes turned upwards until only the whites showed, his tongue protruded between his teeth, and foam gathered at the corners of his mouth. Fabia put a twisted rag between his teeth, rocked him, stroked his head, and murmured in his ear while he writhed and twisted in her arms.

"Fascinating," Marinus breathed. While Pliny, rational man that he was, felt the atavistic urge to spit rise up in him—the ancient apotropaic magic to ward off the Sacred Disease—so strong was the fear of it.

After two or three minutes the boy's tremors subsided. His eyes closed and he went limp as a rag. Fabia continued to rock him.

"He'll sleep for an hour or more," Marinus whispered. "When he wakes up he won't remember what happened."

"Is there something you can do for him?" Pliny asked.

"Nothing that she isn't doing already."

"Then we will wait."

It was well past midday when Aulus' eyelids fluttered open. They had carried him to his own room and laid him on his bed. Fabia sat beside him and hers was the first face he saw. But as his eyes focused and he saw Pliny, Marinus, and Suetonius seated on stools at the foot of his bed, he shrank back.

"It's all right," Pliny said softly. "I have some questions to ask you and you must answer truthfully. Your mother can stay." He looked hard at Fabia. "You will not interfere, do you understand? Otherwise I will send you out of the room."

She met his stare and said nothing.

"We know from the testimony of one of your stable boys that you rode out with your father before dawn on the day he disappeared."

"That filthy little liar!" Fabia cried.

Pliny silenced her with a look. "I've warned you. One more word and out you go. Now, Aulus, what happened out there?"

The boy drew a deep, rattling breath. "I killed my father."

Fabia lowered her head and let out a moan.

"Can you tell me why? Look at me now, not at her. Why did you kill him?"

The boy resembled his father, Pliny noted. The same red hair, the same sharp features. But where Balbus had displayed all the menacing power of a vicious dog, his son had only a squirrel's twitchy nervousness.

"I'm a coward. I was frightened." The voice was barely audible. Pliny leaned forward.

"Frightened of what?"

"The cave. I begged him not to make me go. He wouldn't listen. He said Mithras would make a man of me. Mithras was a soldier's god, he said, and he'd done plenty for Mithras and Mithras could damn well do this for him. He was taking me to be initiated. He said there were seven ranks. He was a Lion, nearly the highest, I would become a Raven, the lowest rank. He said everyone started as a Raven, even him."

"Did he name the other ranks?"

"Yes, but in Greek. I didn't know any of the words."

"Go on with your story."

"Well, he said we would meet the others there. They all approached the cave by different routes to avoid calling attention to themselves because the mysteries of Mithras were a deep secret. He warned me that I should never breathe a word to anyone. They would blindfold me, he said, bind my arms, aim an arrow at my heart, but then it would be all right and I would be raised up to the heavens and see the god. I didn't *want* to. But he slapped my face, told me to stop whining. He was doing it for me, he said, to make me a man at last."

Pliny exchanged glances with his companions.

"It's the curse," Aulus whispered. "You see how I am. I don't leave the house because people spit and make the horns with their fingers when they see me. Even here, no one will drink from the same cup or eat from the same dish as me."

"You've had it all your life?" Marinus asked.

"Since I was nine. If I'd had it as a baby they would have just left me on a rubbish heap and had done with it. I wish they had."

"No, never!" Tears were streaming down Fabia's cheeks. It was the first time Pliny had seen her cry. She had had no tears for her husband, but she was weeping now.

"They tried every way to get rid of it," the boy continued. "Father took me to the temples of Asclepius at Pergamum and Smyrna, the temple of Isis in Rome. I had to smear myself with mud, bathe in an icy river, run around the temples barefoot in winter, wear evil-smelling things around my neck, drink—drink the blood of a dead gladiator, but I couldn't, I threw it up. My father made me sleep outdoors on the ground, made me practice with a sword, slapped me, hit me with his *vitis* when my arm faltered. And finally, after I had a very bad fit, he decided to take me to this god in the cave. I just couldn't stand any more."

Pliny felt a tide of anger rise in him. His heart went out to this tortured child. "By Jupiter, If you suffered all that and lived you're more of a man than most. Now I want you to listen to what my friend here has to say. This is Marinus, my physician."

Marinus pulled his stool closer and looked at the boy gravely. "Your father loved you very much in his way," he said, "but what he put you through is barbarous nonsense. What you have is called the 'Sacred Disease' but it is no more sacred than any other disease, as the great Hippocrates tells us. It is an affliction of the brain. I'll put it as simply as I can. Veins lead up to the brain, the two biggest ones come from the liver and the spleen. These veins carry our breath to every part of the body. Now, there are impurities in the brain of the unborn infant which normally are purged before birth. But if this does not occur then the brain becomes congested with phlegm, which is one of the four bodily humors. If the cold phlegm flows into the veins, the sufferer becomes speechless and chokes, he gnashes his teeth and rolls his eyes—your symptoms exactly. This is all because the phlegm clogging the veins cuts off the air supply to the brain and lungs. The patient kicks when the air is shut off in the limbs, and cannot pass through to the outside because of the phlegm. Rushing upwards and downwards through the blood, it causes convulsions and pain, hence the kicking. The patient suffers all these things when the phlegm flows cold into the blood, which is warm. In time the blood warms the phlegm and the patient recovers his senses. There is no curse. Do you understand me?"

The boy sat up suddenly, wrenching away from his mother's embrace. "Then there is a cure?"

"Ah, well," Marinus stroked his beard. "That is more difficult. Diet sometimes helps. But honestly, at your age, a cure is unlikely."

"Then it's still a curse. How can I live like this?"

"Julius Caesar managed it rather well," Suetonius struck in. "Had it all his life. Most people never suspected. I invite you to read my biography of him when it's published. I'll send you a copy."

"But I've killed my father! That is the worst curse of all. What will they do to me?"

"Tell me," said Pliny, "precisely what happened. Everything you can remember."

"The sun was just coming up. We'd already ridden for two, maybe three hours up into the hills. I was cold, shivering. I begged my father to turn back but he wouldn't listen. Then he said we should dismount and tie the horses to a tree and go the rest of the way on foot. He said the cave wasn't far. "

"Do you know where it is?"

"No. The ground was steep and rocky. There was hardly a path that you could see. I was so frightened I could hardly stand up. I felt a fit coming on. Father grabbed my hand and dragged me along. I was crying and he was saying all these things about Mithras and how I would be a man he could be proud of. I broke away and started to run back. He came after me and threw me to the ground. We struggled and I picked up a rock and I hit him with it as hard as I could, here." Aulus pointed the side of his head. "And then I fainted and that's all I remember. When I woke up, the sun was low in the sky. And my father wasn't there. I thought he had just left me. So I went home. I couldn't find the horses. I had to go the whole way on foot and it was late at night before I got back. I expected him to be there and I was terrified of what he would do to me. But he wasn't there. I must have wounded him mortally and he dragged himself off into the bushes to die. That's where you found him, isn't it?"

"And that's what you told your mother?"

The boy nodded.

Pliny turned to Fabia. "And you kept his secret to save his life."

"Should I have lost both of them?" she cried.

Pliny shook his head in amazement. "It's the stuff of Greek tragedy, like something from the pen of Sophocles! Madam, I admire you—and I never expected to hear myself say that. Now listen to me both of you. We found Balbus buried, with his neck broken. There was no fracture of the skull. I don't know who killed him or why, but Aulus is not guilty of his father's blood."

Chapter Twenty-six

"I once knew a woman," Pliny said to Marinus, "who suffered from falling fits. Hysteria she said it was. When it came on her she looked just like Aulus."

"Ah yes, similar symptoms but quite a different cause. Your woman friend had a wandering womb, or, at least, that's the common theory. Aulus' case is much more difficult. I feel for the lad."

"I think telling him about the Divine Julius cheered him up a bit," said Suetonius.

The three had just returned from Fabia's. They sat in Pliny's office, waiting for the others to join them.

"Where *do* you get these gems of knowledge?" Marinus said testily. "I suspect you make them up."

Suetonius was about to protest when in trooped the swaggering Aquila; Nymphidius, limping on his arthritic knee; Caelianus with precise, small steps; and Zosimus, following some steps behind and looking, as always, as if he were entering a club to which he didn't belong.

Pliny briefed them on the morning's revelations.

"Extraordinary," Nymphidius said. "Sacred Disease? Secret cult? In all my years I've never heard—"

"It does sound like fiction, doesn't it?" Suetonius interrupted. "Which reminds me of a thought I had the other day. To capture this whole mystery—when we solve it, that is—in a work of literature, something quite original. A story where the reader doesn't know the solution until the very end. I don't believe it's ever been done before. You, of course, would be the hero of the tale, Gaius Plinius. I would play a small part. I think it would sell—"

Pliny stared at him without blinking. "You will do no such thing."

"Yes, well, just a passing thought." Suetonius fell into a coughing fit.

Marinus shot him a look of triumphant malice.

"Let us sum up what we know," said Pliny carefully, "and what we don't." He spent a moment minutely arranging the objects on his desk— the ink stand and styluses, the small bust of Epicurus, the cameo portrait of Calpurnia. 'Purnia! It had once warmed his heart, this painting of her touching a stylus to her lips, gazing at him with her big, serious eyes; now he felt like he was looking at a stranger's face. With an effort he dragged his mind back to the present.

"Glaucon feared he would be punished—by whom we don't know—for killing a lion. He was worried enough to consult Pancrates' oracle about it. We now know from what young Aulus has told us that 'Lion' was the title of a rank that Balbus held in an obscure cult. Glaucon and Balbus both owned the same astrology manual—obviously something required of the cult members. Balbus' neck was broken. Glaucon had been a wrestler, notorious for his brutality. Ergo, Glaucon killed Balbus, and at a place and time that only another cult member would know of. The poor lad's confession, while not true, is helpful. It allows us to visualize Balbus' last moments. A rocky path bordered by dense bushes to conceal the assassin. Barely daybreak, the light still faint. Glaucon comes up behind Balbus as he struggles on the ground with his son, gets him in a wrestler's hold around his neck—and at that very moment Aulus loses consciousness. If he saw anything at all, he doesn't remember it now.

"The only problem is that we have no idea why Glaucon wanted Balbus dead. And then someone, who styles himself a

'Persian', killed Glaucon, evidently out of fear that the man was so troubled by what he had done that he might do something rash, like confess."

Pliny paused and took a sip of wine.

"Glaucon's death has opened an unexpected path; one that leads us away from our other suspects. First Silvanus. That man has more than enough motive—personal animosity, fear of exposure as a thief, and perhaps had the opportunity too. But unless we can connect him with Glaucon—which, on the face of it seems unlikely—then we have to remove him from the list of suspects. The same thing holds for Fabia and Argyrus. Did either of them know Glaucon, much less have such influence over him as to get him to commit a murder for them? With Glaucon dead, it's difficult to prove that he did or didn't know someone, but on the face of it all these people moved in quite different circles."

"Unless Argyrus belonged to this cult too" Caelianus offered.

"That is a possibility," Pliny replied, "and one worth exploring. Because that cult is the key to this."

"Mithras," said Suetonius, who had recovered his aplomb and could never resist displaying his knowledge. "An old Persian deity. The Cilician pirates, who terrorized *Mare Nostrum* two centuries ago are said to have worshipped him. But that's ancient history."

"And the Cilician pirates were allies of Mithridates!" said Aquila with a slap of his fist in his hand.

"Let's not start that again," Pliny said firmly. "I don't believe this has anything to do with real Persians plotting to murder us in our beds."

Aquila looked unconvinced.

"And if the cult is anti-Roman," Pliny went on, "how could Balbus have belonged to it? The man may have been many things, but turncoat is surely not one of them.

"And yet," said Nymphidius, "he was knowingly breaking the law by belonging to it. Wouldn't this cult fall under Trajan's ban on voluntary associations?"

"Indeed it does," said Pliny, reminding them that Nicomedia was not even permitted a volunteer fire brigade. "Somehow, we must find out who the other members are. For all we know, they're people we pass in the street every day. What do they do out in this cave of theirs? What purpose binds them together?"

"They're a small group surely," said Marinus. "The boy said there were seven ranks. Lion and Raven are two. Persian and presumably Bridegroom, Glaucon's rank, are two others. Of course, there may be more than one holder of a given rank, but I'd guess there aren't many more to be discovered. How many people can fit into a cave, after all?"

They sat for a minute in thoughtful silence.

"Where do we go from here then, Governor?" Nymphidius said at last.

"I'll interview Glaucon's brother again," Pliny replied. "Is it conceivable that he knew Silvanus, or Argyrus? Who were his particular friends? Although Theron is so embittered that I don't expect much cooperation on that front. And we'll search for the cave."

"A big task. The hillsides out that way are riddled with caves, so I'm told," Nymphidius said.

"Nevertheless, we must try. It's somewhere not far from where Balbus was killed. That leather merchant who brought us to the village where the horses were found. Aquila, go find him again. We're going to need his villagers plus every soldier you can spare. Get started at once."

Aquila stood and clapped his fist to his chest; happy to be doing something at last.

"And," Pliny arched his back and stretched. "I can't think of anything else. Unless one of you—"

"Who owns it?"

"What? What was that?"

Zosimus had been working up the courage to ask his question for some time.

"Owns what, my boy?"

"The land out that way, sir."

Chapter Twenty-seven

"What a question!" Nymphidius shouted. "It's wasteland, scrub, nobody owns it."

"No, wait," said Pliny. "He's got something here. Think about it. These cultists—they aren't peasants, they're city men, wealthy men, if Glaucon is typical. They don't just go out in the woods and squat in some cave. They *own* things, improve them, pass them on. It's the kind of people they are—the kind of people *we* are. I believe this cave *is* on land that someone owns and has used for a purpose."

"It's a long shot," Nymphidius muttered.

"Yes, well what isn't here?" Pliny retorted. "Zosimus, my boy, I'm proud of you. And, as it's your idea, I'm putting you in charge of it. Go off to the city record office tomorrow and start looking at land deeds for parcels east of the city to a distance of, say, a hundred *stades*. If it was legally acquired, there'll be a record. Take Caelianus to help you. Counting the coin in the treasury can wait."

"Of course, I respect your modesty, Calpurnia, but you must understand that I am a physician. If I had a trained nurse, I would employ her. Unfortunately, I do not have such a person. Now please relax, there is absolutely no danger, the pain is slight, and the marks will disappear within a day or two. And you will feel much, much better for it, I assure you."

Calpurnia watched him with staring eyes as he heated the brass cupping vessels over a candle flame. Her hands, white-knuckled, gripped the arms of her chair.

Ione hovered beside her. "I had it done once, *matrona*, it isn't so bad."

"If I refuse?"

Marinus looked at her sternly. "Lady, it is your husband's wish. He's worried about you. We all are. It's plain your humors are unbalanced. Every physician from Hippocrates to our own time has advocated this procedure. Now please let us have no more difficulties." He spread out his instruments on the side table, selected a lancet and tested its edge against his thumb. "Ione, kindly pull your mistress' gown up to uncover her thighs."

Calpurnia looked away. What could she do but submit to this man?

Her flesh quivered under his fingers, touching her where no man but her husband—and her lover—had ever touched her. Brisk, businesslike, Marinus made an incision on the inside of each thigh and, as the blood flowed, pressed a cup over the wounds. She gasped as the hot metal burned her. He took his hands away and cups clung to her.

"So," he said, "we create a vacuum and draw out the bad blood. You're not going to faint, are you? Ione, put a cold cloth on your mistress' forehead. Just another minute now."

She let out her breath slowly.

The cups cooled and loosened. Marinus wiped the blood away with a ball of wool soaked in wine and applied a styptic that stung horribly. "Brave girl. All done." He smiled through the thicket of his beard. "As for the red rings, no one will see them who shouldn't." He chuckled. "You just rest now. With luck, we won't have to do this again. I'll see myself out."

Ione wiped her forehead. "'Purnia, dear, how do you feel?"

"Raped," she said between her teeth.

◇◇◇

The archives of Nicomedia reposed in a colonnaded building adjacent to the council house on the south side of the *agora*.

Zosimus and Caelianus presented the governor's written order to the elderly clerk, who looked them up and down suspiciously and finally stood aside to admit them. It was a grey morning and daylight barely penetrated the cold interior.

"Suppose you'll be wanting lamps," the clerk mumbled. "Mind, you must pay for the oil."

"How are your records organized?" Zosimus asked.

"Organized?" the clerk repeated the word tentatively as though it were a term in a language with which he was unfamiliar. Organized?"

"Yes, organized," said Caelianus. "Kindly show us where the land deeds are kept."

"Land deeds?"

Was the man deaf or half-witted?

"Land deeds!" Caelianus was losing patience.

"No cause to shout," said the clerk. "This way."

He turned and shuffled off, leading them into a long, low room whose corners were lost in shadow. Sagging shelves lined the walls from floor to ceiling. On the shelves were wooden boxes. "Each shelf for a year," said the clerk. "Going back maybe a hundred, maybe two hundred years. Who knows?"

"And different kinds of documents are sorted into boxes?" Zosimus asked hopefully.

"Sorted?"

Nothing, it turned out was sorted. The boxes were loaded with scrolls and papers of every description, both private and public, in no discernible order—treaties, decrees of the assembly, edicts of governors, deeds, loans, mortgages, wills, bills of sale, leases, gifts, dowries. Caelianus sighed.

"We are looking," Zosimus told the clerk, "for a deed to some country property. Is there a cadastral map of the hinterland?"

"Map?"

There was no map. And property boundaries, it emerged, were described in the vaguest terms as so-and-so many *stades* from this or that hilltop, or river, or milestone.

"Mind," said the clerk, "nothing's to leave this room. I'll send the boy for some lamps."

He shuffled off.

They looked around with sinking hearts.

"Let's suppose the property was acquired more than twenty years ago," Caelianus said at last, "and work back from there."

They counted shelves, each bearing the name of the *Archon* for that year. Zosimus reached up and pulled down a box, disturbing the dust of decades. He sneezed loudly.

A day-and-a-half later, the two men, weary and dusty and red-eyed, presented Pliny with the fruits of their search.

"Luckily, Patrone," said Zosimus, "land doesn't change hands very often around here. Once we separated the deeds from everything else, there weren't so many to look at."

"And this one seems the likeliest," Caelianus said. "We sneaked it out while the clerk was asleep." He placed a dusty scroll on Pliny's desk and unrolled it. "A very small parcel, less than a mile square—that caught our eye first of all. What would anyone want with such a small piece of land? And it lies, as near as we can tell, about seventy *stades* east of the city, which puts it right out in those foothills, not far beyond where Balbus was found."

"And the most interesting thing," Zosimus added, "is that it was bought from a larger estate belonging to someone named Hypatius thirty-two years ago for three thousand drachmas by a certain Barzanes. And it says here after his name 'Resident Alien'."

"A Persian!" Pliny thumped the desk.

He poured glasses of wine all around and toasted them.

The two men, who had become friends, went off merrily to enjoy a bath.

Suetonius put his arm around Sophronia's naked shoulder and drew her head onto his chest. They lay on her bed in a tangle of silk sheets.

"That was lovely," she said.

"I have a confession to make, though. I'm combining business with pleasure."

"And you think I'm not? We understand each other, Gaius Suetonius. We're not children."

"Two questions then. First of all, your half-brother, Argyrus. Has he been bothering you?"

"He hasn't shown his face here since you and the governor questioned him. You must have thrown quite a scare into him. Do you think he killed Balbus?"

"Only if he really feared that you would marry him. He says he didn't believe it."

"Oh, he believed it all right. He threatened to strangle me. I laughed at him."

"And when was this marriage supposed to take place?"

"Balbus told me that he had written a new will naming me as his principal heir and providing for Aulus, his son, but leaving Fabia with nothing. He hadn't told her yet. He said he was waiting for the Spring so he could divorce her and put her on a ship the same day. He didn't want her hanging about. He loathed the woman."

Suetonius stroked her hair. "Did you love him?"

"A little."

"What will you do now?"

"What I've always done. Look out for myself. Argyrus doesn't frighten me. You said there were two questions."

"Does the name Barzanes mean anything to you?

"I don't think so, why?"

"Another angle we're pursuing. I'm not to talk about it until we know more. But I think we're going to need the help of your Persians."

"Count on me, my dear."

She kissed him.

"We were told you wanted to see us." Arsames avoided mentioning Sophronia's name.

Pliny explained while Arsames translated for his companions. A minute passed in whispering and gesticulation.

Arsames threw his hands wide. "Barzanes is a common name among us. You say he purchased a piece of land out in the woods somewhere? We are merchants, shopkeepers, not peasants. Why would he do such a thing?"

"What do you know about Mithras?" Suetonius asked.

The black eyebrows shot up. "What do I *know* about him? He is the god of light. He wages an eternal struggle with the forces of evil. He is your Apollo, your Helios. What is that to you?"

"Do you worship him in caves?"

"Caves! Certainly not."

"Think again," Pliny urged, "about this Barzanes. He would be a very old man by now."

Arsames shrugged, turned again to his companions. The whispering grew animated, finally punctuated with a loud "Ah!"

"My father—" he indicated a frail, stooped old man "—once knew a man from the land of Commagene by that name who lived here and mixed with us Persians for a time. A foolish fellow who used to boast that he came of royal stock although his clothes were shabby. People laughed at him, my father says, and, after a time, he turned his back on us. No one has seen him in years. He's probably dead."

Commagene, Pliny knew, was a region in the province of Syria, formerly an independent kingdom, whose ruling caste was culturally Persian. "Does your father know where he lived?" The old man touched his son's shoulder and spoke in his ear.

"My father remembers," said Arsames, "that this man's clothes sometimes had a whiff of urine about them as if he'd spent too much time in a public toilet or a fullery. That's why people laughed. A prince who smelled of piss!"

Chapter Twenty-eight

The day before the Ides of November
The second hour of the night

Pliny and Suetonius trod carefully on the slick cobblestones of the crooked alley. A rivulet of liquid filth ran down the middle of it; rats squeaked and scuttled in its dark corners. The tottering buildings on either side nearly met above their heads. Their way was lit only by the flaring torch of the Night Watch slave who guided them. Behind them, Galeo and three other *lictors* dressed in dark-colored clothing loitered along the way, just close enough to come running if summoned. The damp stones, the sagging tenement walls of rotting timber and crumbling plaster, seemed to exhale a breath redolent of the toilet. Here, on the eastern outskirts of the city, was Nicomedia's largest fullery, where vats of urine and burning sulfur were used in the process of cleaning and whitening cloth. Understandable how, living here, the smell might cling to your clothes, your hair. Doubtless, the inhabitants of the quarter had long since stopped noticing it.

Two days had passed since the meeting with the Persians. Pliny had summoned the city's Night Watch—a score of public slaves, most of them elderly—who knew intimately the city's every corner and cul-de-sac, every wine shop and cook shop and run-down bath house. He had promised a reward to whoever could track down a certain old foreigner, poorly dressed but haughty, living in the vicinity of a fuller's establishment. He hadn't hoped for much.

But then one of the slaves had come back that morning to report that the proprietor of a cook shop knew of a man answering the description. He would come in now and then for a plate of sausage or a bowl of broth, the man said. He was an old geezer who walked with the aid of a stick. He didn't say much but his accent was foreign. He never gave his name. The cook shop man took him for a Jew, but he might be anything. He never mixed with the other customers but ordered the serving girl around as if she were his slave and even slapped her once when she was clumsy. Altogether, a nasty old piece of goods. The cook shop man thought he lived in an *insula* on the corner.

And so here they were, creeping up on the four-story apartment building, its plaster walls patchy and grimy with age, in what was almost certainly a pointless exercise. Pliny could believe that this was the Barzanes that Arsames' father had known. But could such a person be the mover behind a secret cult to which the likes of Balbus and Glaucon had belonged? They would feel like fools when he turned out to be nothing more than a surly old eccentric.

It wasn't the worst tenement Pliny had ever been in—that had been in Rome years ago when he was searching for a runaway murderer— but it was bad enough: dark and smoky and verminous, like all such places.

There was nothing to do but knock on the door of the ground floor apartment. It opened a crack and a man's face, double-chinned and shiny with oil, peered out. The odor of cabbage, burnt oil, and *garum* escaped from the interior, and the sound of a baby crying. The man's eyes widened, seeing the unfamiliar figures of two well-dressed men.

Did an old man live in the building? Foreign accent? Unfriendly?

"Him? Third floor."

A cat fled before them as Pliny and Suetonius mounted the sagging stairs.

There was no answer to Pliny's knock. He put his ear to the door. Did he hear someone breathing? He was almost sure he did.

"Barzanes?"

No sound. Then an explosive, hacking cough.

Pliny put his shoulder to the door; the bolt came away easily from the rotted door jamb.

He was ancient. Bent-backed like the letter C. A nimbus of white hair surrounded a face that was withered and spotted like an old apple. But the forehead was broad and the nose large and strong like an eagle's beak. He might have been handsome once, even kingly. He wore a long-sleeved tunic which hung to his shins; a threadbare shawl around his shoulders. He steadied himself with his left hand on the back of his chair. In his right hand, which shook visibly, was a butcher knife. He held it in front of him

"Who are you?"

"I am the governor of this province. I mean you no harm, Barzanes, put the knife down, please."

The man made no move to obey.

Pliny took in the room with a glance: a table with the remains of a meal on it, one chair, a smoking brazier, a narrow cot with a plain spread, a small wooden chest, a bookshelf with a few scrolls, a cupboard with some plain crockery, a rush mat on the floor. Clean, neat. But so bare. *Surely this is not the man who purchases property for three thousand drachmas.* He was almost tempted to turn and leave. He took another step into the room, Suetonius coming in behind him.

"You own a piece of land on which there is a cave where the rites of Mithras are conducted. I need to know precisely where that cave is and who are the members this cult."

The knife sliced the air. "Get out! I don't know what you're talking about. I have no—" the words ended in a fit of coughing and the old man sank onto his chair. The knife clattered to the floor.

There was fear in those rheumy eyes, and understanding.

It is him. Pliny waited until the coughing fit ended.

"Two members of the cult, the Lion and Bridegroom, have been murdered, apparently by another member, the one called the Persian. You know exactly what I'm talking about. Don't deny it."

He flung out an arm. "No one has been *murdered*. A riding accident, food poisoning."

The shock was wearing off, the man gaining control of himself.

"You don't believe that. Help me find this murderer. Or perhaps you already know, or can guess who it is. Maybe you should fear for your own life."

The old man waved this away.

"You understand you are violating the law on illicit associations. I can prosecute you for that alone. I will overlook it in return for your cooperation. Come now, who is the Persian?"

The old eyes looked fierce. "No. I don't know how you know what you do, but these are mysteries and you are not an initiate. You want to arrest me, torture me? Do so, by all means. It will take very little to separate my spirit from my body and send it flying up to the stars. Do you want someone to persecute?" The eyes narrowed now and there was a hint of a smile around the withered lips. "I know of some who worship a crucified criminal. They meet in secret on the day of the Sun and shamelessly imitate our own rites. And I'm told they refuse to sacrifice to the gods or the emperor. I can tell you where to find them."

"I've dealt with Christians before," said Pliny impatiently. "They are not my concern at the moment. You are. Now, listen to me, Barzanes." There was no other chair in the room. Pliny pulled over the wooden chest and sat down on it. He brought his face close to the old man's. "I know you aren't an enemy of Rome like the Christians. I have no wish to persecute you. What if I were to become an initiate in your mysteries?"

The old man snorted.

"No, I mean it. I am a seeker of ancient wisdom. I've been initiated into the mysteries of Isis and the Eleusinian goddesses." Pliny was never comfortable lying; he could almost feel Suetonius smirking behind his back. "If this Mithras is a great god, I want to know him. As does my friend here."

He'll take the bait. Pliny thought. *Pancrates wouldn't, he's a swindler. But this man is a true believer. He* wants *to convert me.*

Barzanes looked into Pliny's eyes long and searchingly. "I am the Father," he said at last. His bent back straightened, his chin came up. "I am sprung from the prophet Zoroaster. I preach eternal life through the life-giving blood of the Bull, slain by Mithras, the Unconquered Sun, the Light of Truth. He is young and strong, a god of soldiers. Only men are permitted to worship him. The Persians have known him since ancient times." Barzanes' voice was hoarse with age but there was still power in it; the accent foreign, but the Greek excellent. Once, it might have been a commanding voice, even stirring.

"I've spoken to the Persians," said Pliny. "They don't know you."

"I have nothing to do with them, they worship Mithras in their own way. My mission is to the Greeks, and even to you Romans. And I am not alone. There are others of us in every corner of your empire, even in Rome itself, who even now are spreading the Faith. One day soon the whole world will know the power of my god. You want to be initiated? First, you must master the science of the stars. You must pay a fee. You must prepare yourself by fasting and purification—"

"I say," Suetonius spoke for the first time, sniffing and wrinkling his nose. "I would have thought a prophet might live in a sweeter-smelling part of town."

Great Zeus, Pliny cursed silently, *shut up!*

But the spell was broken.

Barzanes blinked. His head swung from Pliny to Suetonius and back. "You're lying! You think you're clever. You've only cheated yourselves. Get out."

Pliny drew a deep breath and stood up. "All right, old man. I leave you with this warning. These rich and powerful men whom you've somehow attracted—don't trust them. They are drawing you into more trouble than you will ever be able to get out of. Think about that, and then come and talk to me."

"I am sorry," said Suetonius as they emerged into the street. "Couldn't help myself. The pretentious old fool. I hate these filthy barbarian cults."

"No more than I do," said Pliny. "Well, what's done is done. But I think we've stung him. He won't sit still now. He'll make a move."

He spoke to his *lictors*, who were waiting outside. "Galeo and Marius will wait here tonight, across the alley where you can watch the building without being seen. I'll send men to relieve you in the morning. You're watching for an old man who walks with a stick. Wherever he goes, follow him."

Barzanes sank onto his chair and stared at the open doorway. He took a rattling breath and tried to still his heart. It fluttered like a trapped bird in his breast. Another fit of coughing seized him and brought tears to his eyes. *Too old, I'm too old. I'll die before my work is done.*

Was it possible, what the Roman said? The Persian a murderer? For what possible reason? He wouldn't believe it. But could it be? He must tell this to the Sun-Runner. He would go to see him in the morning. Risky, to meet outside the cave, they seldom did it, but now he must.

He struggled to his feet and went to shut the door. Seeing that the bolt was broken, he pushed the chest, the small box that contained his few possessions, up against it. The effort brought on another fit of coughing. Then he took his plate from the table and scraped the uneaten bits of bread and cheese out the window and tossed out the lees from his cup of vinegary wine. He closed the shutter and latched it against the night vapors. He shivered. The night was cold and his watery blood had no warmth in it. The coals that glowed in the brazier hardly sufficed to warm the little room. He lowered himself onto his cot and removed his sandals and foot cloths. He rubbed his thin shanks to bring a little warmth to them. He put the butcher knife under his pillow as he always did. He blew out the lamp and eased himself under the covers, his ankles, like sharp stones, grated one on the other.

He had been strong once, equal to the hardest labors. When he and his four brothers—all of them so many years dead—had come here from Commagene, on fire to spread the gospel of Mithras. He remembered how they had bought a piece of worthless land, honeycombed with caves, and with their own hands had fashioned it to their purpose. How, with masons tools and paint and plaster, they had made the image of their beautiful god in the act of slaying the bull; how they had painted the mystery of the zodiac on the walls and ceiling. How they had sought converts—secretly, quietly; only a few, but all of them rich men, important men. Men who gave generously to the work of spreading the Faith. And if they served their own purposes as well, if they conspired to break Roman laws in the privacy of the cave, well, what did that matter to him? And they offered to make him rich too, but he had never taken a drachma for himself. It was all for Mithras: to send missionaries, others from the royal clan of Commagene, to the West, to the army camps—because Mithras was a soldier's god—and to the great City itself, the beating heart of the Empire. To this great purpose he had devoted his life; he had taken no wife, fathered no children. And he would not live to see it, but someday tens of thousands, hundreds of thousands, of men would worship at the altar of his god.

Barzanes lay, lost in his memories, waiting for sleep to come. He heard the ceiling creak as the family that lived above him made ready for bed—a laborer in the fullery and his slattern wife and their four snotty-nosed brats who loved to taunt him. He heard some drunken late-night revelers shouting in the street outside. He heard—what? The chest grating on the floor, his door opening?

"Who is it? Who's there?" The Romans again? He fumbled for his knife under the pillow.

The shadow, black against black, came at him swiftly. He struck out with the knife and felt the point graze his attacker's cheek. Then powerful fingers found his throat, a hand covered his mouth. He felt the assassin's hot breath on his face. He kicked out with one leg, knocking over the brazier, spilling the coals onto the mat of dried rushes.

By the time he was dead, the room was in flames.

Pliny and Suetonius had scarcely arrived back at the palace when Galeo, panting from having run all the way, caught up with them. They returned at once to find the building ablaze, smoke pouring from its windows, flames shooting up through the roof. The inhabitants of the street were fetching buckets of water from the fullery and flinging them uselessly on the flames. The old wooden structure burnt like tinder. Pliny recognized the man whose door he had knocked on standing in the crowd with his wife and baby. The flames lit up his oily face.

"Where are the others, man?"

Tears ran down the man's cheeks. "The couple on the second floor got out, and us. The family on the fourth—all those children…"

"The old man on the third?"

He shook his head. "The stairway was all flame."

Pliny stayed through the night, supervising the bucket brigade, and sent Suetonius back to the palace to fetch Aquila and a squad of soldiers. It would be daylight before the fire burned itself out.

He questioned Galeo and Marius. They had seen a man enter the building, they assumed he lived there. He must have run out with the others who escaped, they couldn't be sure.

◇◇◇

The Sun-Runner was grim-faced. "Idiot! Was is necessary to burn the building down?"

The man held a bloody rag against his cheek. "Was an accident," he mumbled. "Just as well, though. Covers our tracks."

"It was supposed to look like the old man had a heart attack. It's hardly likely that he set his room on fire."

"Could have."

"Let's hope the Romans are stupid enough to think so."

"My silver, sir?"

The Sun-Runner tossed a bag of coin which the man caught in one hand. "Go get your face looked at, you're dripping blood on the floor."

The Sun-Runner poured himself a goblet of wine and drained it in one gulp. He raked his fingers through his hair. He needed to think. Sad, of course, that the Father had to die, but there was no alternative. Sooner or later the Romans would get the old man to talk—if he hadn't already. It was a risk the Sun-Runner couldn't afford to take. And the cult had clearly outlived its usefulness. Mithras, he hoped, would be understanding. Mithras who eternally plunged his dagger into the bull's throat.

More blood than that would be spilled before this was over.

Chapter Twenty-nine

The Ides of November

"…therefore, Sir, if you will authorize the rebuilding of Nicomedia's aqueduct and the refurbishing of the baths, I will see to undertaking these works at once. With respect to the Balbus investigation, I have to report—" Pliny paused, sighed. Zosimus, who sat at the foot of the dining couch with his stylus and tablets in hand, looked up questioningly.

What did he have to report to Trajan? That his procurator was mixed up with some barbarian religious fanatics? That more people had been murdered and he was no nearer the truth? How would all this sound in Rome? Like pure lunacy. Like incompetence.

The embers of Barzanes' apartment were still smoldering. They had gone in this morning and uncovered his charred corpse—which told them nothing.

"Uncle Pliny, play *Latrunculi* with me. Please. You can be the soldiers this time." Little Rufus climbed up beside him on the dining couch. Pliny had given him the board game of Soldiers and Brigands and he loved to spend time, when he could snatch a few minutes, to play with the child. At four, Rufus was an enthusiastic, if reckless, player.

Pliny tousled his hair and kissed him. "I'm afraid you'll beat me again."

"I will, I will beat you. I want a grape. Don't eat 'em all."

"Don't bother master now, he's busy," Zosimus said, trying to sound like the stern father.

"Where's his mother?" Pliny asked.

"With the mistress, I suppose. They spend so much time in the temples these days looking at statues and paintings Ione says she could write a book on the subject, if she could write."

There was a knock at the dining room door. A servant entered followed by a figure that Rufus had never seen before. The child clapped his hand to his mouth and shrank back, trying to hide himself behind Pliny. The figure approached the couch with jerky steps like a puppet on strings. Its face was pinched and pale, its neck ropy, its arms and legs like sticks. Rufus began to whimper.

"Take him away, Zosimus." Pliny handed the child to him with a swift motion. "And leave us for a while."

"Aulus, what a pleasure to see you. Sit down here beside me." Pliny made room for the boy on the couch. "What brings you here? You don't leave home often, do you?"

Aulus sat stiffly, twisting his hands. "I—I haven't told mother. I took a horse from the stable. Asked the way to the palace. They didn't want to let me in until I told them whose son I am."

"Well, I'm very glad to see you. Have you eaten? Try these, they're very good." Pliny handed the boy a plate of grapes. "Will you take some wine? What's that you're holding?"

"A letter, sir. No wine, it does things to my head."

"A letter. What sort of letter?"

"I found it amongst a lot of papers in my father's desk. I am the man of the house now, the *paterfamilias*. I have a right to sit at his desk, look at his papers." He spoke with a fierce insistence as though he expected contradiction.

"And so you do." Pliny took the rolled sheet of parchment from his hands.

"It's in Greek, I can't read it," Aulus said.

"Your education has been neglected."

The boy gave a helpless shrug. "The tutors always run away when they see how—how I am. But I can make out the letters.

There's the word *leon* in it. That means lion, doesn't it? And so I thought—"

Pliny held up a hand to silence him and quickly scanned the page. Then he read it again more slowly, translating it aloud to Aulus.

"*From the Heliodromus*—that's an odd word. What would that be in Latin? *Cursor Solis*—Sun Runner? Something like that. *From the Sun Runner to the Lion, Greetings. You say the Persian has refused to repay you the money he owes you. That is a serious charge, I understand your anger. You demand that we expel him from our worship. This is a drastic step, not to be taken lightly. I have questioned him and he denies your charge, though I made him swear by Lord Mithras, who sees into every heart. I beg you to reconcile with him. You are both too important to our enterprise. I have not brought this matter to the Father and hope that will not be necessary. Farewell.*"

Pliny set the letter down. "I thank you for bringing me this. You can't imagine how important it is. It is dated only a few days before your father disappeared."

"Why? What does it mean?"

"I don't know what it all means, but I begin to glimpse the outlines of what must have happened. This Persian murdered a man called Glaucon, who, we think, murdered your father together with the Persian. You had just lost consciousness, you never saw them, but they were there on the path, waiting to ambush him. The motive, I see now, was a quarrel about money. The Father is, or rather was, the leader of the Mithras cult. He could have named the Persian and the Sun-Runner and all the others had he not died, quite conveniently, last night. All these men, including your father I'm sorry to say, were involved in an illicit cult, as you know. A cult riven by discord, leading to murder. What united them in the first place—this 'enterprise' to which your father and the Persian are so important—I don't yet know, although I have my suspicions. I'm afraid that when we find out it will not reflect well on your father. Are you prepared for that?"

Aulus attempted a smile. "I have no reputation to lose. It will be hard on mother, I suppose."

"How is she? How are things at home?" Pliny put a comforting hand on the boy's shoulder.

"Hard. She cries a lot. Drinks a lot. She claims now that she never really believed I could have done such a terrible thing, but she was afraid I would be accused anyway if it was known that I was with him and there was no other suspect. Now she's tormented with money worries. My father made a second will not long ago. Someone from the treasury brought over a load of papers from his office after he died. She finally got around to looking through them and found it. I thought she'd go mad, raving and screaming. It leaves most of his estate to some woman."

Pliny was suddenly alert. "The woman's name?"

"I don't know, but they fought about him seeing her. It started a couple of months ago when a strange man came to the house when father was out. Why do you look at me so strangely? Have I said something wrong? I don't mean to spy but I couldn't help—"

"Can you describe this man. It's important."

"I hid when he came in but I got a glimpse of him. About your age, I think. Thinning hair. He had a sharp nose and not much chin, he was red in the face—it made him look a little like a ferret. Do you know him?"

"I do," Pliny frowned. "Aulus, do you know the game *Latrunculi*? I fear I've just been sent back to square one."

Chapter Thirty

Aulus looked at him with puzzlement.

"What did this man and your mother talk about?" Pliny asked.

"I couldn't understand them, they spoke in Greek. Mother always says she doesn't know but six words of Greek but she seemed to understand him well enough. And after he left she was furious, and when my father came home that night she attacked him, screaming and crying. He hit her across the head with his *vitis*. He did that when he was angry. After that they seldom spoke. The tension made me very nervous. What would I do without my parents, who would care for me? My fits started getting worse. That's when my father decided to take me to the cave." Aulus' hands writhed and twisted in his lap.

Pliny's brain was in a whirl. *Argyrus and Fabia! Is it them after all? Did they plan the murder together, each for their own reason fearing Balbus' marriage to Sophronia? Was it Fabia's burly slave who was waiting for Balbus in the woods? Do Glaucon and the Persian actually have nothing to do with it? But surely she wouldn't have arranged her husband's murder for the very day that Aulus would be there to witness it? But what about Argyrus? Could he have been out there with Glaucon? Do those two know each other? Is Argyrus in the cult?*

"This man—did you ever see him at the house again?

The boy nodded. "The day of my father's funeral, after everyone else had left. I wasn't allowed to attend the funeral;

mother was afraid I'd have a fit in front of everyone. I came out of hiding after everyone had gone, but then he came. Mother sent me to my room. A little while later, he left."

Pliny gazed at the boy—too hard and too long. Aulus looked away, wrapping his thin arms around his body, hooking one foot behind the other, the knees twisting. "Have I—have I told something I shouldn't?"

The boy looked ill, Pliny was afraid he might have a fit then and there. "No, of course you haven't." He would not tell Aulus his suspicions, the boy was too fragile. "You won't tell your mother you came to see me, will you? I'd rather you didn't. Not just yet."

"Keep a secret from her? I…" The words died in his throat.

For an instant, Pliny was tempted to take the boy home and confront Fabia on the spot. But what would that do to Aulus? This sad, damaged, brave boy, struggling toward manhood, fighting for his place in a world that literally spat at him. No, he wouldn't risk it. There would have to be another way.

"How will you get home, Aulus? I can send you back in a carriage if you like."

"No." He lifted his eyes and met Pliny's. "I can go by myself. I won't tell mother where I've been."

Pliny's heart went out to the boy. "Aulus, have you thought what you might do when you're older? I'd like to help if I can."

"You'll think I'm being stupid."

"Tell me."

"Well, a physician? Like—"

"Like Marinus, of course. I understand completely. I'll speak to him about you. He's often said to me that he needs an assistant. Would you like that?"

Aulus' eyes filled with eager hope.

And inside Pliny a small voice asked, *How much of this is kindness and how much calculation, to win the boy away from his mother?*

He didn't like to contemplate the answer.

◇◇◇

After Aulus had gone, Pliny conferred with Suetonius.

"You must have it out with Fabia, there's no other way. And the sooner the better."

"So I keep telling myself. But she'll deny everything, as she already has, and I can't compel her. And to use her son as a witness against her? I can't tell you how reluctant I am to do that."

"Then go after Argyrus. I remember we decided he didn't look like he had it in him to kill Balbus, but maybe we were wrong. And this time don't just threaten to torture him, *do* it. I know you're squeamish but the man's a weakling, it won't take much. Maybe it *is* him and Glaucon. Maybe Fabia's innocent, after all."

"For the boy's sake I hope so. What will become of him if I have to execute her?"

◇◇◇

For the second time, Argyrus sat on a stool in the palace dungeon, his hands tied behind his back. Pliny and Suetonius watched him tremble and sweat while a jailer heated a pair of iron tongs over a fire until the metal glowed dull red. A shorthand writer sat behind them.

"Show him the tongs," said Pliny, grim-faced.

The jailer held the instrument up to Argyrus' face and opened its jaws—ready to tear off his nose at a word from the governor.

Argyrus twisted away from the heat. "Please—I'm begging you. I'll tell you anything." Tears streamed down his face.

"Let's start with your sister. You told us you didn't believe Sophronia would marry Balbus but that was a lie, wasn't it."

"Yes. Make him take that thing away from my face!"

Pliny nodded to the jailer. "And so you approached Fabia, his wife. Don't lie, we have a witness. What did you talk about? Did you plan how you would murder her husband?"

"Yes, all right, yes. We made a plan. She said how on a certain day each month he rode out to the woods on some secret business or other. I would follow him and she would send her slave too, a regular brute, and we'd—we'd kill him and hide the body. And then she'd have his money and go back to Rome or someplace with her pitiful son, and I'd still have power over Sophronia, the bitch. And I was going to do it, too. But, when the day got closer and closer I began to get pains in my stomach and I couldn't sleep. And finally, I—I just couldn't. And on that day I stayed at home, in bed. I couldn't even get out of bed. You have to believe me."

Suetonius said, "Why did you go back there on the day of the funeral?"

"I don't know. I couldn't stay away. I was curious to know how she had managed to kill him. She told me she hadn't. But why would she admit it to me? I think she did do it."

Pliny and Suetonius exchanged glances.

"This secret business of Balbus'. You know what it is, don't you?" said Pliny. "The cult, the cave of Mithras." It was his last try.

"The what?"

"The cult that you and Glaucon and the Persian belong to."

"I don't know what you're talking about, I swear."

"But you know Glaucon, don't you?"

"No!"

"The tongs, jailer."

"Please! What can I tell you? I don't know what you mean!" Argyrus was shrieking, blubbering.

Pliny lifted a finger and waved the jailer away. He drew a deep breath and let it out slowly. He wanted to get out of this vile place nearly as much as Argyrus did.

"Lock him up."

"Well, that's gotten us nowhere." Pliny pinched the bridge of his nose between thumb and forefinger. His head hurt.

"What now?" said Suetonius.

"Question Fabia. I'll go out there tomorrow. I'm not looking forward to it. For that boy's sake I hope she's innocent."

A fine drizzle was falling as Pliny's coach turned into the drive-way that led up to Balbus' mansion. Almost at once he saw that something was wrong. The gate hung open. There was no sign of the slave who ordinarily guarded it. In fact, there was no sign of anyone on the grounds. He jumped down from the coach and ran up the steps and through the open front door. He stood in the entrance hall and called her name. Only his own echoing voice answered him.

Chapter Thirty-one

Pliny and his coachman ran from room to room. In the dining room plates of uneaten food sat on the table. In the bedrooms the floors were strewn with clothing. In all the house there was not a soul. Pliny cursed himself for allowing Aulus to go home alone. Of course Fabia had made the boy confess what he had told him about her and Argyrus. And now she was on the run. Could there be any clearer proof of her guilt?

Pliny ran back out into the courtyard—and collided with the stableman.

"Where is everyone?"

"Left last evening about dinner time, sir. The mistress and the boy and Lurco."

"Who?"

"The big brute, her factotum. She called us all together—slaves, freedmen, everyone. She looked something awful, like all the Furies of Hades were after her. And the boy, he just stood there like he always does, looking like he'd been hit between the eyes with a plank. She told us to take whatever we liked from the house and run away. But I couldn't leave the horses, sir, with no one to feed and water 'em—"

"Which way did they go, man?"

"Well, sir, they all got in one coach. I had to hitch the horse up for them. And I saw them turn north out the gate, toward the city."

"*Toward* the city?"

"Not the direction I'd go if I were trying to hide."

"Quite. And she didn't say anything?"

The stableman shook his head.

Calpurnia felt like a deer surrounded by baying hounds. The wives had cornered her in her studio, demanding to know what she could not tell them.

"Does Gaius Plinius really think she killed him, then?" asked Fannia, Caelianus' wife, with a tremor in her little girl's voice.

"He hopes not, he—"

But she was drowned out by Faustilla's angry bray: "Of course she killed him, or paid someone to. The woman's a monster. Haven't we all thought so? With all her airs and pretensions, a savage at heart."

There were vigorous nods of assent from Laelia, Cassia, and Gabinia.

"But why?" said Atilia. "She had everything to lose."

Faustilla looked fierce, "Jealously! The oldest reason in the world. Balbus was sticking it where it didn't belong and she caught him at it. Jealousy will drive us to anything, man or woman, doesn't matter. Don't you agree, Calpurnia dear?"

"You seem to relish the thought, Faustilla. I think it's sad, if it's true. And we don't know if it's true." Calpurnia made an effort to speak mildly but she could hardly trust her voice.

"But, of course, you wouldn't know about jealousy, would you, Calpurnia, married to a paragon like Pliny."

"Where could she have run to?" asked Laelia.

"She'll never get away," said Cassia. "The governor's turning the province inside out, my husband says."

But Calpurnia was no longer listening to them. Her flesh had gone cold. *Jealousy*, she thought. *Could it drive even her husband to a murderous rage? Even Pliny? What would he do to her if he knew? No*, she told herself, *he isn't capable of that, he isn't some raving, half-barbarian woman. He's a civilized man. But he is a man…*

Chapter Thirty-two

Silvanus sat at his rickety table in the dark hovel on the outskirts of the city that was his refuge and his prison. His grinding jaws masticated the bread and cheese to a paste, which he washed down with a long draft of wine. He was in the process of getting drunk. How else to pass the long nights? It was nearly a month since the night he had escaped from the treasury with his chests of silver. A month in which he had not put his head out of doors, relying on the hired woman to bring him his food and news of the city. He was beginning to loathe the sight of her. But he would stick it out for as long as he must, until this governor left and was replaced by a new man, until memories grew short and attention flagged, and then he would board a ship and sail away to Arabia, he thought, or any place where Rome's long arm couldn't reach him, and live like a prince.

A rap at the door. What was the damned woman doing here again? She never came at this time of night. With a curse, Silvanus lurched to his feet, crossed the narrow room, and opened the door a crack. He blinked his lashless eyelids. It was a woman, but not his woman. It was Fabia, half-hidden in the folds of a hooded traveling cloak. And behind her, her idiot son, and behind him that monster, Lurco.

"You! What are you doing here?" He could hardly get the words out.

She pushed the door open, driving him back—she was stronger than he was—and the three of them crowded in.

"You actually live in this hole?" She wrinkled her nose. "You told me where it was, you didn't tell me it was a cesspit."

"I said what are you doing here." His voice rose through half an octave.

"Hiding just like you. The governor thinks I murdered my husband. I have no protector, no friends, no money."

"No money? Haven't I given you enough?"

It had started nearly ten years ago in Egypt when Balbus was on the Prefect's staff, handling large sums of money for paying the shippers of grain to Rome and Silvanus was his clerk. Silvanus had begun stealing and, when Fabia became aware of it through a careless remark, he had paid her for her silence. She was a grasping, suspicious woman who wanted money of her own in case her husband should ever decide to leave her. Their arrangement had lasted ever since.

"You can't stay here. You'll bring the soldiers down of all of us! This is a neighborhood of snoops. How many doors did you knock on before you found me?"

She ignored the question. "We're here and you must help us, Silvanus."

"Never! You murdered Balbus, I congratulate you, I suppose the monster there did it for you?"

Lurco, who never spoke, simply glared at him and flexed his huge shoulders.

"You don't scare me. You'll have to fend for yourselves. Get out."

"I didn't kill him," Fabia said.

"Oh? Then why are you running away? Because no one will believe you? I don't blame them."

Like a punctured bladder, the air seemed to go out of her. She sank down on Silvanus' one chair and buried her face in her hands. "I'm afraid—not for me, for the boy."

"A little late for that, murderess," Silvanus sneered. With his small black eyes, beaky face, and thin lips he resembled a tortoise that had bitten into something nasty.

"She didn't kill my father! A—a Persian killed him, I saw a letter—" Aulus shook himself from his torpor with a wrenching effort like the snapping of invisible cords that bound him. For hours he had been going in and out of small seizures, hardly knowing where he was.

"The idiot speaks? Stay in the corner there, you filthy thing, don't come near me." Silvanus spat.

"It's all to do with Mithras," Aulus whispered.

"What's he raving about?"

"Hush, Aulus, that's enough," Fabia warned.

"It's true. We must go back and tell the governor. He understands, he explained—"

"Be quiet! Silvanus, please. We won't stay here if you help us to get away. If you don't they'll catch us all!"

"Murderess!" Silvanus balled his hands into fists as if he would strike her. Lurco stirred but it was Aulus who stepped between them. "Don't you dare!" he said.

"Or you'll what?"

"I am the man of this family." His legs trembled, his head began to jerk. No! He wouldn't faint, he would hold on. He had always needed his mother—now she needed him.

Silvanus snorted. "Fabia, if it were possible to pity you I would, just for having such a son." He paced the little room. "All right. Listen to me. There's a fishing village not far from here. Fishermen won't be happy about putting out at this time of year but enough silver might change their minds."

"You'll guide us there?"

"Certainly not. I'll give you directions."

"The money."

He dragged one chest from under his cot, being careful to place himself between it and Fabia so that she could not see how full it was. He scooped up a handful of coins and, with a sour look, tossed them on the table. "If I were you, I'd make for the coast of Thrace. You're from there, aren't you? Live among the savages. How fitting."

◇◇◇

They were tacking northwest along the coast, nearly out of sight of land, when the wind began to blow strong and the boat to pitch and roll in a confusion of waves. Rain drove in their faces, the deck was awash; the four sailors and their three passengers hung grimly to handholds wherever they could. Aulus' stomach heaved. He felt his bowels loosen. His mouth filled with saliva. Jagged flashes of light exploded behind his eyes. He couldn't breathe. He had fought it down for hours but it would have its way at last. The sailors looked at him with horror, at the whites of his turned-up eyes, his jerking limbs.

"Look, he has a demon in him!"

"Fling him overboard or we'll all drown!"

Chapter Thirty-three

The 14th day before the Kalends of December

Sophronia chose a plump snail from the silver platter, dipped it in savory sauce, and placed it between Suetonius' lips. They reclined side by side on a couch in her elegant dining room. He swallowed and burped appreciatively.

"What's he like, your governor?" she asked.

"Pliny? Hard to sum him up, really. He's one of the most generous men I know. He has a great talent for friendship. If you ever need a favor he's your man."

"Rather dry, though. Not like you."

Suetonius laughed. "He publishes his letters, you know. Quite delightful little pieces, there are even one or two to me. I think they reveal more of the man than perhaps he suspects. For example, he witnessed the volcanic eruption that devastated the bay of Naples when he was seventeen. Terrible calamity. His uncle, who commanded the fleet at Misenum, asked him if he wanted to come with him to help rescue people who were trapped along the shore. And young Gaius said no, he'd rather stay home and finish copying out some passages of Livy! Can you imagine?"

"Because he was afraid?"

"No, it wasn't that. I just think, in a sense, he was never a boy. But he's a good man and, trust me, he will solve this case however long it takes."

"And the hunt for Fabia goes on?"

"It does. We've got every soldier and *lictor* we can spare visiting every inn and post house and village within fifty miles of the city. We've alerted the authorities in Prusa, Nicaea, Apamea. But it's been four days. By now they could be anywhere. I suspect they've put to sea. If they make it across Propontis, we may never find them."

"She killed him, of course. She and my brother."

"He denies it."

"Have you tortured him?"

"Pliny shrinks from it."

"Your governor is too soft. Let me spend half an hour with him in your dungeon."

"You almost frighten me, my dear. I should not like to be your enemy."

She laughed. "Let's hope you never will be."

They were companionably quiet for a while, pleasantly drunk. Then Sophronia rubbed her foot against his and said, "I have a small problem you might help me with."

"If I can."

"There is a banker in the city who owes me money, a rather large sum that I deposited with him to invest for me. It's been months now and he neither returns it nor tells me what he's done with it. A typical Greek male; because I am who and what I am, he thinks he can safely cheat me. Balbus was going to get it back for me but then he died."

"How much money are talking about?"

"Two talents."

Suetonius looked at her in astonishment. "That's a fortune! What were you thinking?"

She pouted. "Balbus thought it was a good idea. He said he trusted the man."

"And who is this man?"

"A wretched little one-armed creature by the name of Didymus."

◇◇◇

"Didymus is his name." Suetonius and Pliny were in the palace baths, soaking in the hot pool. Slaves stood by with armloads of towels. Suetonius knew that his chief was always more amenable to requests when he was warm and wet.

"I know the man," said Pliny. He breathed in a lungful of steam and exhaled it slowly. "I brought him in for an interview two weeks or so ago, just after Glaucon was poisoned. He's the family's banker—the brother's, that is. But it turned out that Glaucon also had invested money with him without his brother's knowledge. I thought it was worth having a chat with him."

"What did you learn?"

"Nothing, really. He struck me as honest, anxious to please. Said he would return Glaucon's deposit to the family."

"They're an important family. He doesn't seem to feel equally obligated to Sophronia, a foreigner, a brothel keeper. And as a woman she can't take him to court."

"You're quite her champion, aren't you?" Pliny cocked an eyebrow.

"Well, I mean she *has* been helpful to us. I think we owe her something."

"All right. Calm down, my friend. I can't officially take sides in a private dispute but I am curious about him—more than curious. Interesting that he's Glaucon's banker and Sophronia's too."

"On Balbus' advice."

"And Balbus said he would get her money back for her and soon after that he was murdered. With so much smoke I think there is bound to be fire. I will pay him a visit."

"On what pretext?"

"Actually, he invited me to visit his premises. He seemed anxious to help me invest my money. I wonder if he did the same for Balbus.

Galeo had been a *lictor* for twenty years. His father had been one before him, and his uncle and his grandfather as well. In fact, the men of his family had attended Roman magistrates going back to the reign of Augustus. It was an honorable profession: to march beside a magistrate, or the emperor himself, clad in a red tunic and white toga, bearing on one's shoulder the heavy ax bundled with rods, emblematic of the power to chastise and execute, ordering the crowd to make way. In his time he had served a dozen or more officials, been entrusted by some of them with important assignments—carrying messages, guarding prisoners. Once he had even deflected an assassin. The profession didn't pay well but the gratuities added up, and the ladies were always impressed. Gaius Plinius was his first provincial governor. He had rejoiced when the lottery selected him from the pool of *lictors*; a chance to see a part of the world he had never visited.

But Galeo was not happy. For a week he had ridden along the coast north of Nicomedia in every kind of vile weather, for winter was upon them; sores on his backside, legs splashed with mud, inquiring in every town and hamlet if anyone had seen a big woman with a sickly boy. This was work for soldiers, not a person of his standing.

Nightfall found him in a tavern, or what passed for one in this piss-poor village, hardly more than a loose construction of boards and thatch that threatened to collapse in the buffeting wind. He stood at the bar, bracketed by a couple of leather-skinned fishermen. Galeo's family were Greek-speakers from southern Italy, nevertheless he struggled to understand the local patois.

He lifted his arm to pour the last dregs of undrinkable wine down his throat, when over the rim of his cup he saw the man coming through the door. The size of him! There was no mistaking him: the monster who had confronted him and his fellow *lictors* when the governor invaded Fabia's house.

And, at the same moment, the man saw him. Unlikely that he recognized him, but he was a stranger to the village and that was enough. The man turned and fled. Galeo tossed his cup aside, lowered his head, and charged after him into the wild night.

Chapter Thirty-four

The 11th day before the Kalends of December

Didymus' round face beamed with delight. The little man bowed, folding himself nearly in two, as he greeted Pliny at the door. "What a pleasure to see you, Governor! We're honored by your presence. I felt when we last spoke that I might have interested you in investing with us. You won't be sorry, sir, you won't be sorry." He put out his left hand to touch Pliny's shoulder confidingly; the stump of his right arm pointed the way within.

The bank occupied the ground floor of an undistinguished brick building on the waterfront. The upper story, Pliny assumed, was the family's apartment. Nothing about it advertised the fortunes concealed in its vaults, the prominent names recorded in its ledgers.

Inside, half-a-dozen clerks hunched over tables, counting sums with their fingers. A rack of scrolls occupied one wall. It was in every way a smaller version of the counting room in the treasury building.

Pliny was ushered into an inner office, seated in a comfortable chair, and offered a cup of wine by a young slave. Didymus stood, rocking on the balls of his feet, his eyes gleaming, his feathery brows going up and down. Of course there would be no more investments in ships' cargoes for the next few months, he said, but there were many, oh many, other attractive opportunities in the meantime—luxury goods brought overland from the

East; slaves, always a sound investment. Was there something the Governor was particularly interested in? Pliny was noncommittal. For a while they discussed interest rates and the deplorable waste of funds on ill-advised building projects, to which Didymus nodded in vigorous agreement. Pliny wondered if Didymus' vault was quite secure. Oh, Absolutely! Would the Governor care to inspect it?

The little man led the way back into the counting room, pulled aside a drapery at one end of it, revealing a heavy door, and produced a large key. As the door swung open, a big brown rat raced across Pliny's foot.

"Forgive me, sir, forgive me!" Didymus exclaimed. "We're infested with them, I'm afraid. So near the wharves, don't you see."

Pliny put his head in and took a quick look around. It was much smaller, of course, than the vault at the treasury, and lined with brick instead of dressed stone, but it had the same metallic smell of stale air. The chests of coin, as far as he could see, were not government issue. He expressed himself satisfied. "And may I ask the names of your principal investors?"

"But, sir," Didymus' face registered alarm, "that would be quite against our rules of confidentiality. You know about poor Glaucon already but I'm afraid I simply can't disclose any other names."

"I ask," said Pliny in a mild voice, "because a certain Sophronia has complained to me that you have refused to return a deposit of hers. Perhaps you knew that she was close to the late procurator?"

The Cupid's bow mouth drew back in a deathly smile. "That woman! I've told her to be patient. I've every intention of returning her money. Honestly, I'm surprised to hear you defending that infamous creature."

"But her money, I suppose, smells as sweet as anyone's?"

Didymus clapped his hand to his forehead. The clerks had stopped working and were staring at them. "The fact is, sir, I've had losses this year. Two ships in which I was heavily invested went down this summer. I have several creditors. She will simply have to wait her turn. Reason with her if you can, sir, I beg you."

"It occurs to me to wonder whether the late procurator, Vibius Balbus, was one of your clients."

"Balbus? Why, no. You asked me that once before. He did no business with me."

"Really?" Pliny looked at him in surprise. "Why not? I assume you made him the same offer you did me."

"Well we simply never had a relationship, that's all. Perhaps he invested with one of the other bankers." Didymus' face was working. "I'm an honest man, Governor. I pay my taxes, I'm straightforward in everything, as fair as I can be to everyone, my hands are clean."

Pliny went to the door and signaled to the two *lictors* whom he had told to wait across the street with his chair bearers. They came at a run. He faced a hard choice. If ever a man looked ready to make a run for it, it was Didymus, and Pliny was determined not to lose another suspect the way he had lost Silvanus and Fabia. Still, he must tread carefully. It was one thing to throw a lounger like Argyrus into a dungeon cell, but this banker was a member of the business community whose good will he needed to conciliate. It wouldn't do to terrorize them. And so far he had no more than a suspicion that Didymus was guilty of anything.

"You will be my guest at the palace today, my friend; and tomorrow, and perhaps the day after. Your family is upstairs, I take it? I'll see that they're informed. Send your clerks home. The bank is closed and I will post one of my men at the door to see that no one enters while you're gone. And you will please gather your books, I intend to go over them with my accountant. I do have the authority to impound them in case you're thinking of protesting."

Didymus groped behind him for a bench and sank onto it. His lips moved but no sound came out. Pliny almost felt sorry for him.

Pliny handed the banker over to his major domo with instructions to find him a comfortable room and serve him a good meal—and post a guard at the door. He would let him cool his heels for a day. Meanwhile, it was imperative to get the whole truth from Sophronia.

Pliny had never been to the Elysium. It was late afternoon when he and Suetonius arrived, too early for customers. They were met by Byzus, Sophronia's accountant, who informed them that his mistress was out but invited them to wait in her private office and take refreshments. Pliny was impressed by the sumptuous décor. He also couldn't help noticing how at home his friend was in this place: greeting the servants by name, exchanging a wink with one of the girls.

"She's out inspecting a property for sale," Byzus explained. "A tenement burned down and the lot's going cheap. It's near a fullery and she might buy that too. Good money to be made in the laundry business." He tapped the side of his nose and looked wise.

Pliny and Suetonius exchanged glances. Barzanes?

Half an hour later, she bustled through the door. Seeing Suetonius first, her lips parted in a smile. Then her eye fell on Pliny and the smile faded.

Pliny wasted no time getting down to business. "I've spoken to Didymus about your deposit. He made excuses, legitimate or not I don't know yet. At the moment he is my guest in the palace and will remain there until I've gotten everything he knows out of him. I've had a quick look at his books and it appears that Balbus never invested with him, which I find odd since he advised you to do so. My question, madam, is this: was any of that two talents you invested actually Balbus' money?"

Her expression betraying nothing. "Forgive me for troubling you with my affairs, Governor. I should never have mentioned it. We'll let the matter drop."

"I'm afraid it's too late for that. More is at stake here than your money. A letter found among Balbus' papers indicates that he had a dispute with someone known to us only as a 'Persian,' who owed him money. He was making trouble for this individual—the details needn't concern you—and soon afterwards he was murdered."

She started to protest but he cut her off. "Yes, I know you favor your half-brother Argyrus as the culprit, and you may yet prove right, but I need to know whether there is a connection between your deposit with Didymus and the sum referred to in that letter. Are they one and the same?"

"Ask Didymus."

"I'm asking *you*!" Pliny was on his feet, leaning over her and staring hard. Despite herself, she shrank back. She looked to Suetonius for help. He studied his wine glass.

"All right." She drew a deep breath. "Some of it was his."

"How much?"

"I don't remember."

"How *much*!"

"Half maybe."

"*Half*! A full talent. Where did he get so much?"

"He wasn't a poor man."

"Why didn't he invest it in his own name?"

"I don't know. It was a personal loan to me. What difference does it make?"

"There are half a dozen bankers in town. Why did he suggest Didymus?"

"I've no idea. He said he was a friend."

"And that was good enough for you? You have a reputation as a shrewd businesswoman. Balbus tells you to invest a small fortune with a banker you've never done business with before and you do it."

"I *loved* him." She was angry now.

"Love," Pliny sniffed. "Indeed it makes us do strange things."

"Is there anything else you want to know about my personal life, Governor?"

He looked at her sourly. "Not at the moment."

"Well," Suetonius sighed as they mounted their litters, "there's an end to a beautiful friendship."

"Consider yourself lucky."

Galeo returned to the tavern. His red *lictor's* tunic was soaked through, his hair was plastered against his head. He had lost the man in the dark—fortunately, perhaps; he wouldn't like to tangle with that brute. He sat himself down at a table, motioned to the tavern keeper to join him, and carefully placed a silver drachma on the scarred table top between them. The man couldn't take his eyes off it.

"Who is that fellow who ran out? How long has he been in the village?

"Calls 'imself Lurco, sir. Been 'ere five, six days, I reckon."

"Did he arrive alone or with a woman and a boy?"

"You know that, do you?"

"Where are they now?"

"Well, sir, I really couldn't say as to that."

Galeo placed another drachma on the table.

"Ah. Well it might be they hired a boat, take 'em to sea, in spite of it bein' filthy weather. You'd best talk to 'er captain."

"Send someone to fetch him. I'm not going out in this again."

"Happens that's 'im over there." He glanced at one of the men at the bar. "Cleitus!"

Cleitus eyed Galeo warily. "'Aven't done nothin' wrong."

"No one says you have." Galeo placed another drachma on the table. Cleitus' eye—he had only one—narrowed. "Tell me about the woman and boy."

"They paid me 'andsomely to sail across Propontis to the Thracian side. Me and the lads agreed though we didn't like the weather. Well, we wasn't far out when the wind picks up and the boy comes all over queer, like maybe he has a demon in him. That's what we thought anyway. I was for pitching 'im over the side but the woman begs me to leave 'em on an island that's out there—just a little speck of rock really, nothin' on it but a few goats. Well, we went in as close as we dared on the leeward side and made 'em jump."

"And?"

"And that's all I know. We sailed back with the big fella, Lurco. He didn't want to jump and we couldn't make 'im." Cleitus' hand shot out and plucked one of the coins off the table. He touched two fingers to his forehead and moved off.

At first light, Galeo was on his horse galloping back to Nicomedia.

Chapter Thirty-five

The 9th day before the Kalends of December

To Aulus the passage of time was formless and endless. He drifted in and out of consciousness. Sometimes spasms shook him, and afterwards he would sleep for hours: sleep filled with dreams of thrashing in icy sea water, of struggling for breath, of his mother's powerful arms around him. And even in sleep the ache of hunger and the ache of cold never abated. In his lucid moments he knew that they drank rain water from a hollowed rock, ate berries that gave him a stomach ache, tried to catch and kill a goat until they sank down exhausted. How long had they been here? How much longer could they survive? *Mother!* She lay beside him on the stony ground, her hair a wet tangle spread out around her, her dress sodden and filthy. Her eyes shut. Was she breathing? *Mother, don't die, don't leave me!* He crawled to her and laid his head on her breast. *It's all right, she's breathing.* He sank again into oblivion.

And then, in his dream, he was being shaken. Hands gripped his shoulders. His eyelids fluttered open and gradually a face came into focus. Not mother's but a man's face. The governor's face! "It's all right, boy, it's all right." Pliny and another man helped to sit up. He knew that face too—the physician. They put a woolen robe around his shoulders, held a cup of water to his lips. He swung his eyes around. A ring of Roman marines stared back. His mother sat on the ground nearby, a rope around her wrists. At the edge of the islet a navy cutter rocked at anchor.

Silvanus was sunk in a pleasantly drunken doze when the soldiers burst through his door and laid hands on him. The next hours were very unpleasant. They bound him with chains and dragged him to the palace dungeon, where the governor stalked up and down the cell, firing questions at him, while a brute of a jailer heated pincers over a flame.

"The procurator caught you stealing, didn't he? What did he do to you?"

"Beat me up. Not for the first time, he loved to hit. Threatened to sack me."

"So you killed him."

"I didn't!"

"But you hated him."

"Everyone hated him."

"Then who killed him?"

"Fabia killed him."

"You know this for a fact?"

"It makes sense, doesn't it?"

"Was Balbus stealing from the treasury?"

"I'm sure he was."

"How?"

"I don't know how. He never included me in that."

"You do know that I can put you to death for what you've done."

"You can't. I'm a Roman citizen. I'll appeal to the emperor."

"All right. I'll send you to Rome for trial, but I promise you you'll find a nastier death at the end of it than the one I'll give you. Now again, how was the procurator stealing?"

"I told you I don't know!"

And so it went until they finally left him alone.

Aulus lay on a soft bed, propped up on cushions as a servant fed him spoonfuls of hot broth. Pliny sat in a chair beside him and spoke in a low voice.

"I honestly don't know what to think about your mother. If nothing else, she had guilty knowledge of Silvanus' whereabouts. I hope it's nothing worse than that."

"But she wouldn't have sent assassins to kill my father when I was with him."

"That is an excellent point, which I take note of. Aulus, I don't *want* it to be your mother, but she did run away."

"She made me tell her everything I told you—about that Greek who came to see her. And then she began to scream and strike her breast. I didn't know what to do…"

"Hush, be calm now. I understand. I'm sending her home under guard until I know more. But what shall I do with you? Do you want to go back with her or would you rather stay here in the palace for a time? I've spoken to Marinus, you know, about you assisting him. He's willing to take you on."

"I—I've never been away from her. What will happen when I…"

"Have a seizure? We'll know what to do. I remember you told me you're the man of the family now. In law, yes. But in fact you never will be as long as you live with her. I'll tell you something. I lost my father early and grew up in the house of my uncle. He was a good man, a tireless civil servant, a prodigious scholar, but a man whose personality absolutely dominated the household. Nothing mattered except his needs. We all tiptoed so as not to disturb him while he was being read to by his slaves and making notes for his *Natural History*, which was literally all the time. Until the day he died, we were almost like prisoners there. It's taken me longer than I like to admit to get over it. Think about it, son."

Mi fili—my son. He had said it without thinking. He felt a sudden pang of longing for the son that he and Calpurnia would never have. Suddenly he wanted very much to be a father to this tortured boy, bring him into his household, give him a better life than he had ever known. He would speak to Calpurnia about it. But what if it caused her pain? They never spoke about their childlessness. And lately, it seemed, they never spoke at all. They had grown so far apart he felt he hardly knew her anymore.

"Sir?" Aulus was staring at him. "Is something the matter?"

"What? No, no, of course not. You rest up, we'll talk again later."

Pliny summoned his staff. He toyed with the objects on his desk while he marshaled his thoughts. "We have, at the moment, four suspects. Silvanus hated and feared Balbus after he caught him stealing, although frankly I don't think the man is capable of murder. Fabia and Argyrus, either together or singly, both stood to lose if Balbus divorced his wife and married Sophronia. In that case I suppose that Fabia's muscular slave, Lurco, was the actual killer. Unfortunately, he gave my *lictor* the slip and we have yet to find him. Finally there is the banker, Didymus."

"That little one-armed runt," Nymphidius snorted. "He couldn't kill my old mother."

"I'm assuming Glaucon did the actual killing. Didymus must have had some influence over him. They knew each other, that much is certain. He wouldn't even have to be there in person."

"And the motive?" Marinus asked.

"A dispute over money. If, that is, Didymus is the Persian that Balbus complained of to this Sun-Runner, whoever *he* is. The same Persian who later poisoned Glaucon to silence him, and burned up Barzanes in his house too, I imagine."

Zosimus spoke up, diffident as always. "Money? Is that reason enough to make a provincial risk murdering a high Roman official? Surely Didymus could have found the money somewhere to pay Balbus back. He *is* a banker with banker friends."

"And speaking of his banker friends," Pliny said wearily, "a delegation of them has been clamoring to see me ever since we brought him in. His arrest has hardly gone unnoticed. Bankers, merchants, and assorted grandees with none other than our friend Diocles at their head, all demanding that I free him. Precisely the people that I do *not* want to antagonize. Unless I can prove something against him soon I'll have to let him go."

"The little banker worshipping Mithras in a cave?" Suetonius put in. "I just find that hard to picture."

"I find the whole thing hard to picture," Pliny sighed. "And that is the crux of the matter, isn't it? Who *are* these people and what are they up to? And we're no closer to learning that than we ever were."

"The cave," said Aquila. "The blasted cave! I've had my men out searching for it for weeks now. They're so tired of tramping through those hills, climbing in and out of one dark hole after another I'm half afraid they'll mutiny soon. And what if we do find it? What'll we learn?"

"It would be pleasant to imagine we'll find a list of the initiates, although probably not." Pliny smiled bleakly. "Anyway, keep them at it."

"Where does this leave us, then?" said Suetonius.

"It leaves us," said Pliny, "with our little banker. I've let him cool his heels for three days while we dealt with Fabia and Silvanus. Let's see if he's ready to talk to us. We'll start on him this evening. Get some rest now, my friend, it may be a long night."

Timotheus tapped his foot, unrolled and rerolled his scroll. The damned woman was late again for her lesson. But, of course, no one in this household minded wasting *his* time, no one bothered about *his* convenience. A Greek tutor in a Roman household was a creature to be pitied. He might wear a scholar's cloak and long beard but in fact he was little better than a slave; a monkey with a collar around its neck, expected to be amusing at the dinner table though fed on scraps of food and bad wine; expected to flatter and praise the master's modest poetical efforts, expected to teach the rudiments of Greek to the master's wife, and to know that while they smiled at him they secretly despised him for a miserable Greekling. These Romans! But Diocles, who was his patron, wanted him here and here he would stay.

He blew out his cheeks. His stomach was hurting him again. He was forced to admit that the lady exhibited some shreds of intelligence—for a woman and a Roman, although she often seemed half distracted. She claimed to know something about art but her taste in literature was execrable. He had given up trying to drag her through Homer and finally consented to read a romantic novel of her choosing. Absolute trash! Pirates, kidnapped brides! Pure torture for a man of his sensibility. And the expressions she came up with—the Greek of the alleys. Where was she learning them? From that slut Ione, he supposed. A thoroughly bad influence.

The library door flew open and Calpurnia rushed in, murmuring apologies.

Timotheus scowled. "Today, madam, I think it best to begin with the finer points of the Greek verb. Its subtlety, its flexibility—"

"Oh, you'll drive me mad with this, Timotheus! O-verbs, mi-verbs, contracted verbs! And the aorist tense—what is it for? And the middle voice and the optative mood? We don't have them in Latin. Your grammar makes my head spin. Why must it be so difficult? Latin is so simple."

"Adequate, no doubt, for expressing simple thoughts, lady. Now, if you will please attend to me—"

There was a knock at the door and Pliny poked his head in. "Thought I'd find you two here. Sorry to interrupt. How are you getting on with your lessons, my dear?" His gaze met hers; she looked away. "Yes, well, I've got a new pupil for you, Timotheus. A young man who's our guest temporarily. Hasn't had much schooling, I'm afraid. I thought he could sit in on Calpurnia's lesson. You won't mind will you?" He opened the door wider and propelled the boy inside, with a hand on his thin shoulder. He was visibly trembling. Calpurnia knew instantly who he was. The tutor started to protest but she silenced him with a look.

"Thank you, Gaius," she said. "I'm delighted to have a fellow pupil. Come, Aulus, sit here beside me." She spoke to him in rapid Latin while Timotheus sat stony-faced. "Don't mind him, he isn't as fierce as he looks. Do you know any Greek at all? Well, I'm still very much a beginner myself. You can't imagine how glad I am to have a companion. We'll make a game of it. I'll bet you're a quick learner too."

Aulus sat carefully on the edge of his chair. His shoulders relaxed a little. He shot Calpurnia a look of almost painful gratitude.

Chapter Thirty-six

The 7th day before the Kalends of December

Pliny had expected that three days of confinement would unnerve Didymus. He realized as soon as the man was brought into his office that he had miscalculated; waiting seemed to have had the opposite effect. Gone was the fawning, anxious-to-please demeanor. In its place, was an expression of stubborn defiance.

"Sit him down." A stool was placed in the center of the room. The *lictor* who had brought him in forced Didymus onto it.

Pliny sat behind his desk, on which he had placed a thick folder of papers. All but two of the sheets had nothing to do with the case at all but made the folder impressively thick. Didymus couldn't take his eyes off it. Pliny opened it and began slowly to turn the pages. The only other persons in the room were Suetonius and a shorthand writer, both seated to one side, beyond Didymus' line of sight. Outside, the night was pitch black and only the uncertain, sickly light of oil lamps, one on the desk, the other hanging from a stand above Didymus' head, illumined the scene.

"How much longer do you think you can keep me here?" The banker's voice was truculent. "I have influential friends, you know. They won't stand for Roman bullying."

"Indeed," said Pliny mildly, "I've had a look at your books, I'm impressed by your clientele. Now this needn't take long at all if you'll cooperate with me." He drew a sheet from the folder and held it to the lamp. "This is a letter from the Sun-Runner to the Lion. It was found among Balbus' papers. The Lion, it appears, had complained that another member of the cult, someone known as the Persian, owed him money and was refusing to repay. The Lion wanted him punished by expulsion. The Sun-Runner is unwilling to do this. 'You are both too important to our enterprise,' he says. And the letter is dated only a few days before Balbus was found dead."

He slipped the page back into the folder and fixed his eyes on the banker. "Vibius Balbus was the 'Lion' in this illicit cult to which you belong. You are the 'Persian' he refers to. You and he quarreled over a large sum of money, he complained about you, perhaps he threatened you physically, we know Balbus was a violent man, quick to use his fists. I sympathize with you, Didymus. You were frightened, anyone would be. Finally, you saw no way out except to kill him. You recruited Glaucon to help you. These facts are not in dispute. I'm giving you a chance to tell your side of the story. It can only help you. Fill in the details for me. Who is this Sun-Runner? Who are the other initiates? Where is the cave where you worship Mithras? What purpose brought you all together? You're a small fish, Didymus. Give me the bigger fish and you may yet save yourself. Unless we can conclude this quickly I will have to leave you in prison for several weeks, even months, while I resume my tour of the province. You don't want that, do you? Come now."

There was a long moment of silence. Outside, a distant trumpet call signaled the changing of the guard. The banker picked an invisible speck of lint from his tunic, shifted slightly on his stool. "I have no idea what you're talking about, Governor. I'm an honest man. I have nothing to do with any secret cult. I worship the same gods as everyone else. And, as I've already told you, I never had business dealings with the procurator. You say you know I killed him? You don't know any such thing."

"Balbus was murdered on the morning of the fourth day before the Ides of October. Where were you?"

"At home or in the bank. Ask my wife and son, they'll vouch for me."

"Oh, I'm sure they will. It's of no importance. We know where you were. You knew exactly where to intercept Balbus on his way to the cave."

"I don't know anything about a cave."

"Let's talk about Glaucon. Where did you get the poison you used on him?"

"I never!"

"His whole family died—wife, children, mother, the lot. Surely you feel badly about that?"

Didymus passed his hand over his eyes. "I didn't poison anyone."

Pliny drew another page from his folder. This is a question that Glaucon submitted to Pancrates' oracle. *Will I be punished for slaying the lion?* Pancrates couldn't understand it, but I do. Balbus was the Lion. It seems Glaucon was suffering remorse, perhaps even on the verge of confessing. I'm less clear about why you set a fire that killed Barzanes, the high priest of your cult."

At the mention of Barzanes the banker sucked in his breath, he hooked a foot behind the leg of the stool and squirmed. "You can't think I...I don't know any Barzanes."

"To kill that venerable old man, that was a desperate step. What did you think he might tell us?"

The night wore on. Pliny and Suetonius took turns firing questions at the banker with such rapidity that he hadn't time to answer one before the next was asked, circling back again and again to the same points: How long had he belonged to this cult? What hold did he have over Glaucon? Where did he get the poison? Who helped him set fire to the tenement? How many initiates are in the cult? What did he do with the money he owed Sophronia? And again and again, who is the Sun-Runner? Through it all Didymus rocked back and forth on his stool, gazed here and there in the room, wiped his face with the back of his hand, and denied everything. The lamps guttered and had to be refilled. Towards dawn his cupid's bow mouth contracted into a tight O and he stared at Pliny with unblinking eyes. Clearly he was done talking. Pliny summoned his *lictors* and had them take the banker away, this time to a cell in the dungeon. He and Suetonius regarded each other wearily.

Suetonius yawned. "I don't know about Didymus, but I'm ready to confess to anything."

Pliny made an effort to smile. "That should be amusing. We'll save that for another day."

"Is it possible he's telling the truth?"

Pliny leaned back in his chair and closed his eyes. "He's lying, I'm sure of it. But I have no proof and he knows it. And with the businessmen baying at my door I need an ironclad case before I proceed against him. I can't hold him much longer or I'll have a riot on my hands.

"What now?"

"Get some rest. We'll have another go at him in a few hours. I have one trick up my sleeve. I'm reluctant to use it but if I have to, I will."

Pliny slid under the covers, careful not to wake Calpurnia. He stretched his legs, arched his aching back, closed his eyes and was instantly asleep. He dreamed of rats. Rats running over his feet, up his legs. In a terror, he sat bolt upright. The first gray light of dawn sifted through the latticed windows.

"What is it?" Calpurnia murmured.

"Rats."

"What! Where?"

"Not here, I didn't mean here. I had a dream about them. Do you believe that dreams tell us things?"

"I suppose so." She looked a question.

Pliny was out of bed and fumbling for his shoes.

"Where are you going at this hour?" she asked.

"To look for rats."

◇◇◇

"Galeo," Pliny said to his *lictor*, "how does a rat happen to get trapped in a bank vault?"

"Sir?"

Pliny alighted from his litter in front of Didymus' bank. Galeo and another *lictor* were with him. He told the soldier who guarded the door to unbolt it. The narrow lane was already crowded with foot traffic; a few passersby stopped to watch. Inside, he surprised the banker's wife, a stout, pale-haired woman, who stared at him with anxious eyes.

"Forgive me, madam," he said, "please go back upstairs and stay there. We have business here."

"My husband—?"

"Is still my guest. Do as I ask."

Pliny had confiscated the key to the vault and now he turned it in the heavy lock. The door swung open and two fat, brown rats scurried out. Galeo jumped back. They had come equipped with torches. Pliny stooped and entered the narrow chamber. In the flaring light more pairs of eyes glittered.

"I hate the damned things," said Galeo, who came in behind him.

"Yes, but they're telling us something. When I was first here and Didymus opened the vault for me, one of them ran over my foot. It didn't occur to me then to wonder how it got there."

"What are we looking for, sir?"

"I'm not sure. It could be I'm letting my imagination run away with me. Hold the torch nearer to the floor."

Step by step they circled the room, shifting chests, peering in the dark corners.

"Sir!" Galeo whispered. "Over here." He pointed to an iron grating set in the floor behind a stack of chests; a hole just large enough for a man to crawl through. As they watched, a frightened rat squeezed between the bars and disappeared.

Chapter Thirty-seven

If Pliny had slept little, Didymus looked like he had not slept at all. His eyes were red and there was a tremor in his one hand. His cheeks were covered with a day's growth of beard and bits of straw clung to his clothes and hair. But his little mouth was set in a stubborn pout.

"This is an outrage. You Romans—"

"I know you're uncomfortable," Pliny cut him off. "Are you thirsty? Suetonius, pour our friend a cup of wine. We needn't prolong this, you know. And you know I'm quite prepared to see you as the victim here. I don't think you instigated any of this. I'd very much like to hear your side of it."

Didymus waved the wine away. "I don't know what you mean."

"I paid a visit to your bank this morning and what do you suppose I found? A tunnel, quite a well-made one, that runs under the street from your vault to a warehouse on the docks. My men and I searched it. There isn't much in the warehouse at the moment, bales of cloth, innocent cargo. But in the tunnel we found a few of these." Pliny held up a silver four drachma piece stamped with the emblem of Heraclea Pontica. "This is tax money, Didymus, conveyed to the warehouse in—I'm guessing, sacks of dried fruit? jars of oil?—and smuggled through that tunnel into your bank vault. Now, my friend, tell me why, tell me who was behind this. Help yourself while you still can."

Behind Didymus' back Suetonius raised his eyebrows in astonishment. He was hearing this for the first time.

"Tunnel? Oh, that. Been there for ages. I didn't know where it went. You said a warehouse?"

Pliny lunged forward. "Stop this nonsense! I already know enough to convict you. Lying only makes it worse. You have one more chance to help yourself. Who dragged you into this mess?"

The little banker stared at the floor. When he looked up his face was white and wet with sweat. Pliny could smell the fear. "Balbus, of course. Who d'you think?" His lips twisted in a sneer.

Pliny leaned back in his chair and smiled. "Excellent! I'm glad you're seeing reason at last. Now, if you would, tell me exactly how it worked."

Didymus answered in a voice that was barely audible. "Four navy ships collect the money from the coastal cities—Heraclea, Sinope, Amisus, the others—and bring it here. One of those ship captains, I don't know his name, was Balbus' accomplice. Somewhere along the coast at night Balbus would meet him in a ship he owns and they'd transfer some of the money, disguising it, like you said, as innocent cargo and offload it at the warehouse, which Balbus also owns. The customs inspector never suspected anything or maybe he was bribed, I don't know."

"The crews of the two ships would have to know what was going on. No one talked?"

"They were paid not to."

"The money chests are tallied at the treasury. Silvanus must have known about this then."

"I don't think so. When Balbus would make up the assessments every year he would levy, say, eight talents from Sinope and write that in his book, but he told the Sinopeans to pay nine talents. The extra talent he would divert; it's like it never existed."

Pliny exchanged a stunned look with Suetonius. The enormity of the thing was almost too much to take in. He would have to arrest all four captains and put them through whatever was necessary to find the guilty one.

"And how did you get involved in this?"

"Well, he needed someplace to keep the money, didn't he? And a way to distribute it. I only did what he told me, I was nothing but his tool."

"Distribute it to whom?"

Didymus shut his mouth tight and shook his head.

"Come now, you've told me this much. This is where the cult comes in, isn't it? That's where you two met. Who are the others, Didymus? What was the money used for? What has all this got to do with a barbarian sun god?"

The banker was silent.

"I can drag in everyone you've loaned money to and question them."

"You think that would be wise, Governor?"

Pliny felt an urge to reach out and grab the little man by the throat and shake him. He took a deep breath and struggled to get himself under control. "It seems you're more afraid of these Mithras worshippers—this Sun-Runner—than you are of me. I can protect you from them."

"But you can't!" The little man's voice rose, the stump of his arm flailed the air. You'll go home in a year or two. It doesn't matter what happens to me but I have a wife and son who have to live here the rest of their lives. My son hopes to follow me in my business." He was near tears.

Pliny held up his hands. "Yes, of course, I see that. You've gotten yourself in quite a fix, haven't you? But let's come back to Balbus. You had a falling out with him and you killed him."

"I deny it and you have no proof."

"Haven't I?" Pliny sighed. He had hoped it wouldn't come to this. "Suetonius, if you would, go out and bring in the witness, he's waiting in the antechamber."

Suetonius led Aulus in.

"You!" Didymus leapt off his stool, knocking it over. He spat and made the sign of the horns with his fingers.

"When we first spoke, I found it curious how you insisted that Balbus' son wasn't right in his head and saw things that weren't there. What were you afraid he saw, Didymus? You and

Glaucon murdering his father? Well, he did," Pliny lied, "and he'll testify to it in court."

"Keep him away from me!"

Aulus blinked his eyes and began to sway; Pliny could see a seizure coming on. "Take the boy out, Suetonius," he said quickly. "It's enough."

Pliny looked severely at Didymus. "I would rather have spared you both this confrontation. Now tell me what Balbus did to you that drove you to kill him."

"He beat me! Me, a one-armed man! Called me a thief, a Greekling, he spat on me! They all looked down on me, those high-and-mighty ones, but where would they have been without me?"

"Why did Balbus beat you?"

"The whore, Sophronia! I'd had reverses, I couldn't pay her back. How was I to know she was Balbus' mistress, that some of the money was his? He said he'd have me expelled from the—the worship. Said they'd find another banker. Not likely! The Roman bully, me a one-armed man— " Didymus was working himself into a fury, red-faced with tears streaming down his cheeks, his one fist clenched white. He spewed a string of curses that was remarkable for its variety and inventiveness. Suetonius, who was contemplating a monograph on Greek terms of abuse, hoped the shorthand writer was getting it all down.

Pliny waited patiently until the banker had worn himself out and sat gasping for breath, beyond speech. "You really must take a little wine, my friend. I understand perfectly how you must have felt. Insufferable the way they treated you. Let us just clear up a few details. You intercepted Balbus on his way to the cave. How did you persuade Glaucon to help you? I don't have the impression that he was much interested either in business or in foreign religions."

"He resented his brother Theron always treating him like a half-wit. He wanted to handle money, lots of it, prove himself, even if it was secret. It was me that brought him into the worship, so he had to respect me. And then he actually started to believe it all. He was afraid Lord Mithras would take away his eternal life for killing one of his devotees."

"But you didn't believe that?"

Didymus shrugged.

"So you were able to persuade Glaucon to help you kill Balbus."

"No, it wasn't like that. It was an accident. I just wanted to talk to him, beg him not to get me expelled from the worship and give me a little more time to repay his whore. I was afraid to go to his house where I wouldn't be welcome so I decided to meet him on the path. I only brought Glaucon along for protection in case he started to hit me again. I didn't know he would have the idiot boy with him. We hid ourselves in the bushes beside the path and we heard them quarreling, the boy whining and pleading. He tried to run away and Balbus ran after him and knocked him to the ground and they struggled. We stepped out and I called him by name. He jumped up and spun around, his forehead bloody where the boy must have hit him. He screamed like some animal and charged at us. I thought he had lost his mind. But Glaucon tackled him and wrestled him to the ground and held him in a headlock. Balbus thrashed about and then suddenly he went limp. When we realized he was dead we were in a panic, especially Glaucon. He kept crying that he'd killed a devotee of the god and Mithras would deny him his eternal life up among the stars. Well, there was nothing to do but hide the body. We dragged it from the path and threw it down a gulley and covered it as best we could. I wanted to do the same with the boy, he looked dead enough, but Glaucon wouldn't touch him because he's cursed and I couldn't manage it alone with my one arm, so we just left him there."

"What did you do then?"

"Went on to the cave. The others all wondered what was delaying the procurator, especially since he had sent word to the Father only the day before that he was bringing his son for initiation. Finally, we went ahead with our service and the sacred meal afterward. I kept my eye on Glaucon all the time. I was terrified he would break down and confess. He didn't, but I had no confidence he could hold out for long. I knew then I would have to get rid of him."

"So you sent him a present of poisoned honey dates. Where did you get the poison?"

Didymus shrugged. "I keep it for poisoning the rats."

"And then you killed Barzanes, the Father, when you learned we'd talked to him."

"No, I never! I swear to you. If someone has killed him it wasn't me."

"Then who do you think killed him?"

"I don't know."

"But you have a suspicion, don't you?" Didymus shook his head violently. "Could it have been this Sun-Runner? Who is the Sun-Runner, Didymus? You've told us this much, tell it all."

"You think I want my family burned up like Barzanes!"

"Poor man, you really are more afraid of your accomplices than you are of me. Rest assured, Didymus, sooner or later I will find them out, with your help or without it."

"But I have helped you all I can. You said if I confessed I'd be helping myself. Was that just Roman lies? What will happen to me now?"

Pliny made a temple of his fingers and rested his chin. "There's death, Didymus, and then there's death. I can spare your family the ignominy of a crucifixion. I can omit confiscating your property. You can't expect more than that."

"Can't I?" The little man was on his feet, spittle flying from his lips. "Will you have me strangled in the dungeon? That's a nice example of Roman justice! Or will you put me on trial and have it all come out, how your procurator has looted the province for two years? I'm sure your emperor will congratulate you for that!"

"*Lictors*!" Pliny shouted. Suddenly, he couldn't bear the sight of this man. Galeo and two others who had been waiting in the antechamber rushed in. "Get him out of here!"

Suetonius crossed the room and put a hand on Pliny's shoulder, easing him back in his chair. He could feel his chief trembling.

Chapter Thirty-eight

"A modest celebration," said Pliny, touching his napkin to his lips, "seems in order."

"Hear, hear," Nymphidius said, lifting his glass, and was echoed by the other staff officers, and Zosimus, and Calpurnia, all reclining round the remains of a frugal luncheon.

"So the banker is the murderer after all?" said Calpurnia. "Who could have imagined it?" She gave her husband a smile that did not rise to her eyes. Tired eyes. The eyes of someone to whom sleep was almost a stranger. "What will you do with him?"

"For the moment, nothing. I will write the emperor for instructions, lay out everything I've discovered. I don't relish it. In the meantime, I intend to issue a statement and have it read out in the assemblies of all the cities that Didymus has confessed to the murder of Balbus because of a personal grudge and is being held for trial. I will say nothing about Balbus' involvement with stolen taxes. I'm not ready to make that public yet. Eventually we must tell the cities how they were cheated and make restitution, but I will happily lay all that in Trajan's lap. I have sent a dispatch to Gavius Bassus, the Prefect of the Pontic Shore, in Sinope to place all our ship captains under house arrest until I have the leisure to interrogate them. Meanwhile all of you will say nothing about this to your subordinates or your wives. Is that understood?"

Suetonius gazed glumly into his wine cup. "Sophronia almost certainly knew about Balbus' stealing tax money and had good reason to suspect Didymus of killing him, but she preferred to see her brother Argyrus go to his death for it rather than tell us the truth."

Pliny agreed. "I've already ordered Argyrus' release. We will leave that charming pair to their own devices."

"Worse luck for you," Marinus leered maliciously at Suetonius, whose dalliance with the lady was the subject of gossip among the staff. Suetonius ignored him.

Aquila gestured with a chicken leg. "Couldn't we just blame it all on Silvanus? We're going to execute him anyway. Wouldn't look as bad as a corrupt procurator."

"An unworthy suggestion," Pliny frowned. "No, this province has seen two corrupt governors already in the past ten years. We will survive a corrupt procurator too when the time comes."

"How long can it be kept secret?" Marinus said. "Young Aulus already has some suspicion, and I'm not convinced Fabia doesn't know something about what her husband was getting up to."

"Maybe, but they are the least likely to talk about it. I dread the day when it does all come out and Aulus has to endure the public humiliation."

"You care for the boy, don't you?" Calpurnia said.

"I do. He has courage. When I told him I wanted him to confront his father's killer, he didn't hesitate for a moment, even though it might bring on a seizure."

"Which it did," Marinus said. "A bad one. He's still sleeping it off."

"I'm fond of him too," said Calpurnia. "I'm glad you brought him to my lesson, although he sat there the whole time staring either at his feet or at me. I'm afraid poor Timotheus was quite disconcerted."

Pliny's heart leapt. Was there something here at last that they could agree on? Some small opening for rebuilding a relationship strained to the breaking point? He covered her hand with his; he didn't risk speaking.

"The money," Caelianus protested with the outrage of a born accountant. "Where did it all go?"

"When we know that," Pliny answered, "we will know everything. Balbus' murder has done no more than lift a corner of the veil that covers his crime. In general, there's no doubt where it went. Didymus was merely a conduit for money which has found its way into the hands of rich men to invest in building schemes out of which they make even more money. Once the money's spent it can't be traced. It's like—like…" he paused, searching for an image."

"Like sending a soiled toga to the fullery?" Zosimus suggested with his customary diffidence. "It goes in spotted and comes out clean."

"Brilliant, my boy!" said Pliny. "Like laundering money! A very apt metaphor indeed."

"And," said Suetonius, "one could easily make a list of the likely recipients. But proving it is another thing."

"Is there no way to make Didymus talk?" Calpurnia asked.

Pliny gave a helpless shrug. "If the man is willing to die rather than expose his family to the wrath of the others, and the Sun-Runner, I don't know what I can do to change his mind."

"With good reason," Suetonius added. "If Didymus didn't murder the high priest Barzanes then there's another murderer out there and he must be desperate, thinking what the banker might tell us. I trust he's safely stowed away where even this mysterious Sun-Runner can't get at him?"

"I'll double the guard on his cell," said Pliny. "*Mehercule*, I almost feel like we're fighting a ghost!"

"And you must be careful too, Gaius. I'm afraid for you." Calpurnia touched his arm.

"Now, now, nothing at all to worry about, my dear." And again his heart leapt.

"So now we just wait to see what will happen next?" said Nymphidius without enthusiasm.

"What I propose to do," Pliny replied, "is resume my tour of the province."

"What?" Marinus was alarmed. "You're exhausted, man. As your physician I can't—"

"Nonsense. Do me a world of good to get back to my proper work again. The weather's turned unseasonably mild again and I shall take advantage of it. Look, we've solved Balbus' murder and that's all anyone outside this room needs to know. If I continue to hang around Nicomedia people will start to wonder why. No, I've made up my mind to set out tomorrow, in fact. Suetonius, as before, I leave you in charge of things here. 'Purnia, I hope you'll keep a kindly eye on Aulus, he—I say, 'Purnia…'"

The next morning

Calpurnia sat at her dressing table while Ione brushed her hair with long, vigorous strokes.

"'Purnia, this is your chance! But no more hanging about the temples, please. I'll take him another letter if you want."

"Oh, Ione, I've given up. It's over," she lied. She'd been badly frightened when she learned that Zosimus had spoken to her husband about Ione. Maybe the girl would never let anything slip, but the less she knew now the better.

"You don't mean that." There was an edge to Ione's voice; something almost accusing in her tone.

"I'm afraid I do."

"But—"

"I'm actually not feeling very well today, dear. I'll spend the day alone with a book. You may leave me now." With her back to her, Calpurnia could not see that look that passed over Ione's face. And if she had, could she have guessed what lay behind it?

"As you wish, Mistress."

Calpurnia had lain awake most of the night while Pliny snored peacefully beside her. In the past month, since she had seen him for that brief moment in the temple of Zeus, she had, indeed, struggled to forget Agathon, had almost persuaded herself that she could. How foolish! She was powerless—a weak, foolish woman, a slave to her love, her *need*. She must see him again, only once, she told herself, just once so that they might part friends. But she knew this was a lie. She would send him another message. Not like the last one, complaining, threatening—of course, he hadn't answered her. No, she would be dignified, reasonable—but not cold, no, she would tell him how much she loved him, she would ask him to spare her an afternoon, an hour even, to be with him. But who would deliver her note? If not Ione, then who? One of the household slaves? Could she trust any of them to keep her secret? They were Pliny's slaves, not hers. She thought for a long time and then she knew whom she would entrust it to. She'd never asked him for a favor but why should he refuse? People like him were useful for this sort of thing. Of course she was taking a risk, but that would be true no matter what she did. She would go out of her way to be charming to him today.

Timotheus sat in his chamber—the mean, shabby little chamber they had given him for his quarters—and eyed the pair of tablets, bound with cord and sealed, that she had placed in his hands, smiling (when had she ever done that before?) and asking, oh so prettily, if he wouldn't mind delivering it to a certain town house. Messenger boy! It had come to this. Bad enough he had to live on their scraps, but to be sent on a slave's errand! What should he do with the thing? He would not stoop to opening and reading it himself. He was a gentleman, after all. But just possibly his patron Diocles would find it interesting. Wasn't it for precisely this that he had been put here?

The 4th day before the Kalends of December

"Ah, darling Agathon, don't stop! I'm dying!" Thais straddled him, brushing his face with her breasts as he thrust into her.

The rays of the setting sun pouring through his bedroom window gave the girl's skin a golden sheen, struck red highlights in her tangled hair. She was his favorite *hetaera* and this was the climax of a long, lazy afternoon of drinking, dicing, and love-making.

Abruptly shattered by sounds of scuffling in the entrance hall below them.

The voice of Baucis, "*Matrona*, no, I've orders not to—please, *matrona*, you can't—" and another voice demanding to be let in. A voice he knew too well. Gods! Agathon heaved the girl off him, sending her sprawling on the floor. "Quick! Get your clothes on." He pushed her through a curtain into a side chamber. He struggled into his tunic, smoothed the bedclothes as best he could. And when Calpurnia burst through the door he was sitting in his chair with a scroll in his lap to cover his still swollen organ, forcing himself to breathe slowly.

With one motion she flung off her hooded cloak, ran to him and threw herself at his feet. He recoiled. Could this be the same woman he had once imagined he loved? It had been six weeks or more since he had seen her at the Roman procurator's funeral, and the change in her was astonishing: her face a dead white, the chin and cheekbones sharp where there had once been soft flesh, and the eyes—the eyes, big and haunted, looking out at him from dark hollows.

Her voice thick with tears, "I waited two days for your answer. I couldn't stand it anymore."

"Answer to what?"

"Please don't lie to me."

"I'm not lying. Here now, get up, don't do that." She wrapped her arms around his knees like a suppliant before the statue of a god. "Look, you can't come here. Your husband—"

"He's gone! He'll be gone for weeks. Now is our chance! Tell me you love me. I know you do, you must. You were only frightened, I understand."

"Calpurnia, it's over."

"You don't mean that! Let me be your Callirhoe again, let me love you." She rucked up his tunic, uncovering him, put her head between his legs. In spite of himself, he swelled again. And sweet little Thais, hidden from them by only the thin fabric of a curtain, was momentarily forgotten. He drew her up and carried her to the bed, still warm from that other body...

When they had finished making love, she lay dreamily with her head on his chest and only then began to take in her surroundings. On the bedside table a tray of half-eaten pastries and two goblets. She sat bolt upright, looking around wildly. "Who's here?"

"What? No one. One of my chums dropped by, left hours ago."

Slowly, she lay down again. "I want to stay here all day and all night," she murmured.

Did he hear a stirring behind the curtain? "Don't be silly, 'Purnia, they'll be missing you soon. You have to go now."

"Say you love me again."

"I love you, I do. Now you have to go."

"I'll come again tomorrow."

"I'm leaving for the country tomorrow. My parents are complaining they haven't seen me in months. I'll be away for a week or more." This was, in fact, the truth, though if it hadn't been he would have said it anyway.

"Oh, too long!" she cried. "I have an idea." She took his face between her hands, her lips parted eagerly. "We'll spend a day in the country, where you took me once before. You can get away, can't you? We'll have a whole day to ourselves. We'll be nymphs and satyrs in the woods. You are a satyr, my beautiful young satyr!"

Anything to be rid of her. And why not? It would be preferable to a day spent listening to a lecture from his father about the planting of winter wheat and why couldn't he take an interest in things like his brothers. And she did excite him even though she knew none of the tricks of a *hetaera*. "Yes, yes, all right. Make it two days from now. Take the road that follows the river up toward the Reclining Woman. You remember? At the waterfall follow the track that goes off to the left about five *stades*. I'll mark the path for you with a cloth tied to a tree branch. It's a steep climb but you can do it. And come alone, Calpurnia. You won't be afraid?"

"I'm not afraid of anything. Only that you won't love me."

"Now go, please."

As the door closed on Calpurnia, Thais rushed out from her hiding place. "So that's your Roman whore?" she screamed. "You poor man, I could hardly keep from laughing, listening to the two of you go at it." She picked up a goblet and flung it at him. "You called her Calpurnia. I'm not stupid, I know who that is. Wouldn't the governor just love to know—"

He hit her in the face with a blow that sent her staggering against the wall. He hit her again and she went down. "You say anything about her and I'll kill you!" He dragged her to the door and threw her down the stairs.

Chapter Thirty-nine

The 6th day before the Kalends of December

Suetonius had promised himself that he would have no more to do with Sophronia, a woman too wily and amoral even for his jaded tastes. But her note had been urgent. And so he found himself again in her private office in the Elysium together with a weeping girl who would have been pretty but for a broken nose and swollen jaw.

"I don't like it when people beat my girls," Sophronia said. "This one is terrified, but I got the story out of her—all but the man's name. You won't like what you hear. What you do about it is up to you. I promise you she will tell no one else, nor will I."

"At what price, madam?"

"That was uncalled for, my dear." She looked at him reproachfully.

Minutes later, he was making his way back toward the palace, his features grim, his head in a whirl. He had devoted years of his life to chronicling, with sardonic wit, the moral lapses of the great and powerful. He had believed himself unshockable. He was wrong.

At the door to Pliny's office, temporarily his own, he was met by a sentry who reported that Didymus' wife and son were waiting on him. "They beg to have a visit with the prisoner, sir. They've brought him a change of clothing, some personal things."

The wife, a stout woman shaped like a flour sack, the son, a younger version of his father, stood in the corner with downcast eyes. A bundle of what looked like rags sat on the floor at their feet.

If Suetonius had been less preoccupied he might have been more cautious. Instead, he waved them away. "Quarter of an hour, no more," he told the sentry.

He sat down at Pliny's desk and remained for a long time with his head in his hands. Finally, he fetched a long sigh, rose, and strode out. He would send a messenger after Pliny of course. But first, he would talk to Calpurnia. For the first time since joining Pliny's staff he devoutly wished himself back in Italy.

But the lady was not in her apartment, or anywhere in the palace, and even Ione claimed to have no idea where she was.

A wintry sun winked through the lattice of naked branches above her head and lit the chuckling water of the river that ran beside the path. The forest floor was covered deep with pine needles and matted leaves so that her horse's hooves made no sound. She breathed in deep lungfuls of the bracing air and shivered inside her heavy cloak—shivers of excitement, of the thrill of danger, of anticipation of the hours ahead with her lover. Not since she was a girl, roaming in her native north Italian hills, had she felt so free. In her whole adult life she had scarcely ever gone out without a train of maids and servants. Now she was that girl again and her heart sang with joy. She had been very careful, saying nothing to Ione and going before dawn to the stables, rousing the boy from his sleep, and giving him a silver denarius to buy his silence. And she wasn't afraid of wild animals or brigands for she knew in her heart that Aphrodite, sweet goddess of passion, was watching over her. And now she saw the red cloth that he had tied to the branch to mark the trail for her. She turned her horse's head and urged it up the steep track toward the distant ridge that people said resembled a reclining woman.

At the clearing she dismounted, spread her blanket roll on the ground and sat down to wait. It was early still. She hadn't expected him to be here before her, he had once told her he liked to sleep late in the mornings. She had wrapped up a loaf of bread with some cheese and olives and a flask of wine. She was hungry and couldn't wait. She took a bite, a sip. Another. He would bring more food. What a love feast they would have!

She waited.

The sun crept across the sky.

Where was he? Why didn't he come? Her nerves were stretched as tight as harp strings.

Ah, gods, had he lied to her? Was he so cruel? Wait—there was a sound, the cracking of a twig. She ran to it. Nothing. Some animal. She shivered again: this time with cold, with fear. With anger. She had humbled herself, a Roman governor's wife, and he didn't care! It was over then. A wail rose in her throat. *Stop it!* She beat hers sides with her fists. *Stop it. Fate has saved you from yourself. What were you thinking? But, not to see him! Where is he? Who is he with? Is he with a girl, some whore? Are they laughing? Is he telling her about me, the governor's wife, his slave? The vulgar, lying little seducer! I'll tell Gaius, confess everything to him, and he'll crush this wicked boy, torture him, make him wish his mother had never borne him.* "No! No!, she cried aloud, "What am I saying? I love him. Juno help me, I love him!"

Weeping, she began to gather her things.

Another sound—the snorting of a horse—and then there he was! She ran to him, threw herself against him. "Where have you been?"

"Sorry, couldn't get away sooner. Had to tour the farm, listen to a lot of boring talk." He unwound her arms from around his neck. "Anyway, I'm here now. Famished actually, let's eat."

"No, make love to me."

"On an empty stomach? I couldn't really. Here, I've brought some venison. Killed it myself, much to everyone's surprise."

They ate. And they made love, rolling and laughing in the crackling leaves. And again he made her feel things that she had never felt with her husband. And she thought she had never been so happy in all her life. Afterwards they lay on their backs under a blanket and Agathon said, "Are you a good climber? I'll take you up to the top of that hill.

"I'm a country girl," she laughed, and jumped up, and started to run. And when they reached the top, panting, their cheeks flushed red, they looked back and they could see the white walls and red roofs of the city, and, tiny as toys, the palace and the temples and beyond them the grey sea.

"What a sight," she said. "I wish I had my charcoal and parchment."

"There are caves all over here," Agathon said. "One just up there. When I was a kid I used to go exploring."

"Let's find one and make love in it," she said, "like Dido and Aeneas."

"Friends of yours?"

"You ignorant boy," she laughed.

But her laughter was cut short by a man's shout. An *optio* and two soldiers were scrambling up the rocky path behind them. They had spent weeks combing these hills, searching for the cave of Mithras. They had spotted the red rag tied to the tree branch and thought it might lead to something.

"They've seen us!" Calpurnia cried.

"Quick!" He pulled her after him around a thorn bush that tore at her clothing and into the dark mouth of a cave, stooping under its overhanging eave.

"Stop there, you!" the officer called.

"Agathon, we're trapped!"

"Follow me." He plunged deeper into the cave, dragging her behind him.

"I can't see anything!"

"Follow the wall."

The floor of the cave sloped downward. Calpurnia slid on loose stones, fell to her knees, tearing them, struggled up again, reached out and felt for the cold stone, slid again. The soldiers had lit a torch. Its light and their echoing shouts pursued them.

"Agathon, where does it lead?"

"I don't know!"

The passage bent to the left, like the leg of a dog, then turned again, and grew lower and narrower until Calpurnia could stretch out her arms and touch both sides. And then suddenly it ended in a wall made of dressed stone blocks. She and Agathon shrank against it, their chests heaving. In another moment the soldiers caught up with them. The officer held out his sputtering pine branch and peered at them. "Lady Calpurnia?" he said.

Authority was her only weapon. "What d'you mean by chasing us? I'll see that you're disciplined for this. My friend is an artist, we came out to sketch. Now leave us in peace."

"But—" He took a step back.

"Look here, would you." One of the soldiers was on his knees, running his hands over the stone wall. There's a ring set into it." He pulled on it. "It's moving, lend a hand." The other knelt beside him and they pulled together. With a screech of stone on stone a part of the wall swung out. The *optio* shouldered them aside and, holding his torch in front of him, crept through the opening. There was a long moment of silence and then a whoop.

"Boys," he shouted, "we've found it!"

Chapter Forty

The cave of Mithras.

The soldiers clapped each other on the back. They were sure to be rewarded for this! They had stumbled on its back door, in fact, which opened into a small chamber behind the bas relief of the bull-slaying. There they found a lamp on a stand, positioned so that its light would shine through holes drilled through the god's eyes. The effect on worshippers must have been spectacular when, at some climactic moment in the ritual, one of the priests, concealed behind the relief, lit the lamp and the sun god's eyes blazed in the darkened cave.

A quick search of the cave proper revealed nothing of interest, at least to these hard-bitten soldiers. No gold, no jewels. When they made their way through to the cave's front entrance they found it so well camouflaged with bushes that you could have stood right next to it and not known it was there. They found they were only some two hundred paces away from the rear entrance, just around the curve of the hill and a little higher up.

The officer told his men to stay there and guard the place. "And I will take these two back to the city." He led Calpurnia and her companion out into the open.

Calpurnia forced a smile. "What is your name?" she asked.

"Marcus Catulinus, ma'am. *Optio* in the third cohort."

"Well, Marcus, just tell them you found the cave. You needn't say anything about my friend and me. You'll have my gratitude, you understand?"

"Ma'am, I can't—"

At that moment, Agathon let out a curse and started to run, bounding down the hillside and dashing into the trees. Before anyone could make a move to stop him he was on his horse and galloping away.

Calpurnia sank to the ground with her face in her hands.

"Come now, lady," the officer pulled her to her feet. "We'd best be off. I'll ride your horse and you'll sit behind me. I want no tricks."

"Take your hands off me!" she screamed. "You'll regret this!"

He looked at her not without a touch of pity. "That's as may be."

Two days later

Pliny stalked up and down the room, their bedroom, clenching and unclenching his hands, fighting to control himself. Calpurnia, small and miserable, huddled in a chair and followed him with her eyes. A winter storm had arrived the night before; Pliny had ridden through it without stopping. Outside, the morning was almost as dark as night and a high wind hurled sleet against the shutters. It was freezing in the room.

"Who is he? Who is this man you betrayed me with?" His voice was thick. He felt he could hardly breathe.

"I haven't betrayed you, Gaius. Don't be silly. We went sketching, he's an artist, nothing happened. We thought the soldiers were brigands, we ran…" Her eyes pleading.

"Don't lie to me! Tell me his name. You made love with him in his house. You were seen there by his *hetaera*. Did you know that? Suetonius knows, Sophronia knows, maybe the whole city knows. How could you do this to me? To us? You think you're the wife of some shopkeeper that you can act like this? I am the governor!" He stood over her, his fists white-knuckled. "Have you lost your mind?"

"Yes! Yes! My mind, my heart, my honor!" She was sobbing now. "Gaius, I love you but I couldn't help it. I was so lonely.

You were too busy for me and then you were gone and I was left alone with these people who hate me. I wanted be the governor's wife, to make you proud of me, but I couldn't. Gaius, you look at me but you don't *see* me. I'm not the woman you think I am. I wish I were, but I'm not. That woman doesn't exist. And so I found a friend. He made me laugh, he flattered me. And I could talk to him just because he was nobody, not one of you. And then the rest—I never meant for it to happen. I beg you to believe me. I'm so sorry."

That woman doesn't exist. He was stunned. She had come to him as a child of barely fourteen—fresh, innocent, unformed. And he, like a father as much as a husband, had molded her into the woman he wanted. Had she always secretly resented that? But she had grown more beautiful and accomplished than he could have hoped for—so much that sometimes it almost frightened him. He knew he didn't cut a dashing figure, had never had great success with women, but he had trusted her, never been jealous of the admiring looks she got from other men.

He turned and walked away, came back. "You understand if this becomes public I will have to divorce you. How can I ever trust you again? How long will it be before you make a fool of me with some other man? *How long?*" He grabbed her by the arm, dragging her from the chair, his fingers sinking into her flesh all the way to the bone. He raised his hand to strike her.

"Yes, hit me, go ahead! Kill me if you like. When my heart was broken you sent Marinus to take my blood. Take it now, take all of it. I don't want to live any longer. I'm no use to you. And *him*, I mean nothing to him. He treated me like one of his whores—you say she was watching us? I'm not surprised. And when we're caught he runs away."

Pliny flung her back. "If you hate him why won't you tell me his name?"

"So you can banish him, kill him? No, despicable as he is he doesn't deserve that. He didn't do anything I didn't let him do."

Pliny felt suddenly empty, eviscerated, no more than a shell, without nerve, without strength. Calpurnia was wrong—he was not a killer, not even a wife beater. But *someone* must be punished. "You didn't do this alone," he said. "Ione helped you. She's been your go-between. By the gods, I'll get the truth out of her."

"Leave her alone, Gaius, please. She only—"

But he rushed out into the corridor, calling a slave and sending him to fetch her. A moment later Ione appeared, with Zosimus at her side. They had been next door in their room, waiting for the summons.

"Zosimus, leave us," Pliny said. "This doesn't concern you."

"I beg your pardon, Patrone." He lowered his eyes. "What concerns my wife concerns me." It was the first time Zosimus had ever opposed his master's wish. It took all his courage.

Pliny turned on Ione. "Tell me the name of my wife's lover, damn you."

"Leave her alone, Gaius," Calpurnia cried. "Don't make her betray me."

"Betray *you*? She has violated the *fides* she owes me, her master. I can have her flung out into the street for this."

"Will you send Zosimus away too, then?" Calpurnia shot back. "Or will you deprive him of his wife and child?"

"*Not* Zosimus' child." Ione's voice was shrill. She pointed a shaking finger at Pliny. "*His* child! Tell her, Patrone, tell her or I will."

Calpurnia stared at her husband wide-eyed, and instantly knew it was true. How could she not have noticed before the growing resemblance between little Rufus and Pliny? How could she not have understood his love for the boy?

He couldn't meet her eyes. A different man would not have cared if he got a slave girl pregnant, and would not have expected his wife to care. But their marriage hadn't been like that. He had been attracted often enough by slave women who would have been happy to share his bed, but he had always exercised the self-control that a man of his education should. And then he had bought Ione from a friend to be his wife's maid and companion. And she reminded him powerfully of that slave woman in his uncle's house who had initiated him when he was thirteen. And Ione was no innocent victim. She soon guessed the effect she had on him and teased him with it. Finally, one day it happened. It was a steamy summer's day at his villa in Laurentum, and he had retired to his bedroom for the midday siesta. He had undressed to let what little breeze there was play over his naked body. Ione came into the room without knocking, claiming she was looking for her mistress. Was that a lie? He never knew for sure. But suddenly she was on the bed and in his arms and he was helpless to resist her.

But that was the only time. And two months later, when she told him that she was pregnant, he had hastily manumitted her and married her to Zosimus.

"Patrone?" Zosimus whispered. "Not my son?" His features twisted in pain. And it was like a dagger in Pliny's heart.

"How long has this been going on, my dear husband?" Calpurnia's voice was heavy with scorn. "She's swelling again, is this one yours too?"

"I only wish it were!" Ione rounded on her like a tiger. "*You* couldn't give him sons but *I* could. I could have been his concubine, given him more sons, I could have been to him what you never can be—the mother of his children! Instead, he used me once and then gave me and our baby away—to *him*." Her eyes slid to the wretched Zosimus.

Pliny sagged, his legs barely supporting him. "I see it now. You hate us. This is all about getting back at me. Such bitterness, so long concealed."

Ione's lip curled. "Oh master," she sneered, "we slaves drink in dissembling with our mother's milk. How else can we survive in your world?"

"And to pay me back for the wrong you think I did you you made my wife a whore?"

Ione scoffed, "She did that herself, I only helped, although she frightened me sometimes with the chances she took. And now see where we all are."

Pliny drew a deep breath. "I ask you again, who is my wife's lover?"

"Don't!" Calpurnia screamed.

But Ione gave him a cunning half smile. "I'll make a bargain with you, master. I'll tell you his name if you promise not to put me out of the house—no, more than that, make me your concubine and acknowledge our son."

"How dare you! I don't bargain with my servants."

"I'll get it out of her, Patrone—" Zosimus, who had stood all the while as motionless as if the eye of a basilisk had turned him to stone, shot out a hand and seized his wife by the throat. "— if I have to strangle her."

But Ione broke loose from his grip, raked his face with her nails, and bolted from the room, leaving the others to stare at each other in mute, unspeakable pain. A frozen tableau. There was no sound but the howling of the wind and a distant mutter of thunder. If some god had struck them all dead at that moment, they would have thanked him.

Chapter Forty-one

The 3rd day before the Kalends of December

"It isn't easy for a man to talk about some things," Pliny said. He gazed down at his breakfast table, the food untouched. "You understand?"

"I'm honored by your confidence." Suetonius looked at his chief with sympathy. The man was unshaven, haggard, his color was bad. Plainly, he hadn't slept all night.

"Well," Pliny forced a weary smile, "you already know the worst. You have a way of knowing secrets, haven't you?"

"I'd rather not know this one. I've never had a high opinion of women. Calpurnia was an exception."

Pliny rested his forehead in his hand. "She's an exceptional woman."

They were quiet for a while.

"What is everyone saying?" Pliny asked.

"They sense something's wrong. The wives, I gather, are desperate to find out what's happened. Harpies. Vultures."

"Well, they won't learn it from Calpurnia."

"What are you going to do with her?"

"She wants to go back to Italy, to her grandfather. He's unwell and needs her. I've told her she can travel by the *cursus publicus*, but it will take some time to arrange. In the meantime, I've put her in another apartment, far from mine."

"I mean, will you divorce her?" Suetonius looked a question at Pliny, waiting for an answer that didn't come. "Of course, you needn't if you don't want to," he went on. "As long as everyone's discreet and the emperor doesn't find out, the Augustan law on marriage needn't be invoked. Sophronia won't talk as long as we're nice to her. And the lover, whoever he is, has apparently kept his mouth shut all along."

"Whoever he is."

"Calpurnia won't name him?"

"No. If she wants to she will. I won't force her, I can't."

"Nor Ione?"

"Do you know she tried to hang herself last night? Zosimus found her in time and cut her down. She'll live, though she doesn't want to. Maybe that's punishment enough for what she's done." Pliny said nothing about fathering Rufus on her. There were some secrets even Suetonius should not know.

"Surely you can force it out of *her*."

"Marinus had a look at her. Her throat's so bruised she can't speak, even if she would. And she doesn't know how to write. So there we are."

"Poor Zosimus."

Pliny nodded. "He has asked my permission to divorce her but I suspect he loves her in spite of everything, and there's the boy to think of. I haven't given him an answer yet."

"There's still the *hetaera*. The girl's scared witless, but we'll lean on her. I'll go back to Sophronia's at once."

"No, don't."

"What? You don't *want* to know?"

Pliny pressed his fingertips to his temples. "Last night, if I had known who he was I might have sent soldiers to drag him out of his house—and it would have been a catastrophe. I'm a little calmer now. You understand the power I have here, my friend. In this province I'm an emperor. I can arrest, I can torture, I can banish, I can execute. I could be a little Domitian, a Caligula, if I wanted to. Plenty of governors have succumbed to that temptation. I'm not sure I could resist."

"I, for one, wouldn't blame you. She disgraced you with a *Greekling*. Because she was *bored*?"

"I never should have brought her here. I blame myself."

"You're not angry?"

"Of course, I'm angry."

"But you still love her?"

"You know that poem of Catullus?"

"*Odi et amo.* 'I hate you and I love you.'"

Yes, that's it. It speaks to me, my friend. Especially the last word, *excrucior*, 'I'm in torment.'"

They were silent for a while. Then abruptly Pliny pushed the table aside and stood up. "It's no use sitting here, I must occupy myself. Come with me, I want to have a look at this damned cave at last."

They left their horses at the foot of the hill and scrambled the rest of the way up, following the *optio*. Pliny stopped at the top to catch his breath. Suetonius shot him a worried look. The soldiers who had been left to guard the place cut back some of the bushes with their swords so that the two men could enter more easily. Pliny ducked under the overhang and felt his way down the seven steps, followed by Suetonius and the soldiers holding torches.

"So this is it," he said. "I imagined it bigger." With a glance he took in the painted blue ceiling with its golden stars, the sculpted relief of the young god with his red cap and blue cloak in the act of stabbing the bull. "All of this the handiwork of Barzanes," he said wonderingly. "Astonishing."

"The signs of the zodiac all along the walls," Suetonius observed. "Clearly their belief has much to do with astrology. That explains those handbooks that Balbus and Glaucon owned. Apparently, you have to study to penetrate deeper into the mysteries."

"That and pay a hefty fee, I don't doubt. I was forced once to learn something about the cult of Isis. They're all the same, they hook you and then they lead you on."

Suetonius touched the desiccated corpse of a squirrel with his foot. "This place hasn't been visited in a long time. At least not since the old priest's death. I don't think we need to keep the guards here any longer."

"No," Pliny agreed. He went up to the relief and examined it closely. "Beautiful workmanship. It's cracked, though. Look here. And the crack runs along the ceiling too."

"The earthquake," Suetonius suggested.

"Yes, probably."

"Do you suppose he's real?"

"What, Mithras?" Pliny shrugged. "I imagine he's just Apollo by another name."

"And eternal life for his worshippers?"

"Frankly, I don't care. I live in this world, the next one doesn't interest me much. Anyway, we know that these particular worshippers, or some of them anyway, were not here to save their souls but to fatten their purses."

Suetonius examined the long stone benches that ran along the sides of the cave. "*Raven*—several of those—*Bridegroom, Soldier, Lion, Persian, Sun-Runner, Father,*" he translated the Greek titles that were inscribed on each place. "This was the hierarchy, then. Half a dozen Ravens and one each of the others, and the remaining places for the common worshippers, I suppose. There isn't room for more than about twenty altogether."

"Unfortunately, no personal names attached," Pliny said. He shut his eyes for a moment, imagining the human forms that had once sat there. "Barzanes, the Father; Balbus, the Lion; Glaucon, the Bridegroom and Didymus, the Persian. That leaves the Ravens, the Soldier, and the Sun-Runner. They could be people we know. Very likely are. My work isn't finished until I can expose them—especially the Sun-Runner."

"And how do you propose to do that?"

"I don't know," he answered wearily. "I simply don't know."

Night. The temple of Asclepius

As ever, the lamps burned late in the chamber beneath the great gold and ivory statue of the god. Pancrates and his assistants labored over the day's haul of questions to the oracular serpent: some deftly removing the seals from the tablets, others concocting crabbed, obscure answers, still others counting the drachmas.

"Have a look at this one, boss." One of the nimble-fingered boys handed Pancrates an opened tablet.

He held it to the lamp and squinted. "Interesting. It isn't a question, it's a message. From Didymus to Diocles. The governor, I hear, has the banker locked up tight. I wonder how he smuggled this out. He asks me to deliver it in person, praises my discretion, my influence." Pancrates' lips moved silently as he read and re-read the words scratched in wax. "The poor fellow is desperate. He begs, he threatens, but without quite saying what he means." Pancrates bound up the leaves of the tablet and set it aside. He smiled to himself. *Where there's a secret to be learned, a favor to be earned, count on me.*

Chapter Forty-two

The 6th day before the Nones of December

"Thank you, my boy, that will do for today."

Three days had passed since his visit to the cave and Pliny was dictating letters to the magistrates of several cities, announcing his impending visit. Once again he was determined to pursue his tour of the province, which seemed always to be interrupted by more urgent business. Zosimus busied himself putting away his tablets and stylus. He avoided Pliny's eyes.

"I'll prepare fair copies, Patrone."

"Thank you, yes, thank you." Thank you and again thank you. How many times would he repeat these empty courtesies, so achingly inadequate to express what he really wanted to say? *Forgive me, Zosimus, for foisting a bastard child on you, for marrying you to a woman who never loved you, for using you as no man should use another simply because I could, because you are weak and I am powerful.* Could they ever be easy with each other again? There were things that had to be talked out; above all, whose son would Rufus be now. But he didn't know how to begin. Too soon, feelings still too raw. Maybe in a few days…

A knock on the door interrupted this desperate train of thought. It was Suetonius, with a rolled parchment in his hand. "A messenger from our friend Diocles has just come with this for you."

Pliny unrolled it and read. "Well. The Golden Mouth is inviting me to his country estate to discuss the affairs of the province with him and his friends. He promises pleasure as well as business."

"I'd rather be thrown into a pit of snarling dogs. Will you go?"

"I don't see how I can refuse."

"I'll come with you, help bear the brunt."

"No, you stay here."

"Gaius, you're not well."

"I'll take Marinus with me, I'll be fine."

"And me, Patrone?" Zosimus had lingered by the door, listening.

"Thank you, my boy." Again, thank you! "Perhaps you'd rather stay with Ione and—" He'd almost said *your son*.

"No sir, I would not."

The following morning the procession of carriages carrying Pliny, his attendants and *lictors*, and the heap of gifts that protocol demanded departed from Nicomedia in a swirl of dancing snowflakes. This was his first visit to Diocles' estate and as they proceeded, guided by the messenger, he saw with surprise that they were heading in the same direction as the cave of Mithras, only veering off on another road while still some miles away.

Pliny owned fine estates in Italy and considered himself knowledgeable about their management. Diocles' well-tended acres impressed him. Fruit and olive orchards; fields of wheat and barley, in stubble now after the harvest; woods full of game; barns and slave barracks in good repair. And the mansion, large and beautifully proportioned, fronted by Ionic columns of pink marble.

Diocles—his bantam cock's chest thrust out and large, leonine head tilted back—stood in the doorway and hailed him in his thrumming baritone. "We're all waiting for you, Governor, come in. So glad you could honor us with your presence. Philemon," he addressed his major domo, who hovered at his shoulder, "see that the governor's retinue are escorted to the servants' quarters."

Instantly Pliny was separated from his *lictors*, from Zosimus and Marinus, as Diocles ushered him into a vast and crowded dining hall that buzzed with conversation. Pliny guessed there must be thirty guests or more, the elite of Nicomedia and nearby Prusa. The big landowners, the richest merchants, city councilors and magistrates, the priests of the great temples—all summoned at short notice by this one man. It was unmistakable how they all deferred to him. Not for the first time, an image presented itself to Pliny's mind of a spider sitting at the center of its web; a taut and sensitive network whose filaments were built of obligation and influence, of favors owed and favors promised. Most of these men he knew, if only slightly. One face in the crowd surprised him—Pancrates. What was that hustling charlatan doing in this sleek and well-fed company? He acknowledged him with a nod.

Diocles entertained like a prince. An army of servants scurried back and forth, bearing course after steaming course of rich food—roast crane and boar, broiled eel and mullet, sow's womb and hare's liver, blood sausage and milk-fed snails, fricassee of veal, truffles in wine sauce, and all of it seasoned with coriander and cumin, fenugreek and silphium and *garum*. Pliny had no appetite for any of it, but ate what politeness demanded. He had no appetite either for the young *hetaera* who reclined beside him and attempted witty conversation. There were more than a dozen attractive women in the company—none of them anyone's wife. Diocles' womenfolk were confined to the *gynekeion* at the back of the house and never seen by strangers

The laughter was forced, the conviviality ice-thin. Diocles' golden throat delivered an unending string of sententious *dicta* on philosophy, morality, and the virtues of simplicity, all adorned with quotations from Homer and other poets. Pliny had never felt more alone. The absence of Calpurnia from his side was an aching wound.

When at last the dishes were cleared away and the *hetaeras* dismissed, the *symposion* began, the serious drinking and serious conversation. After the Greek fashion, wine was mixed with water in a gigantic bronze *krater* of beautiful workmanship and shallow drinking bowls handed round. Pliny had already drunk too much; with an effort he focused his mind. He needed to be sharp now, careful, alert. He, who had interrogated so many in the past weeks, was now to be interrogated.

Why was their friend Didymus under arrest? Surely the charge of murder was preposterous. Had he been tortured into confessing? Were others to be entrapped like this? Were any of them safe? Was Pliny not overstepping his authority? Had the emperor been consulted? The voices grew louder, more insistent, veering close to insolence. Diocles himself was uncharacteristically silent, letting the others talk; his lips relaxed in a half-smile, his gaze fixed on Pliny like a spectator at a bearbaiting.

The hour grew late and Pliny felt his strength ebbing away, his self-control wearing dangerously thin. At last Diocles called a halt. "I'm afraid we're wearying our guest. Where are our manners? Let us retire for the night. We need our rest because tomorrow I have a treat in store for you all. My woods are well stocked with wild pig, you ate a couple of them tonight, but there's one old tusker out there, he's wily and fast and he defies me. Tomorrow we hunt him." He cast a beaming eye on Pliny. "The emperor is a keen boar hunter, I'm told. And you, governor, are no stranger to the sport, or so you say in one of your delightful letters. You see, I know more about you than you think I do."

Pliny's heart sank.

Diocles' smile was wolfish. And then it froze. The room was suddenly very quiet. Pliny looked round to see what was the matter.

An old man had entered the hall. Tiny, wizened, wearing only one sandal, his soiled cloak trailing the ground behind him, his milky eyes staring vacantly. Diocles rushed to him. "Father!"

An elderly slave woman ran in. "Forgive me, master, he wandered, I didn't see where—"

"It's all right, Antiope." Diocles recovered himself quickly. "So glad you decided to join us, father. We're entertaining the governor tonight, did you know that? Would you like to meet him?" He spoke to him as one would speak to a child. He turned to Pliny. "Governor, my father, Hypatius."

Hypatius? thought Pliny. *Where have I heard that name?*

Chapter Forty-three

The 5th day before the Nones of December

Calpurnia sits alone in her room. Not *her* room, a strange room in a distant wing of the palace, her prison cell, though there are no bars or locks. She drinks wine laced with valerian root, hoping to sleep, but it doesn't help. She tries to draw but can't, tries to read but throws the book aside. Finally, she takes up her distaff and spindle and spins thread hour after hour, teasing out the wool with her fingers, watching the whorl spin this way, that way, with no purpose but to find oblivion in that simple, mindless activity. It is the seventh day since she and Agathon were caught in the cave, the fifth since she and Pliny and Ione and Zosimus shed each other's heart's blood in a mutual wounding that will scar them forever.

In all these weary days she has not seen a friendly face. Her new serving women are strangers to her. Ione is not permitted to come near her now—not that she wants her to. None of the wives have called on her—mercifully. No one will risk offending her husband by befriending her. She thinks bitterly how Agathon deceived and abandoned her. Is anything left of her passion for him? It feels now as if it had all happened to some other woman, someone she doesn't even recognize. She has gathered together the dozens of drawings she made of him and has burned them one by one until nothing remains but a heap of ashes.

Ashes. She has the taste of ashes in her mouth. Her heart, her self-respect, her husband's love—all ashes. He will divorce her. How can he not? It's what she deserves. There can be no forgiveness for the pain she has caused him. She has ruined both their lives. All she wants now is to go home and be with her grandfather, in the old familiar surroundings of her childhood.

A knock on the door.

Can it be him? Her husband? Come to forgive her after all? Her heart leaps. If he will let her, she will love him again like the innocent girl she once was. How she longs to be that girl again! "Come in," she says in a tremulous voice.

"Excuse me, lady. They said you were here."

"Aulus?" She tries to compose her face, quiet her heart. "What are you doing here? I thought you were at home."

"I was for a while. I couldn't stand it. I came back to see the governor, but Suetonius says he left yesterday to visit someone in the country."

"Oh, I didn't know." She sees his eyes widen in surprise. He's a sensitive boy, he knows something is the matter, but he is too shy to ask. She must say something. "My husband and I are estranged." She forces a smile.

"I'm sorry, I—"

"It's all right. Why did you want to see him?"

He looks at his feet and grimaces, hunches his thin shoulders, wrings his hands. She's afraid he'll have a fit. "The cave," he says at last. "Everyone says your husband found it. I wanted him to take me there."

"Why in the world?" she asks, astonished. "That should be the last place—"

"You don't understand. I blame myself for my father's death. If I hadn't been a coward, hadn't tried to run away, he would have seen those men who were lying in wait on the path, he could have defended himself."

"Aulus, you mustn't think that." She takes his hands in hers.

There are tears in his eyes. "If I had obeyed him and gone with him to the cave none of this would have happened. And maybe Mithras would have cured me. Maybe he still can. I want to go there now and make a sacrifice to him. I'm a man now, I'll soon be seventeen. I mustn't be afraid anymore. I owe my father that."

"Oh, but you can't, there's no one there, no priest, the cave is empty."

He draws back and stares at her. "How do you know that?"

She realizes too late what she has admitted. "Haven't you heard? I was there—with someone I thought I loved." Why lie to the boy? She's too tired to lie anymore. She sees his confusion.

"And that's why—"

"Why I'm here? Yes."

"I'm sorry for you."

"You're kind to say so."

He looks at her earnestly. "My parents parted in anger too. I will never marry."

"Don't be silly, of course you will."

For a moment he says nothing and then he gathers his nerve. "Could you take me there?"

"No, impossible."

"Who else can I ask?"

"One of the soldiers, Suetonius…"

"I'm afraid of them." He pleads with his eyes. "Only you, lady."

Oh, gods! Could she? Go back to the last place where she and Agathon had made love and face whatever feelings assail her? Is she brave enough for that? Is she as brave as this poor boy? It must be right now, before she loses her courage.

"Come with me to the stables," she says.

The air was as sharp as a knife. A morning mist lay in the hollows and the ground was white with hoarfrost. Dressed in woolen breeches and thick cloaks, their legs encased in leather puttees, Pliny, Zosimus, and Galeo tramped along in single file, stepping carefully over fallen branches in the dense underbrush. The stout, long-bladed boar spear was heavy in Pliny's hands. From somewhere ahead of them came the baying of the Laconian hounds. They had found the scent. Diocles' huntsmen were busy stringing up the nets of woven flax, hanging the meshes on the forked branches of trees.

Diocles—where was he? He and the other Greeks had been within sight only a moment ago—Diocles had assured him he wouldn't have to use his spear; the huntsmen would do the dangerous work. But surely a noble Roman must relish the excitement of the chase? What would people think if their governor showed himself lacking in manliness? And Pliny, like a fool, had allowed himself to be imposed on, although Marinus had tried his best to dissuade him. The physician would have nothing to do with such foolishness himself and had stayed behind in Diocles' house.

Pliny slowed his pace and waited for Zosimus to catch up. The young man was even less accustomed than Pliny to physical exertion. He looked half frozen. "Something's been bothering me all night," said Pliny, his breath coming out in white puffs of steam. "I was introduced to our host's father last night. Poor old fellow's lost his wits. Name's Hypatius. Seems to me that name has a familiar ring but I can't place it. Mean anything to you?"

Zosimus stopped in his tracks and turned worried eyes on his master. "Patrone, we should leave this place. Now."

"Why, what is it?"

"Hypatius was the name on the deed, the owner of the estate who sold Barzanes the plot of land with the cave. Patrone, they're all in this together. They've lured you into a trap!"

"*Mehercule*! The Sun-Runner? Diocles?"

The snarling of dogs was suddenly loud in their ears. Branches snapped. The boar burst out of the thicket in front of them, two dogs hanging from its bristling neck, others snapping at its legs. Two hundred pounds of muscle balanced on tiny feet. It charged, bursting through the net that should have drawn tight around it and ran straight at Pliny. Where were the huntsmen? He crouched and tried to take it on the point of his spear but the beast flicked the weapon out of his hands with a toss of its huge head. Pliny threw himself on his stomach, pressed his face against the frozen earth, scrabbled with his fingers. The boar worked at him with its wet snout, grunting and snuffling, he could feel its steaming breath on his face and smell its stink. If it got those wicked, upcurving tusks under him—

"Patrone!" Zosimus had been given a javelin to carry—useless in his unpracticed hands. He threw it and missed, then snatched up a fallen branch and brought it down with all his strength on the animal's shoulder. The boar turned and slashed at him, ripping open his belly, flinging him aside like a rag doll. Then Galeo was standing over the boar with Pliny's spear in his hands. He thrust it down between its shoulder blades up to the cross piece and held on until the animal sank to its knees and fell over. He helped Pliny to his feet.

A moment later three of Diocles' huntsmen appeared as if from nowhere. "Are you all right, Governor?" said one. "Looks like your companion is…well, too bad."

Zosimus lay on the ground, clutching his belly, a grey bulge of intestine showing between his bloody fingers.

"Calpurnia, where are you going?" Suetonius had been alerted by one of the slaves and had followed her and Aulus out to the stable.

"Are you my jailer now?"

"No, of course not, but—"

"Then get out of my way."

"Not until you tell me where you're going."

She made an angry gesture with her hand. "To the cave, then."

"With the boy? Why?"

"Because he asked me to."

"At least let me come with you."

"So you can report on me to my husband?"

Marinus' arms were bloody to the elbows. He had done what he could, gently replacing the large intestine, trimming the ragged flesh around the wound and bathing it with vinegar and verdigris, then suturing it with the complicated double stitching recommended for belly wounds. Zosimus lay on the blood-soaked bed, scarcely breathing.

"He won't live, will he?" Galeo had just come into the room and leaned over the physician's shoulder.

"Not likely." Marinus wiped his face against his shoulder. Though it was cold in the room he was sweating. He had been working for an hour.

"Where's the governor?"

"With Diocles, I think. Why?"

"Because I went back out to the woods and had a look at the nets. In the excitement nobody bothered to take them down. I know a little bit about boar hunting."

"And?"

"And they were only tied to bushes at the bottom, not to the tree trunks as they should have been."

Marinus answered with a wordless stare.

"Do drink some wine, Governor. And please sit down. You're badly shaken, of course. Quite understandable."

Diocles' private study, which overlooked a spacious courtyard, was a virtual museum of Greek culture. Centuries-old Athenian vases sat on antique tables; busts of Plato, Socrates, and Homer stood on pedestals. On one wall hung ancient weapons and pieces of armor. He pointed to an ivory-hilted short sword in a jeweled scabbard. "Said to have belonged to Mithridates the Great. The bane of the Romans. He was a hero to us, you know."

Pliny said nothing.

"Yes, well," Diocles' genial smile faded, replaced by a look of concern, "terrible business this morning. But boar hunting is a dangerous sport and no place for a scribe. You really shouldn't have allowed him to go along. I expect you're blaming yourself."

"I'm blaming *you*! Where were your huntsmen, where were *you* when it happened?"

Diocles' eyes narrowed. "I hope that isn't an accusation of some sort? You asked to speak with me privately. Was it only to complain about my huntsmen?"

"Diocles, man, come out of there"—the distant, boisterous shout of one of the guests—"we're waiting lunch for you."

"I have more to accuse you of than that," Pliny said. "You're a thief and a murderer, Diocles. You were in league with the procurator and the banker Didymus to steal tax money. Tell me, how did you all come together? Balbus needed a place to hide the money he planned to steal and a way to invest it secretly. A crooked banker like Didymus was the obvious choice. And was Didymus already a member of your cult? Did he bring Balbus to you? How convenient for all of you. A cave, a meeting place where money could be distributed in return for favors, and all of you bound to one another in secrecy by the mystery of initiation, and poor Barzanes imagining all along that it was for the glory of his god! And you, Diocles, pretending to resent Roman rule while you profit from its corruption. How much of that money flowed into your coffers? And what did you give in return? The support of your faction? A docile city council that would ask no questions, make no complaints? Was my predecessor part of this too? I was sent here to clean up the financial mess in this province and who do I find at the heart of it? None other than you. I'm placing you under arrest. You will accompany me back to Nicomedia for trial."

"Remarkable." Diocles' golden voice flowed like honey. He leaned back in his chair. "What an imagination you have. I wouldn't have suspected it. I can see you aren't well, Governor. I urge you not to excite yourself. An imbalance of the humors can affect the mind, produce strange fantasies. I think you should ask the emperor to relieve you at once."

"You'd like to see the last of me, wouldn't you? The cave of Mithras, where Balbus was going when he was killed, is only a few miles from here. In fact a certain Hypatius sold Barzanes the land. Hypatius, your father."

"But this is absurd. I don't know any Barzanes and we don't sell land, with or without caves. I'm neglecting my other guests. If there's nothing more—"

"I have the bill of sale to prove it, thanks to my secretary, who now lies dying. You used that religious zealot for your own ends, and finally you had him killed when you realized I had found him. *You* are the mysterious Sun-Runner that Balbus wrote to, complaining about Didymus. And Didymus has confessed to everything, even though he fears you. I know how you and your friends stole the money, how you invested in aqueducts, temples, and baths that would add to your glory as benefactors and philanthropists—although often enough, in your greed, you pocketed the money and never even finished the buildings. And I might never have uncovered any of this if Didymus hadn't quarreled with Balbus. Didymus has given you up."

"That greedy, stupid little man!" Now the golden voice grated like iron. The pretense of civility was gone. "I admit nothing, and you are bluffing, Governor. Didymus hasn't named me and he won't. Pancrates is a most useful man. Did you imagine he peddles his secrets only to you? I, too, was anxious to know who killed our friend the procurator. And I thought that you, with your power to summon witnesses, and that charlatan, with his network of informants, might discover the truth together. And you haven't disappointed me. Naturally, Pancrates has kept me informed. You say Didymus has implicated me? Not true. Pancrates has just delivered to me a letter from him, vaguely threatening that he might talk if I don't rescue him. But I will rescue him, you and I together, Governor. Let me suggest that you arrange to leave his cell door open one night and a carriage waiting, and I will see that he and his family are taken care of somewhere out of the province."

"Or have him quietly murdered like you did Barzanes? And why would I leave his cell door open?"

Diocles sighed and ran a hand over his silver mane. "We wondered what to do about you, Governor. Some were for bribing you but I knew that was pointless. Unlike our previous governor, you are incorruptible. The boar hunt, as you may have guessed, was also a bad idea. I was against it, too much could go amiss. As usual, I was right. Poison would have been simpler, but I suppose you've been careful to dose yourself with *theriac*, and, if not, it would raise suspicions if you succumbed at my dinner table. But, in fact, I know exactly how to deal with you. I'm not a violent man. Information is my weapon. Excuse me a moment, will you?"

Diocles went to the door of an antechamber, and opened it. "Join us," he commanded. "Yes, now. And do try to act like a man."

A young man stepped through the door, his eyes, like a frightened deer's, looking everywhere but at Pliny.

Diocles smiled. "Here's someone I want you to meet, Governor. You may recall you met him briefly at Balbus' funeral. Our estates neighbor each other and his father, as it happens, owes me quite a lot of money. See how pale and trembling he is. Allow me to introduce you, once again, to Agathon, your wife's lover. Ah, you know I'm telling the truth, I see it in your eyes. Agathon has told me how they were found together in the cave. She's been carrying on an affair with him for months right under your nose, you poor man. And he will declare it publicly if I tell him to. And, if you think his word isn't enough, I happen to possess a letter to him in your wife's handwriting. Foolish woman, she made the mistake of entrusting it to her tutor, who brought it to me instead. He resented being treated as an errand boy, you see, though that never would have occurred to her. Would you care to read it? Do sit down, Gaius Plinius, before you fall down. Women!" Diocles spread his arms in a theatrical gesture, "Zeus only made them to cause us grief, all the poets say so, no? And yet we love them anyway. The boy is good-looking, I grant you, though not very bright. Really, I don't understand what your wife sees in him."

Pliny felt the breath go out of him. *This* was his rival? He had tried to imagine her lover—a handsome older man, he supposed;

strong, with a noble face. Not this *boy*! Anger and shame filled him all over again. He tasted bile in his throat.

"I had hoped this wouldn't be necessary," Diocles murmured. "I'm not a cruel man, I don't relish the spectacle of humiliation. But think of the scandal if you should become the laughing stock of all Bithynia. The governor with a cuckold's horns because his wife preferred a Greek lover—and not any Greek but this unimpressive youngster. We Greeks are a virile race, whatever you may think. Among us there is no greater shame than being cuckolded. You won't be able to show your face, much less govern. The emperor, who will learn about it from my Roman friends, will, with many expressions of regret, be forced to recall you. And he will force you to divorce your wife. I've done my homework, you see. I'm familiar with your Roman laws. They even compel you to kill the lover with your own hands. What an appalling piece of folly, but there it is. And you, of all men, Gaius Plinius, are devoted to the law.

"Your wife is not exactly the faithful Penelope, fending off the suitors—how far we have sunk since the days of Homer!—still, I suspect that you don't want to divorce her. She's a charming and beautiful woman, after all. Your man Suetonius was good enough to lend me his copy of your published letters. I had them translated and read them with interest. You see, I believe in knowing my adversary. I was impressed by the touching love letters to your wife. The picture of domestic bliss you paint! Did she really sleep with your speeches when you were away from her, and set your poetry to music? I can scarcely credit it. Young love! Indeed, I envy you. Now surely those tender feelings aren't entirely extinguished? You and she may yet spend many happy years together with this unpleasantness forgotten. And I suspect you are not prepared to play the outraged husband now and disembowel young Agathon here. Are you? Let us see."

He went to the wall of weapons, took down the sword of Mithridates from its peg and tossed it on the table in front of Pliny. Agathon blanched. Pliny did not move.

"Well? Have you the stomach for it? No? I didn't think so."
Diocles seated himself again, not bothering to look at Agathon.
"You've done an admirable job here, Gaius Plinius, helping us
poor Greeklings to put our sorry affairs in order. But your labors
have taken a toll on your health. Time to rest on your laurels
then? Time to return home after a job well done? The emperor
will understand if you beg to be relieved of your post. You and
I are reasonable men, we don't need to resort to violence. You
may frighten young Agathon here but you can't frighten me."

"You have misunderstood our law," Pliny said very softly. "I
can only kill him if I actually find him in my bed." Then with
one swift motion he seized the sword, drew it from its scabbard,
and struck at Agathon's head with the flat of the blade. The boy
let out a scream and fell backwards, clutching his head. "If you
ever approach my wife again you will wish I had killed you!"

Agathon scuttled crab-like toward the door.

They dismounted at the foot of the hill.

"It's halfway up the hillside and to your left. You can almost
see it from here." She pointed.

"Come in with me?"

"No, you go, I'll stay here with the horses." She felt the panic
rising in her breast again. This was close to the spot where the
soldiers had surprised them. She pulled her hooded cloak tighter
around her shoulders. "It's cold. Don't be long."

Aulus held a trussed up cock in his arms; it struggled and he
felt its heart beating as fast as his own heart. Over his shoulder
he had slung a wineskin. His offerings to the god.

He found the entrance and descended the seven steps. A
dim and dusty light sifted through the cave's mouth. He looked
around in wonder at the dully glowing stars strewn across the
walls and ceiling. What message might they hold for him if only
he knew the key? Slowly, feeling his way, he walked down the
nave, forty paces, until he was face to face with Mithras. The
beautiful youth—manly, fearless, plunging his dagger into the
bull's neck, shedding its blood for him, for *him*. Aulus sank to

his knees in front of the altar. With what words could he pray to this strange god? His yearning was beyond words—an end to shame, an end to self-loathing. Mithras would hear him and understand. He drew a knife from his belt and cut the cock's throat, letting its blood spurt over the altar. "Are you here, Lord Mithras? I give you this. Help me, come to me…"

And he *felt* it, he felt the god near him, felt his power and his indescribable sweetness. And he understood in an instant of clarity that all his visions, the exploding bursts of light inside his skull had been mere glimpses of this reality beyond reality, of Mithras' starry realm. And the lights were exploding in his head now—he was shaken, he was lifted up, his chest swelled with such joy that he thought it would burst…

And as Aulus slumped, twitching and jerking, before the altar, the earth did rumble with the bellow of a subterranean bull, and shake and split open, and the roof of the cave came down on him, burying him under a ton of rock.

◇◇◇

The horses reared and screamed as the earth heaved under them. Calpurnia was thrown to the ground half-stunned. Was this her punishment? Were the Furies coming for her? She looked up in time to see a tree—the very tree under which she and Agathon had coupled—lift its roots from the quivering earth and slowly, slowly fall toward her.

◇◇◇

"Well, Governor, you surprise me. But you should have killed him, you know. It's too late now. This is your last chance to be reasonable. I'm offering you a way out. Simply resign and go home, with or without your wife, it's up to you. But if you refuse, consider that you are in my house, far from home. And though, as I have said, I personally dislike violence…"

The antique vases began to vibrate.

A bronze shield fell from its hanger with a ringing crash.

The bust of blind Homer, leapt from its pedestal and rolled crazily across the floor.

Diocles looked around, wild-eyed. "No!"

With a groan of splitting timbers, the floor buckled and the ceiling cracked. Pliny and Diocles were both on their hands and knees, Pliny nearest the door, which hung from one hinge.

Diocles, crouched against the farther wall, was trying to get to his feet when the wall fell inward, pinning him under a weight of brick and plaster. Pliny, in the doorway, glanced back and, through a choking cloud of plaster dust, saw Diocles stretch out his arm. "Help me!"

Pliny crawled back, picked up the marble bust of Homer where it lay and lifted it high. Their eyes met. "You won't kill me," Diocles whispered.

Pliny brought it down on his head. Again. And again.

Then he dashed for the door just as the ceiling collapsed in a cloud of choking dust.

Chapter Forty-four

One week later
The Nones of December

Pliny sat in his office—its walls disfigured with cracks and fallen plaster—numb with exhaustion, trying to pull his thoughts together as he dictated a letter to the emperor. Philo, his new secretary, sat beside him with his stylus poised. Zosimus had died on the journey back to Nicomedia without ever regaining consciousness. In the chaotic aftermath of the earthquake there had been no time to build him the splendid tomb he deserved. His ashes rested, for the time being, in an underground crypt on the palace grounds. Pliny had composed the epitaph himself.

DEDICATED TO THE SPIRIT
OF GAIUS PLINIUS ZOSIMUS . FREEDMAN OF GAIUS .
WHO LIVED XXXIV YEARS . VIII MONTHS . AND XV DAYS
BEST OF SCRIBES . BEST OF FRIENDS
MAY THE EARTH REST LIGHTLY ON YOU

How inadequate those formulaic words to express his sorrow. He would have other secretaries, but never another Zosimus. He felt lost without him. He had decided to acknowledge little Rufus as his own son and raise him with all the advantages of his rank and fortune. That meant, of course, that Ione would have to stay on. He found her presence distasteful but the poor child, having just lost the man he believed was his father, could hardly be separated from his mother as well. If only he and 'Purnia could have raised the boy together...He drove his thoughts back to the task at hand.

...and so, Sir, the city is in need of architects and engineers to repair the damage to buildings which were already in a ruinous state from the previous earthquake. Destruction in the countryside is widespread too, with several villages obliterated. I am making what provisions I can for the refugees...

He had been in constant motion day and night, surveying the damage, issuing orders. It was the only thing that was keeping him sane.

...The province is mourning the loss of one of its leading citizens, Diocles, son of Hypatius, called the 'Golden Mouth', who died when his house collapsed. I have issued a proclamation in his honor...

In a moment of murderous rage he had killed a man with his bare hands. Was it possible? He had discovered something about himself that he would far rather not have known—how little it took to strip away the thin skin of civilization, of humanity and reveal the savage that lives in all of us. He knew it would haunt his dreams for the rest of his life. The body was eventually found, crushed almost beyond recognition, and given a public burial. To expose Diocles publicly as a criminal now would be impolitic. The cult of Mithras was no more. Some of its members had escaped detection but in time he would find them out. Pliny had already written to Trajan informing him of Balbus' corruption and the arrest of Didymus for his murder. More than this he would not entrust to a letter; time enough when he returned to Italy (which he prayed would be soon) and made his report to the emperor in person.

Balbus' widow has asked me to intercede for her. I suspect she was not innocent in his corruption but now she has lost not only a husband but a son as well. It think it befits your magnanimity not to confiscate her property...

He hoped he would never lay eyes on the woman again. Where she should have begged, she demanded. And she seemed, in some unreasoning way, to be blaming him for Aulus' death.

That poor boy. In all this sad business his death seemed to Pliny particularly tragic. What might he have made of himself if he had lived?

...I am deeply indebted, Sir, to my senior lictor, Titus Asinius Galeo, to whose courage and quick thinking I owe my life twice over. I ask that you enroll him in the equestrian order. I myself will endow him the necessary four hundred thousand sesterces...

A soon as the ground began to shake, Galeo had raced to Diocles' apartment, where he found Pliny staggering through the doorway. He had half carried him to the courtyard and then, leading the other *lictors*, gone back inside for Marinus and Zosimus and got them out before the whole building fell in.

There had been many dead among the guests—not, however, Agathon. Ironically, Pliny mused, he had probably saved the boy's life himself by driving him out into the courtyard just before the quake hit. And what should he do about him now? Banish him? Have him murdered? The act of a tyrant. No, he would not stoop to that. And any move he made against Agathon might only bring the whole story out into the open. For the moment he would do nothing and rely on the boy's innate cowardice to seal his lips.

...finally, Sir, I have dealt with a most troublesome character—one Pancrates, an oracle-monger who dabbled in sedition. I have arrested him and, with your permission, will have him taken under guard to an island in the Propontis where he will live out his life.

Pancrates had a large and loyal following in the city. Pliny knew he was taking a risk. But perhaps this was the best time to strike, when the people were distracted by their own misery.

"Thank you, Philo. You'll see that that's sent off at once."

The young man bowed himself out.

And now for the letter that he dreaded writing—the one he must write to Calpurnia's grandfather. He would write this one with his own hands; he did not want the scribe to see him weeping.

Calpurnia had vanished.

Suetonius said she and Aulus had gone out to the cave, but when he went with a search party to look for her they could find no trace. The cave itself had vanished. He had lost her already in a way—lost her love—but that was no consolation. Her death was more than he thought he could bear. He would forgive her her infidelity a thousand times over if he could only see her dear face again, hear her voice…

Suetonius knocked and came in. "Is this a bad time…?"

"No, it's all right." Pliny wiped the back of a hand quickly across his eyes.

It pained Suetonius to see him like this, grey-faced with grief and exhaustion. He wanted to put an arm around his shoulder, but he was afraid he might not tolerate the familiarity. He had tried once before to talk to him about Calpurnia but Pliny had cut him off. For a man with such a talent for friendship, Pliny was the one now who needed a friend—and yet he couldn't allow anyone into his private world of pain.

"At last, we've had a letter from the emperor!" Suetonius did his best to sound enthusiastic. "The courier says the Via Egnatia has been blocked for weeks by one blizzard after another."

Pliny touched the familiar objects on his desk, avoiding his friend's eyes. "Read it."

Suetonius unrolled the scroll, studied the page for a moment, and cleared his throat. *I am delighted, my dear Pliny, to hear of your safe arrival in the province. You must be diligent in examining the financial accounts of the cities, for it is clear that much is amiss. Still, in every province trustworthy allies can be found if you carefully seek them out. I needn't tell you what great confidence I place in your judgment. Please do not hesitate to consult me when questions arise. Trajan.*

Post scriptum: The empress sends her fondest greetings to your lovely wife who, we both feel, will be a support to you in the difficult days ahead.

Suetonius went out, closing the door softly behind him.

◇◇◇

"She still doesn't speak?"

"A god has taken away her wits."

"Broken her shoulder and one leg too. Scratched up her face pretty badly."

"All that, I can mend," the healing woman said. "Was it you who found her?"

"My son. He and his brother were out looking for our scattered livestock."

"Here, dearie, sip this." She held out a cup of boiled herbs to the figure that lay on a bed of rushes in the little hut

"So many of our own are injured, why bother with her?"

"Money in it maybe? Look at her fine clothes."

"If we knew who her people were." The headman got off his haunches and went out.

"Now, dearie," the healing woman leaned close and whispered, "just who are you?"

FINIS

Appendices

I. The Roman Calendar

In the Roman calendar, each month contained three 'signpost' days: the Kalends (the first day of the month), the Nones (either the fifth or the seventh), and the Ides (the thirteenth or fifteenth). After the Kalends was past, the days were counted as so-and-so many days before the Nones, then before the Ides, and then before the Kalends of the following month.

The story takes place from the second half of September to the beginning of December. The signpost days with their English equivalents are as follows:

The Kalends of October	October 1
The Nones of October	October 7
The Ides of October	October 15
The Kalends of November	November 1
The Nones of November	November 5
The Ides of November	November 13
The Kalends of December	December 1
The Nones of December	December 7

II. Roman Time-Keeping

Romans divided the day, from sunup to sundown, and the night from sundown to dawn into twelve *horae*. As the length of the day and night varied throughout the year, one of these 'hours' could be as short as forty-five minutes or as long as seventy-five. In September, when the days and nights are of about equal length, the *hora* came closest to our standard sixty minute hour. The first hour of the day in September was about 6 am. The sixth hour was noon; the twelfth hour, sundown. And similarly, the first hour of the night was about 6 pm, the sixth hour was midnight, and the twelfth hour was the hour just before dawn. By December, the daylight hours were several minutes shorter and the nighttime hours correspondingly longer.

III. Greek and Roman Money

The smallest unit of Greek coinage was the obol. Six obols = one silver drachma. 100 drachmas = one mina. Sixty minas = one talent. A Roman silver denarius was roughly equivalent in value to a drachma. Four bronze sesterces = one denarius. Large amounts of money were generally expressed in sesterces.

Glossary

Agora: marketplace in a Greek city

Archon: a senior magistrate of a Greek city

Capsa: a cylindrical tube for holding scrolls

Chlamys: a Greek man's cloak

Cursus publicus: the public post

Eques: a member of the equestrian order, the lower rung of the Roman aristocracy

Fasces: the bundle of rods enclosing an ax carried by *lictors*

Fides: faith, loyalty

Garum: a condiment made of fermented fish parts

Gynekeion: the women's quarters in a Greek house

Hetaera: a paid female companion/entertainer

Insula: a tenement building

Janitor: a door slave

Krater: a large bowl for mixing wine and water

Latrunculi: Literally 'brigands', a board game something like checkers

Lictor: a Roman magistrate's bodyguard

Ludus Magnus: the imperial gladiator school in Rome

Mathematicus: astrologer

Matrona: a married woman

Megaron: the central hall in a Greek house

Mehercule: by Hercules!

Mentula: penis (vulgar)

Mare Nostrum: Our Sea (the Roman name for the Mediterranean)

Mystes (plural *mystae*) : an initiate in a mystery religion

Nymphios: bridegroom

Optio: a Roman army rank second to a centurion

Palaestra: exercise ground

Palla: a Roman woman's mantle

Paterfamilias: the oldest male in a Roman family

Secutor: a heavy-armed gladiator

Stade: Greek unit of distance, approximately an eighth of a mile

Synposion: a drinking party

Tabellae: a pair of wooden leaves coated with wax and joined together with string

Tablinum: the office or study in a Roman house

Theriac: a compound believed to be a universal antidote against poisons

Tribunal: dais on which a magistrate or judge sat

Triclinium : dining room; arrangement of three couches, each holding three diners around a rectangular table

Univira: a woman who has known only one man

Venator: a gladiator who fights wild beasts in the arena

Vitis: Centurion's cudgel made of a vinestock; his symbol of authority

Author's Note

Bithynia-Pontus

Pliny served as governor of the province of Bithynia-Pontus (in present day Turkey) in AD 109 or 110 with a special commission from the emperor to bring order to that troubled province. His dispatches to Trajan, and Trajan's replies, are recorded in Book Ten of the *Letters*. Although our plot is fictitious, the background of embezzlement, waste, financial mismanagement, and political turbulence is abundantly documented, not only by Pliny, but in the orations of Dio Chrysostom ("Golden Mouth"), who is the model for the character of Diocles. It may be mentioned in passing that Nicomedia did suffer a severe earthquake while Pliny was governor. He describes it in a letter to the emperor and notes that the absence of a volunteer fire brigade (forbidden by Trajan's injunction against voluntary associations) made the destruction that much worse.

Mithraism

There is, at present, no archaeological evidence for the practice of Mithraism in Bithynia. Our cave and its locale are entirely fictitious. Nevertheless, one leading scholar of the religion places its origins in the Persian influenced region of Commagene in south-eastern Anatolia, and it would be odd if the cult entirely leapfrogged Bithynia on its way west. In any case, the early second century AD saw the remarkable burgeoning of the cult in areas as distant as Africa, Germania, Britain, and Italy. What we don't know about Mithraism is a great deal more than what we do, and no detail of its ritual and theology is beyond dispute. If there were Mithraic scriptures, the Christian church made sure that they did not survive. If there was a Mithraic Saint Paul, he is unknown to history. Yet it is hard to imagine that the religion was able to spread as far and as fast as it did without energetic proselytizing by someone. Christians regarded Mithras as a blasphemous imitation of their own savior god (who also has strong solar associations). Although vestiges of the cult may have lingered in some places, it had effectively ceased to exist by the end of the fourth century AD.

Suetonius

Gaius Suetonius Tranquillus (circa AD 69 to circa AD 140) is well-known only as the author of *The Twelve Caesars*, the biographies of the emperors from Julius Caesar to Domitian (the principal source for Robert Graves' *I Claudius* novels). But among the many other works attributed to him are *Lives of Famous Whores*, *Roman Festivals*, *Roman Dress*, *The Physical Defects of Mankind*, and *Greek Terms of Abuse*. None of these has survived in more than fragments. What a loss! Suetonius did serve under Pliny in Bithynia, though precisely in what capacity is not clear. In a letter to Trajan (X 94) Pliny writes: "For a long time now, my lord, I have admitted Suetonius Tranquillus, that most worthy, honorable, and learned man, into my circle of friends, for I have long admired his character and his learning, and I have begun to love him all the more, the more I have now come to know him from close at hand" [Trans. P. G. Walsh]. Suetonius went on to serve as private secretary to the emperor Hadrian—a post from which he was eventually dismissed for some impertinence to the empress.

Pancrates

The name is borrowed from a famous magus of Hadrian's reign but I have modeled him mainly on the oracle-monger, Alexander of Abonoteichus, who flourished in the later second century AD. The Greek satirist Lucian, in a delightful essay, describes his encounter with the man and his oracular snake (see Bibliography). I have given to Pliny the stratagem Lucian employed to expose the charlatan.

The Sacred Disease

Epilepsy was described by Hippocrates (circa 5th century BC) in his essay *On the Sacred Disease*. The Father of Medicine argued that the disease was not 'sacred' at all but the result of an imbalance of phlegm, one of the four humors in his system of physiology. Needless to say, it continued to be regarded with superstitious dread up until the dawn of modern medicine (see Bibliography).

Bibliography

Primary sources:

Dio Chrysostom. *Discourses*. Translated by H. Lamar Crosby. Loeb Classical Library, 5 vols. 1946

Lucian. "Alexander the Oracle-Monger" in *The Works of Lucian of Samosata*. Translated by Henry Watson Fowler and Francis George Fowler. Forgotten Books, n.d.

Pliny the Younger, *Complete Letters*. Translated by P. G. Walsh. Oxford U. Press, 2006

Selected secondary works:

Andreau, Jean. *Banking and Business in the Roman World*. Cambridge U. Press, 1999

Beck, Roger. "The Mysteries of Mithras: A New Account of Their Genesis." *Journal of Roman Studies*, 88 (1998), 115-128

Idem. "Myth, Doctrine, and Initiation in the Mysteries of Mithras: New Evidence from a Cult Vessel." *Journal of Roman Studies*, 90 (2000), 145-180

Burton, G. P. *Proconsuls, Assizes and the Administration of Justice under the Empire*. Journal of Roman Studies, 65 (1975), 92-106.

Clauss, Manfred. *The Roman Cult of Mithras*. Translated by Richard Gordon. Routledge, 2000

Jones, A. H. M. *The Greek City from Alexander to Justinian.* Oxford U. Press, 1940

Jones, C. P. *The Roman World of Dio Chrysostom.* Harvard U. Press, 1978

Knapp, Robert. *Invisible Romans.* Profile Books, 2011

Pomeroy, Sarah B. *Goddesses, whores, Wives, and Slaves: Women in Classical Antiquity.* Schocken Books, 1995.

Schachter, Steven C., ed. *Brainstorms—Epilepsy in Our Words: Personal Accounts of Living with Seizures.* Raven Press, 1993.

Temkin, Owsei. *The Falling Sickness: A History of Epilepsy from the Greeks to the Beginnings of Modern Neurology.* 2nd ed. Rev. Johns Hopkins U. Press, 1971

About the Author

Bruce Macbain has earned a B.A. in Classical Studies from the University of Chicago and a doctorate in Ancient History from the University of Pennsylvania. He has taught Classics and Greek and Roman history at VanderbiltUniversity and BostonUniversity. His special interests are religion and medicine in the ancient world.

To receive a free catalog of Poisoned Pen Press titles, please contact us in one of the following ways:

Phone: 1-800-421-3976
Facsimile: 1-480-949-1707
Email: info@poisonedpenpress.com
Website: www.poisonedpenpress.com

Poisoned Pen Press
6962 E. First Ave. Ste 103
Scottsdale, AZ 85251